"I'm fine. We're fine."

Melody swung the scraper and Brad had to duck to avoid getting it in the side of the head. "*Everything* was fine," she added, "until you showed up here as if you owned the town."

"Fine? Really? That's not exactly the word that comes to mind when I think about your situation, Mel." If it took cold hard truth to wake her up, then so be it. He had nothing to lose at this point.

"What do you know about it? You're back in Brookhollow for all of three days and all of a sudden you know something about my life? You know nothing." Opening the back sliding door, she tossed the snow scraper inside and shoved the door shut.

"I know you're losing the house."

Dear Reader,

The holiday season can mean so many things to different people. For some, it is a season of love, laughter and making memories with family and friends. For others, it is a time of reflection and forgiveness. For single mom Melody Myers, the holidays are a struggle both financially and emotionally and, when Brad Monroe appears three weeks before Christmas, things get even harder.

Learning to confront past mistakes and learning to forgive are two of life's greatest challenges, and Melody and Brad are forced to decide whether they can move forward or if some things simply cannot be forgiven...not even for love.

Brad and Melody's story is one that is very close to my heart and one that I hope you will enjoy. Happy Holidays from my family to yours. Wishing you a season of love, laughter, hope and forgiveness.

xo

Jennifer

HEARTWARMING

The Mistletoe Melody

———

Jennifer Snow

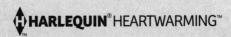

Recycling programs
for this product may
not exist in your area.

ISBN-13: 978-0-373-36700-9

The Mistletoe Melody

Copyright © 2014 by Jennifer Snow

Printed in U.S.A.

JENNIFER SNOW

lives in Edmonton, Alberta, with her husband and four-year-old son. She is a member of the Writers Guild of Alberta, the Romance Writers of America, the Canadian Author Association and shewrites.org. She is also a regular blogger on the Harlequin Heartwarming Authors site and is a contributing writer for *Mslexia* magazine and *RWR*. She has offered online courses on writing sweet romance through several RWA local chapters and has written articles for *Avenue* magazine. An active volunteer with Frontier College, she is an advocate for literacy programs worldwide. More information can be found on her website, www.jennifersnowauthor.com.

Books by Jennifer Snow

HARLEQUIN HEARTWARMING

THE TROUBLE WITH MISTLETOE
WHAT A GIRL WANTS
FALLING FOR LEIGH

For Jacob—you're the coolest kid I know,
but you'll never win the "I love you more" game.
Mommies always win that one.

Acknowledgments

Thank you to Stephany Evans, the best agent in
New York—xo. Thank you to my wonderful editor,
Victoria Curran, for ignoring my pouting and
helping to create the best version of this book
possible—as always, you were right :). Thank you so
much to Doug Organ for the music industry
insights—amazingly cool guy and recording studio.
I could have stayed there all day! Special thanks to
recording artist Joal Kamps and his wonderful
manager Laurie Brown for their help and support
with this book. And thank you to Reagan for never
giving up on my dream, even when I do.

CHAPTER ONE

MELODY SNEEZED AND reached for a tissue from the magazine table of the walk-in medical clinic's crowded waiting room. Then she promptly pumped her hand sanitizer.

Lindsay Harper, the clinic's head nurse, looked over at her from where she was plugging in the artificial Christmas tree in the corner. "Not you, too, Mel," she said. The white, five-foot-tall decoration began to rotate, its multicolored LED lights twinkling in time to the sound of "Jingle Bells," which suddenly filled the air.

Melody could do without the reminder of the upcoming season. Christmas used to be her favorite time of year, but since Patrick's death, it only caused her stress—emotionally and financially.

"'Tis the season," she mumbled, sitting back in the plastic waiting-room chair she was sharing with her eight-year-old son,

Josh. Every year around this time, they both seemed to get sick. She could mark her calendar by it. December first—first day of the flu.

Josh's head fell against her shoulder, and with a scratchy voice he asked, "How much longer, Mom?" The fit of coughing that followed gained him sympathetic looks from some of the other waiting patients.

Melody wiped the boy's dark hair off his hot forehead and checked her watch. "Soon, sweetheart." She hoped. Her evening shift started in less than an hour. Thursday was one of the busiest nights at the bowling alley.

Josh's twin brother, David, who had been sleeping curled up in the chair next to them, stirred and opened his eyes slowly. "Mom, I don't feel so great."

"I know, sweetheart. We'll see the doctor soon."

Lindsay reappeared with their file and a sympathetic smile. She leaned close to Melody as she whispered, "I know you have to get to work, so I'm bumping you guys ahead."

"Thanks," Melody said, grateful for the gesture. Despite Lindsay's reputation as a party girl, she took her job seriously, and her affection for her patients, especially the young children, was obvious. Helping Josh to his feet and taking the hands of both her sons, Melody followed Lindsay down the hallway to an empty examination room. "Dr. McCarthy will be just a moment."

"Okay," Melody said, helping Josh onto the examination table, as David sat in the chair near the door. She buried a throaty cough in the crook of her arm and cringed. Each time she coughed, her chest hurt and her throat felt rawer than ever. If she was feeling this awful, she hated to think how Josh was feeling.

She yawned, shaking off a wave of exhaustion. She'd spent the night before sitting on the edge of Josh's bottom bunk, one hand propping up his pillow while he slept and the other continuously checking his forehead for a fever.

"Where are our pictures, Mom?" David asked, slumping against the back of his chair and studying the wall of photos of newborns. Dr. McCarthy was one of two pediatricians in Brookhollow and was essentially always on call. She'd delivered almost every baby born in the small New Jersey town in the past decade, including Melody's boys.

"Just look for the cutest ones," Melody whispered with a wink at the older twin, who had been born six minutes before his brother on November 2, in the middle of a hail-and-sleet storm. Patrick, a guitar player in a country band, had been performing in Beach Haven that night, two hours away, and had almost missed the delivery, rushing in just minutes before David's arrival. But he'd been there…

"There we are," David said.

Melody's heart swelled as it always did at the sight of the boys' baby photos. They'd looked so much like her husband in that first year, with their light hair and bright, crystal-blue eyes. Over time, their hair had darkened to the same chestnut-brown color as hers, minus the ever increasing gray ones that seemed to have arrived in the three years since Patrick's death. Despite the passing of time and the deepening lines on her face, it still felt as if he'd died yesterday. Seemingly overnight, she'd transformed from a stay-at-home mom with virtually no professional skills, to a working woman holding down several jobs and supporting a family on her own.

Dr. McCarthy knocked once on the door before walking in. "Hello, Myers family," she greeted, setting their files on the tiny desk in the room. "Let me guess—coughing, sneezing, fever and muscle aches?"

"Been seeing that a lot today?" Melody asked.

"When one person in Brookhollow gets sick, we all get sick," Dr. McCarthy said, placing a hand on Josh's forehead. "Part of small-town charm, I guess. Has he taken anything for his fever?" she asked as she reached for a tongue depressor. "Say 'aaah' for me, okay, buddy?"

"Children's Tylenol about two hours ago," Melody said.

Dr. McCarthy nodded as she looked at Josh's throat. "Strep is my guess, but we'll send a swab to the lab just to be sure." She swabbed his throat and placed the pad in a tube, which she then sealed and labeled. She turned to David. "Him, too?" she asked, sympathetically.

"I think so... Not as bad, yet," Melody said, before another sneeze escaped her.

"You don't sound too good yourself," the doctor said. She checked David's throat.

"I'm fine… I'm too busy to be sick." It was true. Three jobs didn't afford her the luxury of giving in to sickness, even if it meant she was spreading the contagion.

"I think it's strep over here, as well." Lifting the back of David's shirt, Dr. McCarthy listened to his breathing. "I'll give you a prescription for antibiotics for both of them." She scribbled a prescription. "And just continue the Tylenol every four to six hours for the fever… Do you want me to take a look at you, as well? I've heard you cough."

Melody shook her head as she accepted the prescription slip and helped Josh climb down from the table. "Thank you, Dr. McCarthy." Antibiotics for the boys would be expensive enough, and they needed the drug more than she did. If only her pending promotion with Play Hard Sports, the big sporting-goods store in town, could happen a little sooner. Medical coverage was a benefit enjoyed by a full-time management employee, which she hoped to become in a few days, after she'd completed the training course and written the final exam. She hoped the three months of study would pay off. With the raise in pay, she could quit her two evening jobs bartending—as long as she passed this one last exam.

She began to collect their belongings. She had half an hour to pick up their babysitter, Lauralee—a high school girl who'd been babysitting the boys for years—drop them all off at home, put their dinner in the oven and then get to the bowling alley. She'd be lucky if she had time to change out of her Play Hard Sports uniform. She prayed the predicted snow hadn't started yet. Her old minivan still had its summer tires and it would be at least a few weeks before there was money in her tight budget to take the vehicle into Bailey's Place to have new winter tires put on. She knew the mechanic, her future sister-in-law Bailey, would do the work without charging her, but she couldn't accept charity.

When Patrick was alive, he'd taken care of such things as the upkeep of the vehicles, or repairs to their old bungalow, which they'd bought as a fixer-upper ten years ago. As much as she loved the character-rich home, in recent years the maintenance had drained her limited funds. Still, the idea of selling the home where her family had made a lot of happy memories wasn't one she liked to entertain.

"Come on, guys," she said, taking Josh's hand.

"Mel, hang on a sec." Dr. McCarthy opened a locked mini fridge in the hallway near the file cabinets. Removing a white plastic bottle, she checked the label before handing it to Melody. "Here. This is essentially the same antibiotic I gave the boys— just a stronger dose. It's FDA-approved, but it's still in the clinical-trial stage, so it isn't being offered in pharmacies yet. It'll help with your cough."

Melody hesitated.

Dr. McCarthy reached for her hand and forced the medicine into it. "Take it. It's really not a big deal—I've been handing it out all week. Unfortunately, the dosage is too strong for the boys," she said, stopping in front of the door of the next examining room and turning her attention to a file.

"Thank you again, Dr. McCarthy," Melody said. Exchanges like this were so awkward. She longed for the day when her financial struggles weren't obvious to everyone in Brookhollow. But today wasn't that day. She was sick and she was expected to be behind the bowling alley bar in twenty-five minutes.

"THE KEY STEPS in performance-based management are…defining missions and goals," Melody muttered as she stacked clean beer mugs on the glass shelves behind the bar. The Thursday-night crowd at the bowling alley was full of the usual suspects. To her right, the over-thirty men's bowling league occupied eight of the twelve lanes, and to her left, several off-duty firemen played pool at the corner table. The front wooden doors opened and a group of twentysomethings entered. "Be with you guys in just a moment," she told them, turning to grab menus.

She noticed her brother approaching the bar. "Hey, Ethan, another round?"

"Just for those guys," he said, pulling out his wallet and nodding toward his fellow firefighters. "Bailey's off in ten minutes and I'm picking her up from the shop. I finally talked her into storing her motorcycle a few weeks ago."

Melody nodded her understanding. Ethan's fiancée, Bailey Sheppard, loved her motorcycle, and since Brookhollow had been blessed this year with a mild fall season, she had been able to ride the bike longer. "Have I mentioned how happy I am that you two finally got together?" Melody said, drawing the beer.

After years of friendship, Bailey and Ethan had finally realized what the whole town had known for years—they were perfect for each other. They'd gotten engaged three months before during a trip to Venice.

Ethan tossed enough cash on the bar to cover the group's tab, and added several additional bills to Melody's tip jar. "You and me both. I can't believe it took me so long to see how amazing she is." Then, noticing the textbook on the bar, he asked, "How's the studying?"

"A lot tougher than I'd expected." It was true. The three-month management-trainee program had included ten different instruction manuals, four exams and weeks of on-the-job training, in which she'd had to shadow a Play Hard trainer in his management role. "But it's worth it," she was quick to add. "I just wish I had more time to study. A lot is riding on this last exam."

"Well, you know Bailey and I would be happy to babysit the boys if you need some extra time."

"Thanks. I appreciate the offer. I wish it was just the boys keeping me busy, but honestly, I've been working such long hours lately, I barely have enough time with them as it is. I really hope I'll be able to give up these evening shifts soon."

The strong early December wind caught the front double doors as Heather, the part-time bartender, walked in, her long, dark hair blowing wildly around her pink cheeks. Tugging the doors closed behind her, she mumbled something unintelligible. "Sorry I'm late, Mel," she said, panting.

"Don't worry. It's just starting to pick up." She watched as Heather struggled to catch her breath. "Did you run here?" She shot a glance at Heather's feet. She was wearing five-inch-heeled, red leather, pointy-toed boots. Still, if anyone could run in them, the tall, slender, feisty brunette probably could. A New York City girl, she'd come to Brookhollow for the wedding of her friend Victoria

Mason, the owner of the B and B in town, to Luke Dawson, and had decided to stay. She said she'd taken a liking to small-town life. Melody was grateful to have someone to train to take over the bar once she left.

Heather took off her coat and hung it on the hook behind the kitchen door. "Practically. That piece-of-crap car I bought broke down again yesterday—it's still at the shop." She wrapped the black apron around her thin waist and smiled at Ethan. "Thank God for your fiancée. She rescued me from the side of the highway again last night."

"Bailey picked you up in the tow truck?" Ethan's annoyance was pretty obvious.

Heather hesitated and Melody waved her arms, shaking her head behind Ethan's back. Heather shot her a puzzled look as Ethan swung around to face her. "I saw that. She was supposed to have Nick doing the evening highway tows."

"Oops," Heather said sheepishly. "Didn't mean to get her in trouble."

Ethan grabbed the tray of drinks from the bar. "Don't worry. I suspected she was still doing the towing herself. Bye, ladies. Mel, good luck on the exam. Tell the boys I need them next week at hockey practice, so they should take it easy this weekend and get better."

In addition to working as a firefighter, her younger brother coached the junior boys' soccer, hockey and football teams. "Thanks. I will, but you know the boys—they'd play even if their limbs were falling off." Her twins had been born with athletic genes, and they rarely missed a practice.

She hoped they'd feel better once the antibiotics kicked in. Already her own symptoms appeared to be easing, for which she was grateful. Customers rarely appreciated being served by someone at death's door...

Heather saved Melody's textbook page with her finger as she closed the book to see the cover. "*Essentials of Management...* yuck." She wrinkled her nose. "How's that going?"

"It was going terribly. But it's much better now that I took your advice about writing my notes on index cards and leaving them all over the house. Now as I'm cooking or getting the boys ready for bed, I'm memorizing information." She covered a cough as she opened the dishwasher and loaded in the empty beer mugs. She'd never been great at academics, barely getting by in school, but this management course was important to her. The past three months, she'd pushed herself harder than she ever had before. She'd passed the three previous exams with a B average.

Heather collected more empty cups from around the bowling alley and set them on the bar before reaching for the television remote control. "Well, take a break. It's eight o'clock. Our show is on." She flipped through the stations on the flat-screen television above the bar. She passed the hockey game, ignoring the cries of protest from the men playing pool, and stopped on *American Voices*, the reality television competition they'd watched every Thursday night together since she'd started training at the bar.

A young woman wearing a black leather jumpsuit, was crooning a Sheryl Crow song. Heather folded her arms and leaned against the bar as she watched. "I still think you should have tried out when they were holding auditions in New Jersey, Melody. You can sing circles around these contestants."

She winced as the redhead struggled to hit a high note.

Melody took several shot glasses down from the shelf and refilled them with tequila as Mark Adams, a local firefighter and the biggest flirt in town, approached the bar. He asked for another round of shots. "Good luck, Heather. We've been trying to convince Mel to try out every season for three years."

"I'm too old, guys," Melody said, sliding the shot glasses toward him. She tossed her long, wavy chestnut hair over one shoulder as she added, "Besides, I gave up on that dream a long time ago."

At twenty-one, all she'd wanted to do was leave Brookhollow and move to Nashville to pursue a career in country music. But then she and Patrick had gotten married and the boys had arrived…and the dream had turned into more of a quiet longing.

She held up her textbook. "I have a new dream now." One that made sense. One she could depend on. One that would provide a secure future for her children. Nothing kept her more firmly planted in reality than two boys who needed new clothes, school supplies, sporting equipment and medicine.

Heather scoffed. "You'd be an instant star in Nashville and you know it. And you're always writing your own songs."

Melody's shoulders tensed. She wished Heather would drop the subject. She hadn't written a new song in a long time. Sure, she often hummed original tunes that popped into her head, or made up random lyrics, none of which she could ever remember afterward, but she hadn't actually put pen to paper in more than three years. Not since the last song she'd cowritten with Patrick.

After Patrick's death, a record label had approached her, offering to buy any original material Patrick may have had, but she'd been unable to sell the music they'd written together. She only had a few mementoes left of him—his lyrics and musical scores were vital to her.

"Oh, I love this guy," Heather said, her attention captured by the screen. "Victoria and I saw him in New York last summer when he opened for Toby Keith."

"Who?" Melody asked, turning to look at the television.

She lost her grip on the wet beer mug in her hand and it crashed to the floor, shattering in a million pieces at her feet.

Brad Monroe, her husband's former bandmate and friend, sat in the guest judge's seat on the critique panel, commenting on the girl's performance.

Her mouth went dry. She held on to the edge of the bar as the deep, husky voice she hadn't heard in years filled the heavy air around her.

"Mel, you okay?" Heather asked. She reached for the broom behind the kitchen door.

"I got it," Melody insisted, taking the broom from Heather with a shaky hand. "Um…do you mind if we turn that program off?" She knew her request would sound odd and would require an explanation, but she wasn't sure she could handle seeing Brad's carefree, handsome face at that moment— or ever. She'd been successful in avoiding that face for the three years since Patrick's funeral. She was sure she'd done the right thing by keeping Brad completely out of her and her sons' lives. The man had been responsible for her husband's death, and she felt unnerved enough just by the sight of him on television.

"Oh, sure." Heather quickly changed to the channel showing the hockey game and held the dustpan for Melody as she swept the broken glass onto it.

Heather's lack of protest spoke volumes. "Who told you?" Melody asked.

"Told me what?"

"About my late husband and Brad Monroe...uh...Jackson." The smug jerk had changed his last name to Jackson to sound more "country" when he'd left Brookhollow to pursue a record deal with Propel Records, a record deal that had launched his career. A career that should also have been Patrick's.

"I remember Victoria mentioning something about it after the concert when we bought his CD from the merchandise table. He'd mentioned your family in his acknowledgment section, and Vic recognized the connection."

Melody hadn't known. She'd refused to even look at his CD cover in the music store at the mall or talk about him with family and friends over the three years. So he'd acknowledged them—big deal. It didn't soften her feelings toward him, not one little bit. As she often told the boys, saying sorry might be the right thing to do, but it didn't erase the deed.

She emptied the broken glass into the trash can and leaned the broom against the bar. "What did Victoria tell you, exactly?"

"Not much," Heather replied. "Just that the three of you had a history."

History was an understatement. "We went to high school together, but Patrick was four years older than Brad, so they were never really friends. Brad and I were in the same classes, but I never knew much about him. I certainly wouldn't have expected him to be interested in music—he was always hanging around with the jocks and cheerleaders. Anyway, after one of Patrick's gigs about nine years ago in Beach Haven, where Brad happened to be vacationing with his girlfriend of the week, they caught up on old times and somehow the discussion turned to Brad's interest in music. Next thing I knew, Brad was joining the band." She couldn't keep the disdain from her voice.

She'd liked Brad just fine, but she'd always worried about his playboy influence on her husband when they were on the road—groupies were a simple reality. Her trust in Patrick had been unwavering, but his being with Brad had caused her concern. She wasn't thrilled about her husband playing wingman for the free-spirited bachelor, no matter how innocent the situation.

"Were you okay with that? Taking a step back?"

Not exactly, but she wasn't about to tell Heather about all of the arguments she and Pat had had over the decision. The decision that meant walking away from music. "I was pregnant with the boys at the time, so we'd decided it was best for me to step away from performing. Patrick was amazing on the guitar, but even he recognized they needed a new singer. Brad took over the microphone and we all became close friends as well as musical collaborators. Brad is even the boys' godfather." She paused. That had been Patrick's choice, not hers.

"Wow," Heather said. "But then the accident happened?"

Melody nodded. "The accident report revealed they'd both been drinking—they'd been celebrating the signing of their contract with Propel Records in New York." She paused, the words still hard to say, "Brad survived. Patrick didn't."

In truth, Brad had barely escaped the same fate. He'd suffered critical injuries and a severe concussion that had left him in the hospital for weeks. At Patrick's funeral, he'd been in a wheelchair.

"Brad was driving?" Heather guessed.

Melody nodded, clenching her hands into fists at her sides. How many times had she told Patrick that Brad couldn't be trusted when he was drinking? His judgment when sober had been questionable enough.

"And then he left town and that was it? You haven't heard from him since?" Heather frowned, her expression a mix of anger and sympathy.

"Yeah," Melody answered, avoiding Heather's gaze. It wasn't exactly the truth. Brad had attempted to contact them over the past three years, offering to help in any way he could—emotionally, financially— but Melody had put an end to the contact by changing the family's phone number and blocking any incoming emails from him.

She didn't want anything to do with Brad

Monroe or Jackson or whatever he called himself.

All she wanted were the things he'd taken away and couldn't give back—her husband and their dreams for the future.

"How did you get in here?"

"Oh, honey, please. I'm a publicist. I can talk my way into anywhere."

From the hot tub in the men-only section of BodyWorks, a therapeutic spa and chiropractic clinic in downtown Nashville, Brad watched as Roxanne Klein kicked off her designer shoes. Grabbing a towel to sit on, she lowered herself to the edge of the tub, sinking her tiny feet into the water. He rolled his eyes and then lowered his head back against the towel he had positioned behind him.

"Don't look at me like that," Roxanne said. "I asked the last guy I saw coming out if there was anyone else in here before going in."

And that made it okay? The woman was terrible. She had no sense of boundaries, although in truth, it was no doubt the reason she was so fantastic at her job. As one of Nashville's most sought-after publicists, she could turn acts no one had ever heard of into overnight successes. As much as he hated to admit it, she was worth the astronomical fee she charged—a fee he really couldn't afford. That's why he had put the fate of his career in her hands a year before.

So far she'd changed his hair color from light brown to blond and had forced him to buy colored, non-prescription contacts to hide the fact that his eyes were different colors—one a deep blue, the other a sea-foam green. She'd also changed his stage name from Monroe to Jackson and had ordered the name switch on his first CD cover before it had hit store shelves. He'd found out a week later when he'd seen it advertised in a flyer.

"Besides, I wouldn't have to resort to these measures if you'd stop avoiding my calls," she said, a chill in her Southern accent.

He felt it, despite the heat of the water. "I got your voice mails and I left you one of my own." He stood and pushed himself out of the hot tub. There was no relaxing around Roxanne.

Already, he felt his muscles tightening again after the two-hour session with his physical therapist. In the three years since the car accident, he had been going to therapy twice a week to build up the strength in his legs and back. Besides the countless broken bones, he'd had torn muscles and five dislocated disks in his spine.

Yet he'd been the lucky one.

"But you didn't give me the answer I wanted to hear." Roxanne kept her eyes on him as he made his way to the towels and wrapped one around his waist. Luckily, he always wore his swim trunks.

"Well, it's the only answer you're going to get." Brad raked a hand through his high-lighted hair and watched her as she swung her legs over the side of the tub and stood up. With her shoulder-length blond hair and big blue eyes, he might have found her attractive if she weren't always trying to convince him to do things he didn't want to do—such as her latest request.

Even in bare feet, Roxanne was almost as tall as the five-foot-eleven Brad. "Think about this rationally—it's television. So far, we've done the magazine articles, the talk radio, that one-time appearance on that music reality show, but we haven't been able to secure a prime-time spot focused on you as an artist. This is the opportunity we've been waiting for."

"Heartland Country Television is the opportunity we've been waiting for?" He raised an eyebrow. Roxanne could talk, and he suspected 99 percent of the time people bought everything she said. But even *she* had to know that calling Nashville's local country television station *prime time* was a stretch.

"Okay, so it's not Oprah—and don't think I haven't tried calling her—but it's a start. And their 'Home for the Holidays' episode is one of the most watched Christmas Eve programs. Apparently, people love seeing how stars spend their holidays," she insisted, following him to the men's change-room door.

"You can't come in here," Brad said, pausing with his hand on the door.

"Try to stop me."

He let out an exasperated sigh. "Roxanne, I won't do it. 'Home for the Holidays'… Do you even know what that means for me?" He shuddered at the thought of returning to his family home in Brookhollow, a place he hadn't dared visit in three years. He'd tried the year before when he'd been performing an hour from his hometown, but as the town-limits sign had come into view, he'd pulled a U-turn and hightailed it out of there. Facing his past, especially this time of year, would have destroyed him.

"Let me guess—your family's crazy? So? Whose isn't? Country music is about crazy mothers, alcoholic fathers, hillbilly farm life and broken-down trucks. Be the stereotype. Embrace it. Trust me, it will surprise you how fans love humble beginnings. It makes you more relatable—"

"Forget it, Roxanne. I don't think my family would go for it."

That was a lie. His mother and five older sisters would have eaten it up. Brookhollow did Christmas in a big way, with the color-fully decorated storefronts on Main Street, the twenty-foot evergreen erected in the town center, the parade and the horse-drawn sleigh rides through the park. He didn't even want to *think* about his own family's extreme holiday traditions. At Christmas, not an inch of wall space inside the home was visible beneath the garlands and wall hangings. Outside, the twelve thousand multicolored lights stapled to the roof lit up the entire neighborhood, and the large evergreen trees around the family farm were decorated with hundreds of baubles and bows. *Overdone* was an understatement. *Tacky* was more the word.

"Let me talk to them." She offered him a confident smile.

"No. And besides, you've changed my last name, remember?" How did she expect to pull that off?

"So, we'll change the name on your family's mailbox. I'm not seeing an issue here, Brad."

She was unbelievable. He didn't doubt for a second she would force his entire family to assume the surname *Jackson* for this publicity stunt. "Can we talk about this later? I'd like to get dressed now." He had no intention of resuming this conversation, but goose bumps were covering his bare skin now that he was out of the hot tub. Or maybe it was the icy chill he always felt around his publicist.

"Go ahead," she said with a shrug, daring him to force her to follow him into the change room.

"You're unreal, you know that?"

"It's called being persistent. It's why you hired me. I'm going to take your wavering resolve and lack of a snappy retort as agreement." She opened her shoulder bag and pulled out the contract for the television spot.

He accepted it with reluctance and scanned the pages. "You forged my signature?" Why her behavior still shocked him, he didn't know. By now, he knew there was no point in putting up a fight. Roxanne Klein didn't know the meaning of failure.

"Don't get caught up on morality," she said. "We needed to secure the last-minute spot before they gave it to some adorable seventeen-year-old kid who writes all his own songs and plays like eighteen instruments. I did what I had to do. I've also confirmed your travel arrangements to Brookville…"

"Brookhollow."

"Whatever. Middle of nowhere, New Jersey…" She positioned her aqua-blue heels on the concrete floor and held his shoulder for balance as she slid her feet into them.

"Are you going with me?"

"It's the holidays. Are you kidding? No." Her eyes fell to his torso and she frowned. "Have we talked about getting a plastic surgeon to look at those?" she asked, pointing to the scar tissue on his chest and upper abdomen.

"No, and we won't." He hoped his voice held enough conviction to make her drop the point.

"Fine. I'll take my victories where I can get them—we'll discuss it another time. You fly out on Monday morning. Bye, Brad."

Brad watched her saunter away. He ran a hand over his damaged skin.

He didn't doubt she would bring it up again, but removing the scars was something he would never consider. They were a permanent souvenir from a bad decision that had cost him so much, as well as a constant reminder that life was short.

Besides, unless the surgeon could remove the scars he carried on the inside, what would be the point?

CHAPTER TWO

"DAVID, COME ON. You're going to be late for school," Melody called down the hallway of her two-bedroom bungalow to the room the boys shared. Opening their matching superhero backpacks, she tucked their lunch tins inside before adding juice boxes and sandwich meat to the grocery list on the fridge. She hated running out of things on a Monday, which called for a between-jobs run to the grocery store. But with the three of them recovering from illness all weekend and her shifts at the bowling alley, there really hadn't been time.

"Worry about Josh!" David called back. "He's out in the shed again."

Melody moved to the kitchen window and looked across her backyard. The light in the shed was on, and through the open door she could see Josh sitting on the tiny sofa in what had once been the family's makeshift recording studio, his father's electric guitar on his lap. She sighed. He spent so much time out there trying to learn to play. She wished she knew how, but she'd never bothered to learn. Patrick had been playing since he was four years old, and he could play anything simply by hearing it. He'd taught Josh a few simple chords.

If only music lessons weren't so expensive, she would have signed both boys up for them. She was struggling just to keep the equipment. She hated the idea of selling Patrick's things, a few times in the past couple of years the idea had tempted her. She didn't go out to the shed anymore. The sight evoked memories that were too much to take, longings that were too hard to face. But she couldn't sell the equipment if Josh wanted to use it.

Leaning forward, she opened the window. She shivered in the blast of cold air. "Come on, Josh. Time for school," she called.

A minute later, the kitchen door opened and Josh entered, leaving a trail of wet snow on the floor. "Here's the mail, Mom."

She chose to ignore the mess and thank him for the gesture. Eight-year-old boys were oblivious to things like tracking mud or snow through the house. "Thanks, honey," she said, accepting the stack and tossing it into a bin on the counter. She unrolled a sheet of paper towel and bent to wipe up the clumps of snow.

"Aren't you going to check the mail?" Josh asked.

"I will later. We're in a bit of a hurry now." She didn't need to look through the stack to know it held an overwhelming number of overdue notices. Besides, this was exam day, and she was trying her best not to let anything frazzle her.

"But there might be something important in there," Josh persisted.

He was up to something. "You're right. I should probably check it now." Picking up the stack, she noticed a piece of blue construction paper sticking out of one corner. She pretended to flip through the rest. "Bills, bills…ah, what is this?" She shot a glance toward him, then pulled out the construction paper, which was folded like a greeting card. She read aloud, "'Good luck, Mom.'" On the front was a drawing of a bouquet of flowers and on the inside the boys had signed their names.

Josh's smile reached from ear to ear. "David and I made it with Lauralee last week. We didn't actually mail it," he confessed.

"Thank you, Josh. I love it." She gave him a hug. She didn't doubt the card had been his idea. Her boys may have been identical in appearance, but they had different personalities. Josh was more thoughtful than David, whose hardheadedness she knew he'd inherited from her. David kept his emotions to himself most of the time, while Josh was more like his father—open and kind. Tucking the card into her purse, she said, "Can you please go get that brother of yours? We're going to be late."

She checked her watch, noticing the slight trembling of her hand. She didn't feel nervous about the exam, though she suspected she must be, subconsciously. A lot was riding on this opportunity. She would feel much better about things once it was over. She was the only employee at the Brookhollow store who had completed the course, so she was confident the position would be hers if things went well today.

Flipping through the rest of the mail only reinforced how much she needed this promotion. The envelope for her power bill was stamped with a huge red *Final Notice*. The overdue stamp on the cable-bill envelope was smaller—it would have to wait. The boys would lose their minds if the cable was shut off, but sleeping in a cold, dark house would have been far worse. Hopefully, she'd be able to catch up on the outstanding debt in the first half of the new year.

As she placed a stack of flyers on the edge of the counter for recycling, another envelope fell to the floor. When she picked it up, her heart rate soared—it was from the Brookhollow Trust, her bank. It wasn't her usual bank statement, which always came in a white envelope, or the mortgage bill, which came in a small tan one. This was a thick, heavy legal-size manila envelope.

"Ready, Mom!" David announced, appearing in the doorway of the kitchen. He grabbed his backpack and tossed Josh's to him.

"Okay, take the keys and go get in the van. I'll be right out. Don't forget your hat and gloves." She returned her attention to the envelope as the boys disappeared down the hall. She waited until she heard the front door close before she opened the mailing. She paused. Did she really need to read this now? Maybe she should wait until the evening. But if she didn't, it would be on her mind all day, anyway.

Inside was a copy of the mortgage and a statement summary showing the current balance and payment history. She swallowed hard. Six missed payments that year. Had it been that many? She'd expected two, maybe three, but six? She scanned the missed months. Yeah, six was correct. Money had been tight that year, especially with David needing glasses for school and the front window of the house needing replacing after Josh had thrown a baseball through it that summer.

She turned to the last page, which was a letter from Jeff Thompson, the bank's branch manager and a guy she'd gone to school with. Now their boys played together on the same hockey team. Her knees all but gave way beneath her as she read.

Dear Ms. Myers,

We regret to inform you that due to the arrears owing on your mortgage, we are obligated to ask for payment to bring your account up-to-date. If you are unable to settle the debt, we will be forced to foreclose on the property as of January 1…

The letter continued, but that was all she needed to read. They were going to take her house? The room around her began to spin, and the little blue flowers on the outdated wallpaper she'd loved when they first moved in danced around her. She closed her eyes in a desperate attempt to stop the spinning. January 1 was less than a month away. Even with the promotion, she wasn't sure if she could settle the debt that quickly. Thirty-two-hundred dollars just to bring the payments up-to-date. She folded the letter and slid everything back into the envelope, then hid it under the stack on the counter. She forced herself to take several deep breaths as the van's horn sounded outside. The exam needed to be her only focus. She would figure this out. She always did. There was no way she was losing her family's home.

THE STAFF LUNCHROOM in the back of the Play Hard Sports store served as the exam room. Melody and two other management trainees competing for the same position at the Newark store sat in the overheated room waiting to begin. Again, she was relieved there had been no one else interested in the position in the Brookhollow store. The whole process had been stressful enough, and she'd have hated to compete for the promotion. Staring at the closed booklet, she replayed over and over the things she'd studied. Heather had taught her to visualize charts and definitions in order to recall them more easily during the test, but today whenever she closed her eyes, all she saw was the notice from the bank. She forced all thoughts of that morning's disturbing news away. The exam facilitator, a woman from head office, checked her watch and told them to begin.

Melody opened the exam booklet and scanned the first section. She felt the tension in her shoulders begin to melt. Product knowledge—her strongest subject. Not only had she worked in the store for eight months, but she also had the advantage of growing up with two athletic brothers. Now her boys were playing on every sports team in town. Sports equipment was something she knew. She flew through the hundred multiple-choice questions quickly, never second-guessing her answers.

The next section was tougher—questions about the principles of management—but as she skimmed them, images of the cue cards around her house popped into her mind. *Thank you, Heather.* Furiously, she scribbled detailed responses and even provided examples that weren't required. Better to give too much in the way of an answer than not enough.

As she turned to the last section an hour later, she felt her cell phone vibrate. She'd put the cell in her purse, which was sitting on the floor against the chair leg. Who was trying to reach her at twelve-thirty on a Monday afternoon? Everyone knew she was writing an exam at that time. She contemplated not reaching for it…but what if it was an emergency? When the boys weren't with her, she liked to be available. Lowering her right hand, she slid the zipper open on the purse and glanced down to see the caller ID. Brookhollow Elementary. The boys' school never called unless they were sick or injured.

"Um, excuse me," she said to the exam moderator.

"Yes?" The woman looked up from the home-and-garden magazine she was reading.

The other two employees glanced up from their exams.

"Sorry," Melody said. "It's my son's school. Can I take it outside?" She held the vibrating phone.

The woman shook her head. "I'm sorry, but if you leave the testing area, you can't reenter."

"Well, can I answer it quickly here?"

"No."

Melody stared at the vibrating phone. She was almost done the exam. Another hour at most. Could the call wait? The exam was too important to mess up, especially now, but family always came first. What was she supposed to do? If she left the exam, she wouldn't get the promotion and the kids would suffer...but what if one of them were hurt? Damn it. "I'm sorry, I have to take this." She grabbed her purse and rushed from the room, dropping the unfinished exam on the facilitator's desk as she passed. "Hello?" she said as the room door closed behind her.

"Melody?"

She recognized the school secretary's voice. "Yes, Amy. Are the boys okay?" She pushed her purse strap up her arm as she rushed down the hockey stick aisle in the showroom toward the front doors.

"It's David." The woman paused.

If only I could reach through the phone and strangle this woman. "Is he hurt?"

"No. He's suspended."

Melody struggled to catch the phone as it slipped from her fingers. David was suspended? How was that possible? He was a good kid. Sure, he'd been going through a bit of a rebellious phase lately, but that was normal for a boy his age, wasn't it? Brookhollow Elementary never suspended anyone. At least this was the first suspension she'd ever heard of. "Why?"

"I'd rather tell you in person. Can you come to the school?"

Did she have a choice? "Yes, of course. I'll be there soon," she said. She disconnected the call.

Outside in the parking lot, she struggled with the stubborn handle on the minivan, her anxiety making her oblivious to the bitter cold whipping through her long-sleeved, ribbed shirt. She'd forgotten her winter coat in her haste to leave the exam room and answer her vibrating phone. "Come on," she muttered, yanking the handle and steadying herself as the door flew open. Inside, her hand shook as she shoved the key in the ignition and reached for her seat belt. The strap wouldn't budge, and glancing down, she saw it was trapped in the door. "Seriously?" Swinging the door open again, she freed the seat belt and slammed the door shut.

She tore out of the parking lot. The tires spun on a snowy patch and she cringed. She really couldn't put off getting those winter tires any longer. Maybe she needed to allow Bailey to do them for free. If the boys got hurt because of the useless vehicle, she would be devastated.

As she drove, her mind reeled. Her son

was suspended. Of all things. Of all days. What possibly could have happened that would have warranted a suspension. Lost in thought, she almost didn't hear the wail of a police siren behind her. That couldn't be for her…but a glance at the speedometer confirmed it was. She checked the rearview mirror, hit the brake slowly and pulled the van to the side of the road. She rolled down the window and waited, rubbing her arms for warmth. The van's heater was useless.

"In a rush?" her father asked, coming up to the open window a minute later.

As the town police chief, her father took his job seriously. She just hoped he'd give her a break this time. A speeding ticket was the last thing she needed. "Hi, Dad. I'm sorry. I wasn't really paying attention to the speed."

"A tip? That's not the best response to offer a police officer who pulls you over for dangerous driving, Melody."

"Sorry," she mumbled, shivering.

"Where's your coat?" He frowned.

"I forgot it at work—I'm on my way to Brookhollow Elementary," she said reluctantly. Her family members were always offering unsolicited advice on her life choices and the way she was raising the boys. They criticized her independence, claiming she should ask for help more often.

Her father's face changed in an instant from annoyed cop to worried grandfather. "The boys okay?"

She hesitated. She hated to tell anyone, including her family, if one of the boys had done something that appeared to be less than perfect. In their eyes, it was a reflection of her lack of parenting skills. "David has been suspended."

"What did he do?"

She stiffened. Without the details, she refused to judge her son's actions as being right or wrong. "I don't know, but I'm on my way there now, Dad."

"Do you want me to come with you?"

She shook her head. She didn't want her son to feel ganged up on. The boys were close to their Grandpa Bishop, and she knew they would hate to disappoint him. Besides, having the town's squad car parked in front of the school would just cause panic. "No, thank you. I've got it under control."

"Okay," he said, "but please slow down. You're lucky it was me on patrol."

Who else would it have been? Her father's partner had retired two years before, and he'd been the only law enforcer in the town since. Finding a new sheriff was proving to be difficult. "You're the only one in town."

"For now," he said, sounding noncommittal. "Anyway, slow down. I *will* give you a ticket next time."

He didn't make idle threats. "Okay. Oh, and, Dad, don't say anything about David…"

"You know I won't. If you need anything…" He shrugged and shook his head. "You still won't call," he finished. "Bye, darling."

"Bye, Dad." Melody rolled up the window and waited until he was back in the squad car before pulling the van onto the road. She wished her family could understand her need to do things on her own. It was against their advice that she'd started dating Patrick…and then married him. They'd claimed that as a musician, he didn't have a steady income. When she'd gotten pregnant with the boys, they'd questioned his commitment to his family, what with him being on the road almost every weekend. But she'd believed in him. In them.

Pushing the thoughts away, she parked the van in the parents'-pickup-only parking near the front of the school. She jogged through the slushy puddles of melted snow and ice in her running shoes, toward the entrance. Inside, she stomped her feet on the mat before making her way to the principal's office. Michael Thompson sat on the bench outside the door, an ice pack pressed to his eye. *Oh, no,* she thought as realization dawned on her. The two boys had been on the outs lately. She'd noticed the looks between them at hockey practice, and David hadn't invited Michael to their house since the first week of school. Come to think of it, Michael hadn't attended the boys' birthday party last month, either. "Hi, Michael," she said.

He ignored her, simply turning his tear-stained cheeks away.

Entering the principal's office, she saw David, head in his hands, slumped over in a chair across from the secretary. His eyes met Melody's and a look of sadness flickered in them momentarily before it was replaced with stubbornness and anger. She was taken aback—she'd never seen such a look on his young face before. But she was relieved to see he wasn't hurt. Michael was much taller and heavier than David.

Melody directed her gaze at the secretary, Amy. "So what's going on?" She resolved to give David the benefit of the doubt. Let him explain what had happened between Michael and him. Her own parents had always treated their children fairly in disciplinary situations, and it was a practice she'd adopted with her own children.

"Principal Andrews has ordered a two-day suspension for David," Amy said as she stood and slid the paperwork toward Melody.

Melody stared at her. "Why?" She could guess, but she wanted to know for sure.

"Physical violence against a classmate. The school has a zero-tolerance policy." Amy pointed to that section of the report.

That was all it said. No explanation of what had transpired between the boys to cause the fight. "Do we know what happened?"

Amy shook her head. "It was during lunchtime, and the teacher on duty arrived after it occurred. Principal Andrews questioned David a few minutes ago, but David refused to say what had provoked him."

Well, something clearly had. Neither of her children had ever demonstrated violent tendencies before. Not even in sports. "Is Principal Andrews available?" Melody refused to sign the suspension form without first receiving more information. A suspension stayed on the child's permanent school record—it wasn't something to be taken lightly.

"He's with the Thompsons now. I can schedule you for tomorrow sometime," she said, glancing at her calendar.

Melody had to work the following day at Play Hard Sports, and after running out on the exam, she couldn't ask for more time off. "That won't work. I'll have to call in the morning to set up a meeting later in the week." Inwardly, she winced. Because of her busy work schedule, things like this were always being put off—important things, things that should be top of her priority list. But then where would eating and having a roof over their heads fall?

"Okay. I'll still need your signature on the suspension form, though."

"I'll sign it once I speak to Principal Andrews." She turned to David. "Let's go."

David stood, pushing the chair roughly against the wall behind him.

"You're on thin ice," Melody warned.

He scowled as he left the office and glared at Michael as he passed him.

Melody waited until he'd climbed into the van beside her before she spoke. "What happened?"

David only stared outside, his lips locked.

"I can't talk to Principal Andrews about lifting the suspension if I don't know what happened."

Still nothing.

"Did Michael hit you?" David didn't appear to have any marks, but maybe…

Nothing.

"Did he say something to upset you?"

Silence.

Melody fought to keep her exasperation at bay. Today was not the day for her son to be stubborn. She couldn't help him if he refused to talk. "David, talk to me."

"He deserved it" was all David said.

"No one deserves a black eye. Not for any reason. You know that. I thought Michael was your friend. What's been going on with you two?"

"None of your business."

Melody gaped. Who was this kid in her van? Not the child she'd raised to have manners and be respectful. "Excuse me? It *is* my business when my son gets suspended for violence." She took a deep breath. Stay calm, she reminded herself. She'd get nowhere by yelling. "I can't help you if you won't talk to me."

"You never have time to listen, anyway."

The hurtful words tore a hole through her heart. She knew he missed having her around, the way she had been when Patrick was alive, but what choice did she have? She had been so close to changing things. Hadn't she explained that to him? With the promotion from Play Hard would have come the opportunity to make things better with her children. To spend more time with them. "I'm listening *now.*"

His defiant stare met hers and sent a shiver through her. "I've got nothing to say *now.*"

"SO TELL ME about your family," Bridget Marilyn asked in her smooth Southern drawl. She had warm, chocolate-colored eyes and dark hair that curled around her shoulders, which were only partially concealed by her pink tank top. Under any other circumstance, sitting next to the beautiful woman with the sun-kissed skin and Southern manners for two hours on the plane from Nashville to New Jersey would have been Brad's idea of the perfect way to travel. Now he just hoped the woman had packed a warm coat and wouldn't bail on the interview the moment she arrived in cold Newark, only to learn there was still an hour's drive to Brookhollow. "Roxanne says y'all are very close."

Roxanne. The definition of a troublemaker. "Uh…she may have stretched the truth a little. I haven't been home in a while, but we used to be close." When the brunette's perfectly arched eyebrows met in the middle, he added, "I've just been so busy these last few years." As much as he'd initially been opposed to the idea of this television segment, after he'd agreed, he'd done his research. It turned out Roxanne may not have been lying about this "Home for the Holidays" Christmas Eve program having done wonders for the careers of several other up-and-coming performers. He'd found three separate lesser-known acts that had become headliners after appearing on the show. Of course, they'd also recorded breakout hits shortly afterward, something else Brad had yet to do. His first CD was good, but none of its singles had skyrocketed to the top of the country music charts.

"That's only natural," Bridget said, smiling once more as she crossed one long leg over the other. She wore a pencil skirt and stilettos, and Brad had a difficult time picturing her in his mother's messy home. Of course, Beverly Monroe preferred the term "lived-in" when referring to the state in which she kept the family's two-story farmhouse. He hoped she allowed the staging crew to make the necessary changes for filming. "And it's yourself and five older sisters?"

"Yes, that's right. Bobbi, Becky, Brooke, Bethany and Breanne."

Bridget laughed. "And your parents, Beverly and Bernie. I assume the B names were on purpose?"

"Yes. You'll fit right in." Brad liked how

at ease she made him feel. He'd expected the famous Heartland Country Television host to be standoffish, but she was anything but. "We're all about two years apart, with Bobbi being the oldest—though she will deny having just turned forty-five until she's blue in the face—and me being the baby."

"Five girls and finally a boy."

"I love to tease my sisters that my parents had been hoping each of them were a boy." He stretched his legs out in the limited space in front of him. His right shin ached as it always did when he sat for long periods of time. The muscles in the front of that leg had taken a lot longer to heal than the others, and they still gave him trouble.

"And the family home is…"

"It's a farm on the outskirts of Brookhollow. Three hundred acres of land. We grow crops and Christmas trees. As a kid, I worked the Christmas-tree part with my father." It had always been one of the highlights of the season for him. Away from the house of six women, Brad and his father had bonded in those silent moments on the farm.

"I can't say I've ever been to a Christmas-tree farm. Growing up, we had an artificial tree—not quite the same experience, I bet."

Brad grinned. "Yeah, that's a little different. My youngest sister, Breanne, and her husband, Troy, took over running the farm during the holidays four years ago when my dad got sick. Of all us kids, she's the only one who still lives in Brookhollow. She and Troy live in the family farmhouse with my mom and their two children, Gracie and Darius." The mention of his young nephew made him pause as a wave of guilt washed over him. The six-year-old boy suffered from what the doctors called select mutism. He refused to talk to most people, with the exceptions of his older sister, Gracie, and for some reason, Brad. It had made Brad's absence from home over the past few years that much tougher, especially on Darius.

"I did my research on Brookhollow last night," Bridget said, "and it seems the town has some impressive holiday traditions, as well—sleigh rides, an ice-sculpting contest…"

The small town of less than ten thousand did indeed do Christmas in a big way. As a kid, Brad had loved the festivities, and spending the holidays in Nashville the past three years just hadn't been the same. Still, returning home hadn't felt like an option. His past mistakes haunted him even more the closer he got to town. He let out a deep breath. Like it or not, he would have to face them now.

"Yeah, if it's Christmas spirit you're looking for, Brookhollow's the place."

ARRIVING IN HIS HOMETOWN four hours later, the television camera crew and Bridget had gone straight to the Brookhollow Inn, the local B and B, to check in. Brad had continued on in the rental car toward his family home. Now as he drove the familiar roads, the knot in his stomach grew tighter. The last time he'd gone through this area was the day after Patrick's funeral. Despite his still being confined to a wheelchair in a disoriented state, he'd known he had to get away. Against the doctor's recommendations and his family's protests, he'd enlisted the help of his good friend Luke Dawson. With Dawson's Architecture working on large projects in New York, Luke had sublet an apartment in the city for himself and his crew, and he'd let Brad stay there during his recovery, to be closer to Propel Records. It was that fragile period during which Brad had feared the record company might cancel the entire recording deal. He owed a great deal to Luke. He pulled onto the shoulder to dial his friend's number, and then put on the headset and pulled back onto the road.

Luke answered on the third ring. "Hey, man. So, are the rumors true?"

"Depends on which ones you're referring to," Brad said, slowing again as the two lanes narrowed to one leading onto Main Street.

"Well, my beautiful new bride is now co-owner of the Brookhollow Inn, and their reservation system shows three rooms currently being held for Heartland Country Television—I know they're not here to interview me."

"That's right, I'd heard Vic bought the old inn last year. And again, I'm so sorry I missed the wedding." Luke's high school sweetheart had returned to Brookhollow last Christmas after twelve years in New York City. Soon after, her and Luke had gotten married. Brad had been performing at a

Labor Day Red Cross charity event in Oklahoma and hadn't been able to make it to the September long-weekend wedding. He chose to believe he would have manned up and made it for his good friend's wedding if his record contract hadn't demanded otherwise.

"Believe me, your gift made up for it." Luke laughed. "Victoria said the day at the Mandara Spa in the Bahamas was exactly the relaxation she'd needed. So, when do you arrive?"

"Just got here," Brad said, taking in the festive sights lining both sides of Main Street. The lampposts, decorated in large, white snowflakes, were coming to life as dusk fell over the town, and the storefront windows on both sides of the street were illuminated with holiday displays. He waved as he passed Mr. O'Hanlon, owner of the horse stables in town, who was waiting near the town park's entrance for the sleigh to arrive so he could fill it for the first ride of the evening. As Brad approached the corner of Main Street and Commerce Avenue and the bowling alley's neon sign came into view, he couldn't help but ask Luke, "Hey, does Melody still work at the alley?" The last he'd heard, his old friend was working several jobs, and bartending at the local hot spot was one of them. He prayed that was no longer the case, that things were getting easier for the Myers family. He'd respected Melody's wishes and had ended his attempts to contact them, but time had yet to erase them from his thoughts.

"I think she might've quit last week—got a promotion with Play Hard Sports. At least that's what Vic's friend Heather said. Heather's taking over Melody's job at the bar."

Relief flowed through Brad. Maybe Melody was doing okay. "I guess that store wasn't such a bad idea, after all," he teased his friend. The big-chain sporting-goods store had been the reason Victoria Mason had returned to Brookhollow the year before. She'd been working for an acquisition firm that was looking to buy out the town's local store in order to open Play Hard. At the time, Luke had owned Legends Sporting Goods and had been reluctant to sell it— though his success rate in refusing Victoria anything she wanted had never been great.

"Yeah, yeah, like I haven't heard that a million times in the last year. I can admit when I'm wrong. So how long are you in town?"

The million-dollar question. The recording was scheduled to be done in three days, and he'd planned to leave as soon as they finished. He knew in three days, he'd probably see a lot of old faces, but he hoped to avoid as many confrontations as possible. He doubted Patrick's family and friends had forgiven him for the accident. Hell, he hadn't forgiven himself. And he didn't want his presence in town to ruin anyone's holiday season. "Just a few days," he answered.

"Well, I hope you weren't planning to leave without playing a few rounds of pool."

"Of course not." He checked the time on the dash. It was after seven already. His niece and nephew would probably be in bed. One quick game with Luke might be just what he need before facing his family. He wasn't sure what kind of welcome they'd give him after him being away for three years and now expecting them to go along with this publicity stunt. He swallowed yet another pang of guilt. Yep, he was definitely too chicken to go home just yet.

CHAPTER THREE

"'NONE OF YOUR BUSINESS.' Can you believe he said that?" Melody asked, hanging a tangled set of white Christmas lights on the mirror behind the bar. If she'd had her way, they would have been in the trash can. But the bowling alley's owner, Mr. Ericksen, who lived just outside of Brookhollow and rarely visited the bar, had of course decided to make an appearance earlier that day and had wondered why the festive decorations had yet to be hung. With the week she was having, Melody marveled at her restraint in not telling the older man where he could put his decorations.

"Kids are getting lippier all the time," Heather said, pouring several beers for the over-sixty men's bowling league, their only patrons on the slow Monday night. "I'm just so disappointed you didn't get to finish that exam. It sounds like you were doing well. And you're sure you have to wait three months before writing it again?"

"That's what my boss's assistant said when I called this afternoon, but I'm not done trying to convince them otherwise," she said. She climbed down from the bar stool, only to notice the string of lights wasn't straight. "Seriously, these lights are going to be the death of me."

"Here, let me do it." Heather moved Melody aside.

"Thanks," Melody muttered. "I'm not exactly in a fa-la-la kind of mood." After the events with David, she hadn't had much time to think about the consequences of not finishing the exam that afternoon, but now she was desperate to come up with a way to save her family's home. Christmas was the furthest thing from her mind. "I was hoping to be done working here this week." That wouldn't be happening now, and that meant fewer shifts for Heather, who'd mentioned her own savings were quickly depleting from her lack of steady work.

"Hey, don't sweat it," Heather said. "I'm not kicking you out." She studied Melody for a long moment. "I know this may be a dumb question given the day you've had, but are you okay?"

Melody knew where the question was coming from. Normally, these small setbacks were things she could deal with. The challenges of raising the boys on her own or working hard and long to make ends meet were things she dealt with every day. Obviously, Heather could sense there was more she wasn't disclosing. Melody hesitated, not sure whether to mention the foreclosure. The two women had grown close in the three months that Heather had been in Brookhollow, and Melody already counted her among her good friends. "Can I tell you something?"

"Without everyone in Brookhollow finding out by morning? Of course."

"I got a foreclosure notice from the bank today."

Heather's face fell as she slid off the stool. "That's awful, Mel. I'm so sorry… And now the promotion…"

Melody nodded. "Yeah, I'm in a tight spot." She leaned against the bar. Exhausted and defeated, she barely had enough energy to hold herself up. "They've given me until

January 1," she said through a yawn. "And honestly, I have no idea what to do. I don't think I can physically work any more hours, and with Christmas coming up…" In the past few years, when met with adversity, she'd always figured something out. But in this case, she wasn't sure she could. Thirty-two-hundred dollars for the mortgage might as well have been a million. She could work twenty-four hours a day for the rest of December and still come up short.

"I know you may not like what I'm about to suggest, but have you considered asking your parents for a loan?"

She had considered it a hundred times that day. She'd also dismissed it a hundred times. The day she'd married a broke musician, she'd given up her right to her family's financial support. Besides, her parents weren't exactly rich. They just lived within their means. Going to them looking for a handout was out of the question. Hadn't she been the one to say she could take care of herself and the boys? And after David's suspension, the last thing she wanted was a lecture about her parenting skills. "I can't."

"They are your family. They are supposed

to help you…to support you," Heather insisted.

"They would if I asked, but I have my pride, you know," Melody replied. "They didn't approve of Patrick, or of us buying that old house. I can't bear the thought of them saying, 'I told you so.' I'd have to admit to having made mistakes."

"It wasn't any mistake of your own that landed you in this situation, Mel," Heather said.

No, it was Brad Monroe's mistake that had caused her life to start spiraling out of control. "Anyway, I'm sure I'll figure this out… I do have a few options." A few options she'd never been in a tough enough spot to consider until now.

She saw Luke and Victoria walk in, and noticed the buttons on Victoria's coat were undone. The pretty blonde co-owner of the Brookhollow Inn was the definition of a blushing bride—though Melody suspected her new glow was from something else entirely. "When is Vic going to tell everyone she's pregnant?" she whispered to Heather. She waved to the couple, her troubles momentarily put aside.

Heather laughed. "She won't even admit it to me. I think she's terrified to say it out loud."

"Well, she can only hide it for so long," Melody said as Victoria approached her, a worried frown on her face.

Luke waited by the door. He opened it every few seconds to glance outside.

"Hey, Victoria. What's up with him?" Melody nodded toward Luke.

"Oh, nothing. We just stopped in to say hi, but we're probably not going to stay. I, uh, thought you were done here at the bar." Victoria kept glancing nervously toward the door.

"That wasn't a sure thing…"

"She didn't trust me to work here alone just yet," Heather said, coming to her rescue. "You okay, Vic?"

The front door opened again, and Victoria didn't have time to answer, as all three women turned toward it.

Luke's eyes widened and Heather gaped, but Melody stood frozen, calmly fighting her desire to escape the room as soon as Brad Monroe entered it, dusting snowflakes from his blond hair. He turned toward the bar, and when his gaze met hers, it looked panicked. What was Brad Monroe doing in Brookhollow? He hadn't come home for Christmas or for anything else, much to her relief, in three years. Now here he was, on one of her worst days, standing right in front of her, bringing the day down to a whole new level of awful.

No one moved. No one spoke for a long moment.

Heather broke the silence. "He shouldn't be here," she hissed to Victoria.

"I know. We're leaving." She looked at Melody. "We didn't expect you to be here, Mel." Her tone was apologetic.

Tearing her gaze from Brad's and remembering to breathe, Melody said, "No, it's okay, really. Stay." The words were said through clenched teeth. She picked up three menus and slapped them onto the counter in front of Victoria. The bar was a public place, after all. Brookhollow was Brad's hometown—this had been bound to happen someday. She'd have preferred it not be today, but she refused to give Brad Monroe the satisfaction of seeing her become frazzled by his sudden appearance.

"No, Mel, we don't want to upset you…" Victoria stammered. The men were still standing near the door.

Mel forced a cold smile. "Do I look upset? Please stay."

Victoria hesitated before shaking her head. "Okay, I guess we will."

Melody watched as Victoria approached the men, said something and practically dragged them to a booth in the corner. She slid her damp palms down her black apron and steadied her shaky knees as she went around the side of the bar.

"Where are you going?" Heather blocked her path.

"To take their order."

"No way. I can't believe you even let him stay. And that's my table, anyway, so get back behind the bar."

"Seriously, Heather, I've got this. I'm fine," she said firmly.

Heather touched her arm. "No one's buying it, Mel."

Why should they? She was not fine. Her life was slowly unraveling, and Brad Monroe's appearance had just severed the last remaining tie.

"I THOUGHT YOU said the coast would be clear," Brad said to Luke as he watched Melody and the other bartender talking across the room. Her cold, hard stare had rattled him. His worst nightmare had come true.

"I thought it would be," Luke said. He helped Victoria remove her coat and hang it on the side of the booth. "Uh-oh, that's Heather coming to serve us. She's Vic's New York friend."

"She and Mel have grown close, but don't worry, her bark is worse than her bite," Victoria said quickly. She slid into the booth next to her husband just as Heather stopped in front of the table.

"Are you crazy, Luke?" were Heather's first words.

"Hi, Heather. Nice to see you, too," he said.

She placed her hands on her hips. "You need to leave. He isn't welcome here." She shot Brad a piercing glance.

Wow, Brad thought, *her bark is pretty bad.*

"Heather, this is my friend Brad Monroe," Luke continued, unfazed.

"Well, we have the right to refuse service…" Heather said.

"Don't worry about me—I don't drink," Brad said, leaning back in the seat. He brought his gaze to Mel across the bar, searching her face for any sign of peace or forgiveness, but couldn't find even the smallest trace in her disapproving glare.

He'd often seen the same glare in the past, albeit for far less reason. She'd never fully trusted him or approved of his playboy lifestyle, and she'd been worried whenever he and Patrick had been on the road together. Like the day they'd met with the Propel Records executive in New York.

He'd been a mess of anxiety and excited nerves as they'd waited for the executive, Hank Miller, to finish listening to their demo. Six months of daily phone calls from Arnie, their manager, to the guy who had finally landed them an appointment in Hank's New York office three weeks before Christmas.

Hank had sat quietly as the first three songs played from start to finish. There'd been no indication as to whether he'd liked or disliked them. Somehow Patrick had remained calm and cool, at least on the outside, but across from him, Brad was sweating. When the fourth song started and the executive reached forward to shut it off, staying quiet proved impossible for Brad.

"That's the best one on the CD," he'd said. The man had to listen to that one. Turning them down without hearing their best song would have been torture. Damn it. He'd told Pat to put that song first.

"I've heard enough," Hank had said, his face still revealing nothing.

Brad had glanced at Patrick. Man, his friend should have played poker. His face, too, had been unreadable. How had those guys been so good at hiding their emotions? Brad had stood and started pacing behind their chairs.

"Brad, have a seat," Hank had said. "Is he always this wound up?" he'd asked Patrick.

"He just needs a drink—he'll be fine," Patrick had answered.

The truth had been he'd already had two, compliments of the flask in the glove compartment of his Mustang. Brad had then sat down.

"I like what you guys are doing," Hank had finally said. "It's fresh and different."

Fresh and different. That was good. So why had his heart begun racing even faster?

"Give me an hour," Hank had said, "and I'll send the contract paperwork to Arnie."

Brad's mouth had fallen open. Patrick had smiled. And then Hank had ushered them out of his office.

"Did that just happen?" Brad had asked as they'd exited the building on Fifth Avenue into blowing snow that had started while they'd been in the meeting.

"Yes, my friend, it did." Patrick had hugged him.

"How are you still so calm? I was totally losing it up there. What if he'd said no? Were you really that confident?" Brad had asked as they'd made their way into a small pub a block away.

"No, but as they say, you fake it till you make it, man. And we made it." Patrick had reached for his phone as they'd settled into a corner booth.

"Calling Mel?"

He'd nodded and a second later a wide smile had spread across his face as he'd said, "Hey, baby, we got it."

From across the booth, he'd heard Mel's

excited squeal and then tiny voices on the line. He'd looked away and flagged the waitress.

"What can I get you boys?" the pretty red-headed waitress had asked with a flirtatious smile.

"Four tequila shots and your phone number, please," Brad had said with a wink.

He heard Patrick say on his phone, "Yes, we're just grabbing a quick drink and then we will be on the road…No, just one…It's fine…"

Brad had shifted uncomfortably in his seat. He'd known Mel liked him enough, but he'd also known she saw him as a bad influence on her husband. Maybe he had been, but she had absolutely nothing to worry about. Patrick hadn't been able to see past his wife and kids. It would have surprised the couple to know that Brad was jealous of what they had. Their life had seemed so perfect, and their dream of a future in music had been finally happening, as well.

"I promise you, there's nothing to worry about," Patrick had said. "I'll be home soon."

Brad had been responsible for making Patrick break that promise to his family.

Seeing Melody now made it hard to breathe. She'd been right. They should have listened to her, skipped the drink and headed straight home after the meeting. Patrick would still have been there if they had. Clearing his throat, Brad said, "I think we really should leave."

Heather looked relieved. "I think that's a good idea."

A few moments later they were standing outside, Luke's arm draped around Victoria's shoulders as the three walked to their vehicles in the parking lot. "Sorry about that, man. We thought she was done working there."

"Yeah, it's strange," Victoria said. "Heather told me her promotion with Play Hard was to take effect this week if the final exam went well." She frowned.

"It's my fault," Brad said. "And I wasn't exactly expecting a warm welcome from anyone in town, anyway." He'd reached the passenger door of Luke's truck and opened it for Victoria.

"Thank you," she said, hoisting herself up.

He closed the door and turned to Luke.

"Well, thanks for trying, man." He shoved his hands into his pockets.

"You're welcome to come back to our place…"

Brad glanced to where Victoria was resting her head against the seat and closing her eyes. His friends may not have told anyone yet, but it was pretty obvious they were expecting their first child. "Maybe not tonight. She looks exhausted. I'll stop by before I leave town," he said.

"Okay." Luke extended his hand. "And hey, man, I didn't know you were sober…"

Brad gave his friend a quick hug. "Two years, eleven months and four days." Every day brought its own challenges and rewards. Many times since the tragedy, he had been tempted to indulge the urge to drink himself stupid, to forget, to find momentary relief from the guilt. But then he'd remind himself that it was alcohol that had cost him so much. Alcohol couldn't make anything better. "Drive safe," he said now to Luke.

Then his friend jumped into the driver's seat and started the truck. Brad made his way through the blowing snow to his rental car on the other side of the lot. He shouldn't have been surprised by the less-than-pleasant greeting he'd received in the bar. He expected Heather wouldn't be the only one with something to say…or nothing to say to him, as the case may be. He just needed to finish the filming for the TV show and get out of town before his presence hurt anyone further.

A noise at the side of the building caught his attention, and he turned. Melody was leaning against the back door of the bar, arms folded against the cold air. Something about how she was standing there filled him with a mix of anxiety and compassion. *Don't make things worse. Just get in your car and leave.*

Ignoring the voice in his head, he slowly approached her. His legs felt heavy. Apprehension grew in his chest with each step across the snow-covered parking lot. Her eyes were shut, and he stopped several feet in front of her and said her name.

She opened her eyes, and the pain he saw in them mirrored his own.

The guilt he struggled with every day choked him, and he clenched his jaw as a wave of despair coursed through his body. He'd ruined her life. He'd been responsible for taking away her husband, her boys' father. It was hard to breathe as he stared at her. What did you say at a moment like this? A moment that was long overdue, but one he knew they both wished they could have avoided forever.

"Mel, I'm sorry." How empty the words sounded. He was sorry? Who cared? Sorry he couldn't bring Patrick back? Sorry he'd been drinking? Sorry didn't ease her pain.

She didn't say anything, just lowered her head and placed her hands over her face.

Without thinking, he closed the gap between them in one quick stride. Taking her shoulders, he moved her away from the building, and then brought her fully in his arms. She didn't fight—she sank into him, letting her weight fall against his frame. "I'm sorry, Mel," he said again uselessly. "I'm so sorry..." He said the words over and over into her hair, holding her tight.

Time seemed to freeze in the cold evening air as they stood there, his arms around her in an embrace that should have been uncomfortable, but instead felt natural. The only sounds were her soft sobs against his chest, each one feeling like a knife through his heart. At one time, they'd been good friends. His favorite memories of making music in the small town always included her, and so much of his past revolved around her family. Now she refused to allow him to be a part of her or her sons' lives anymore. And it was his fault—all his, no one else's.

A long time and a tsunami of emotions later, her sobbing eased and her weight shifted. She broke away from his arms, wiping at her cheeks. Releasing her, he waited for her to break her silence, desperate to hear from her lips absolution, forgiveness, all the things he knew he didn't deserve, to free him from his own self-loathing.

At last she spoke. Her voice strong, unfeeling, unwavering, she uttered words he knew he would never be able to forget. "I'd like to forgive you, Brad. But as hard as I've tried over the years, I just can't."

AFTER RETRIEVING THE key from under the welcome mat, Brad unlocked the back door of his family home and quietly turned the knob. It was much later that same evening. Unable to shake the feelings his encounter with Melody had left him with, he'd just driven aimlessly through whatever streets he could navigate without much attention. Trying to feel like anyone other than the worst human alive, he'd surrounded himself with landmarks that spurred memories of less complicated times—but the holiday decor on every corner only made him feel worse. This would be the Myerses' third Christmas without Patrick. Brad didn't imagine it ever got easier, especially on the boys.

Inside, the only light came from the living room down the hall. The house was quiet. He knew by now most everyone would be asleep, but he knew who would be waiting up for him. He removed his boots and carried them down the hall, setting them on the drying rack near the front door before heading into the living room. "Hi, Mom," he said.

Beverly Monroe was sitting in her favorite armchair next to the woodburning fireplace, her latest cross-stitch pattern on her lap. Her warm smile of welcome did wonders for his frazzled nerves. "Hi, honey," she said. "Everyone tried to wait up for you, but they were all too exhausted."

"Yeah, sorry I didn't phone. I met up with

Luke and Victoria for a bit. I had planned to be here sooner." It wasn't a complete lie. He had seen his friends for a few minutes at least. He kissed his mother's cheek before collapsing onto the sofa.

"Are you hungry? Do you want something? I can make you a sandwich."

"No, I'm good, thanks." He was starting to get a headache, and he massaged the back of his neck.

His mother studied him with keen eyes. "You've been in town less than a few hours and the stress is already mounting, isn't it?"

"Nah, I'm fine—but I just saw Melody Myers."

His mother set the cross-stitch aside. "You don't waste any time torturing yourself, do you?"

"I didn't mean to run into her, and I think the impromptu meeting stressed her out more than it did me." He'd been able to dull his guilt and pain by staying away from Brookhollow, but what had given him that right to run away? Every day the people he'd hurt had to face the bitter loss of someone they had loved deeply.

"You know, son, it's okay to acknowledge

your own pain. You lost Pat, too. And you continue to suffer a lot of physical pain. It's been three years—I think it's time you start forgiving yourself just a little."

He shook his head. "There's a long list of other people who would have to forgive me before I could even start to forgive myself."

"You made a mistake, Brad."

"Yeah, one that cost everything."

"Not everything. You're still here. You were graced with another chance."

"While my best friend died. It's hardly a consolation that I'm still here, Mom." How many times had he wished he'd died on the side of the highway along with his friend? Most people saw his second chance at life as a gift, but he saw it as a punishment. A lifetime to reflect on the damage he'd caused.

His mother stood and kissed the top of his head. "Well, I almost lost my son that night. I thank God every day that I still have you, even if you don't."

CHAPTER FOUR

THE DOOR TO Leigh Norris's home-based day care opened just as Melody raised a hand to knock on it. "Hey, Melody. David," Leigh's new husband, Logan Walters, said as he moved aside to let them enter.

"Hi, Logan. You heading out already?" It was just after seven. Her shift at Play Hard started at eight, and Leigh had agreed to watch David for her that day while she worked. But Melody was surprised to see Logan, a bestselling author who'd recently moved to Brookhollow, planning to start his day so early. "I thought writers slept in and wrote into wee hours of the night."

Logan laughed. "I'm not sure about the sleeping-in part, but the staying-up-all-night part is true enough. I can't tell you how many times I've fallen asleep at the office during the day. Good thing Ginger's furniture is still there."

After Leigh's grandmother had suffered a heart attack and decided it was time to move into a seniors complex, Logan had rented her apartment. "Hi, guys," Leigh met them in the hallway, her newly adopted baby girl in her arms. She leaned forward and kissed her husband. "See you at dinner?"

"You bet." He bent to kiss the baby's forehead, and with another quick kiss to Leigh, he left.

Melody touched the baby's cheek. "Look, David, how tiny she is."

The little boy ignored her and kicked his feet out of his boots. "Can I watch TV, Miss Leigh?"

"Sure."

"No!" Melody said. "He's grounded. That means no television."

"Mom, that's not fair!"

How many times had she heard that in the past twenty-four hours—when she'd taken away his video games, when she'd insisted he eat at the table and not in his room, when she'd told him he couldn't stay home alone while she went to work. "Here's your backpack. Go do the set of math pages you're going to miss at school today."

He stomped away, dragging the backpack behind him.

"Wow, he's angry," Leigh said, bouncing the baby on her hip.

"I can deal with anger, but what's bothering me is he won't tell me why he's angry, why he hit that other boy." She'd told Leigh the whole story on the phone earlier.

"Given time, he will."

Melody wasn't so sure. This was a side of her son she hadn't seen before. It worried her, especially since she felt helpless to do anything about it. She decided to change the subject. "So have you and Logan decided on a name for her yet?"

Leigh rolled her eyes. "No. Poor baby girl, who knows when we'll be able to stop calling her that. Every time I suggest one, it reminds Logan of a character he's written in one of his novels." She laughed.

"Well, good luck."

"Thanks. We'll need to decide in the next few weeks, because her christening is the first week of January. By the way, we wanted to ask if you would sing at the church. Would you?"

Requests for her vocal talents were frequent in the small town. Whenever there was a wedding, she was usually asked to sing at it. She didn't mind being a part of her family's and friends' special life moments, but since Patrick's death, it had gotten harder to watch couples in love. A christening might be easier. Besides, how could she say no to Leigh, who never charged her for watching the boys? "I'd be happy to."

"Great."

"I better go." She called to the living room, "David, I'm leaving. Can I get a hug?"

"Can I watch TV?"

"No."

"Well, then, no hug."

Melody glanced at the baby girl. "Enjoy her while she's small and can't fight with you." She opened the front door. "If David gives you a moment's trouble…"

"He never does. Don't worry."

"You'll have to share with me your secret someday." As she made her way to her minivan parked in front of the house, Melody heard voices coming from the B and B next door. Three men she didn't recognize were loading camera equipment into the back of a dark SUV. As one turned, she could see the logo on the back of his jacket: Heartland Country Television.

Of course, she should have known. Brad hadn't made any effort to visit his family before now. Only a publicity stunt could have brought him home.

THE ICY GROUND beneath him sent chills through his torso beneath his soaked cable-knit sweater. He blinked several times before finally opening his eyes. He was staring up at the cloudy night sky, big wet snowflakes falling onto his face. His body was lying on an angle and a sharp rock was biting into his right shoulder. He attempted to push himself up, but the searing pain of his muscles contracting took his breath away, and he fell back against the frozen ground. Where were his legs? He couldn't feel them. In his mind, he tried to move the lower half of his body, but nothing happened. He glanced down and his stomach turned at the image of his legs crushed beneath the metal car several feet away. Oh, God... He closed his eyes as waves of nausea hit. Behind his closed lids he saw again the dark ice patch, the sharp curve in the road, felt the wheel spinning beneath his hands as the car jerked into the opposite lane and then the plunge over the side of the cliff into darkness. His thoughts grew hazy and consciousness started to slip away...

The sound of moaning to his right snapped him awake. Someone else was there... Patrick. Turning his head and forcing his heavy eyes to focus, he looked for his friend. The headlights of the vehicle shining on the glistening snow made it impossible to see past a few feet. "Patrick!" he called, the effort shattering his lungs. He felt blood trickling down the side of his face as he continued his frantic, immobilized search of the area around him, trapped as he was by the weight of the vehicle. "Patrick!"

He made no response other than to moan weakly. Brad heard the sound of sirens wailing. Saw flashing lights in the distance. At last came the noise of people talking... What were they saying?

"You can't move that."

The sound of his mother's voice shook him from the dream, and Brad opened his eyes to see the familiar spiral design on the stucco ceiling of his old bedroom. Instinctively, he reached his arms out around him, only to feel the floor beneath the deflated air mattress next to Darius's race-car bed. He let out a choked breath. He was home in Brookhollow, in his old room.

"That nutcracker statue has stood at the base of that staircase every Christmas for over forty years…"

Oh, no. Tossing the handmade quilt to the side, Brad jumped to his feet, ignoring the pain shooting through his right shin as he stood. His muscles always took time to warm up. First thing in the morning was the worst. Grabbing his T-shirt from the bean-bag chair in the corner of the room where he'd left it the night before, he opened the bedroom door and painfully made his way to the middle landing of the stairs, tugging his shirt over his head as he went.

"Mrs. Jackson…" said a young man Brad recognized as a member of the staging crew.

"It's Monroe," his mother said.

"Right, sorry, Mrs. Monroe. We need to make space for the cameras and lighting equipment."

Each had a hand on the four-foot nut-cracker statue, which had indeed sat in that spot every Christmas for as long as Brad could remember. His mother was holding it in place, while the man was attempting to move it. Good luck to the guy.

"What's wrong, Mom?" Brad asked, raking a hand through his disheveled hair.

"You didn't say anything about rearranging the decorations," she told him, a deep frown wrinkling her forehead.

The young man looked at Brad. "We need to set up in this foyer in order to get the best angle shots into the living room," he said. "This tin soldier thing has to go."

"It's a nutcracker, and it's not going anywhere." Beverly's voice was firm.

This was going to be worse than he'd expected. "Mom, can't we move it to the dining room...just for a few days?"

Beverly looked ready to argue, but Darius ran into the hallway and postponed her response.

"Uncle Brad! You're awake," he said, running up the stairs to meet him.

Brad's mother's face immediately softened and her shoulders relaxed. The entire family cherished the rare sound of the little boy talking. "Hi, buddy," Brad said, bending to pick up Darius. The boy had been asleep, sprawled across his bed, when Brad had finally made it upstairs the night before.

"Mom and I cooked breakfast. Your favorite—blueberry pancakes with whipped cream." His nephew's eyes lit up as he revealed this.

Brad didn't have the heart to tell him his rigorous diet and exercise routine didn't allow for refined sugars and carbs. "Sounds delicious. I'll be right there—as soon as Grandma agrees to move the nutcracker." He shot his mother a pleading look.

She folded her arms across her chest. "It's not the way we do things."

"Can it be the way we do things…just for a few days?"

His mother still hesitated. Brad set Darius down and whispered, "Go give Grandma a hug and say please."

The little boy did as he was told, and Beverly's eyes watered. "That was a new low, Brad," she said.

"So, are we moving it?" the guy from the crew asked impatiently, checking his watch.

"Fine, go ahead," Brad's mother said. "But, Brad, *you* are putting everything back once they are done." His mother pointed a finger at him.

"Yes, ma'am," Brad said. He tapped the man on the shoulder as he passed. "I warned you this wasn't going to be easy."

In the kitchen, his sister Breanne was standing at the stove, a reindeer apron hung around her neck. She was flipping the next batch of pancakes. Gracie and her father, Troy, were sitting at the table with stacks in front of them. "Morning, everyone," Brad said, setting Darius down on his chair next to his sister. He kissed the little girl's cheek.

She smiled, her mouth full of pancake.

"Hey, Brad. I hope you slept okay. I wasn't sure how that air mattress would hold up." Troy took a sip of his coffee.

"It was fine," Brad said, sitting next to him on the wooden bench behind the table, near the large bay window that overlooked the yard. The bare maple trees were already decorated with lights, and garlands, bows and holly adorned the white picket fence surrounding the property. Several cars were parked along the gate near the Christmas tree–farm entrance, waiting for the business to open. "Wow, they're lining up already."

A quick glance at the time on the stove revealed it was just after eight.

"Every day," Troy said, tucking in a last mouthful of pancake and standing up from the table. He poured his coffee into a travel mug and kissed Breanne's cheek. "See you out there."

"Okay, sweetie," she said, carrying Brad's plate of pancakes to the table. She set them in front of him with a raised eyebrow.

"What?"

"I'm just waiting to see if you're really going to eat these."

"Of course I am," Brad said, picking up the fork and mentally calculating the caloric intake of six blueberry pancakes topped with a mound of whipped cream. He could work out later by helping at the tree farm. Besides, it was the holidays. Everyone deserved a break from their diets this time of year. Cutting into the pile, he took a big bite. He could feel whipped cream smearing his lips and chin.

The children giggled. Breanna removed her apron and sat across from him. "So… Jackson, really?"

"I know. Look, it wasn't my idea. Please

just bear with me for three days. That's all I'm asking," he said as he chewed. The blueberry pancake was heaven.

"All I'm saying is, you're lucky the other four couldn't be here on such short notice," she said, referring to their older sisters. They'd all left Brookhollow for different reasons over the years. While they usually made it back for the holidays, it was only early December now, so the recording for Heartland Country Television would be without them—to his relief. Six Monroe women on that show? The country wouldn't have been able to handle it.

The sound of his mother's voice drifted into the kitchen. "But the Christmas tree always goes in that corner…"

He shot a pleading look at his sister. "Help me out here."

Breanne stood and pointed a finger at him. "You owe me. I expect a really good Christmas gift."

"Done. Name it, and it's yours. Just get her to cooperate. Three days, that's all I'm asking for," he said, savoring another bite of his breakfast. He would enjoy it while he could. Turning to his niece, he asked, "So, how's school?"

"It's good. We're getting assigned parts for the Christmas play this week. I'm probably going to be a donkey in the Nativity scene again," she said. She poured maple syrup over the whipped cream on her pancakes.

He winced. If her mother saw her do that… Then he reached for the syrup and did the same. "So you were a donkey last year?" He hadn't been able to attend, but he'd seen the photos Breanne had posted online of his niece's school concert.

"Yes. I've been a donkey the last three years." She played with the rim of her glass of milk.

"Do you want to be something else?"

"She does, but she always chokes," Darius said, fighting to remove a paper napkin from his sticky, maple-syruped fingers.

His sister kicked him under the table. He shot Gracie a look and rubbed his knee.

Brad reached over and freed the little boy's hand from the sticky mess. "What do you mean?"

Gracie sighed. "Every year, I practice for

one of the speaking roles, but then when it comes time to audition, I freeze. I forget the lines."

"Stage fright?"

She nodded.

"That's normal," he said.

"Do you get stage fright, Uncle Brad?" Darius asked, his eyes wide over his glass of milk.

"Of course. Every time. You just need to remember certain tricks to get over it." He stood and poured a cup of coffee.

"Like what?"

"Well, I always find one friendly, smiling face in the crowd, and for the first few minutes, until I get comfortable onstage again, I just look at that person whenever I start to feel nervous."

"That works?"

"Always."

"Well, if I decide to try out for a different part this year—and I'm not saying I will— but if I do, I'll try it," the little girl said.

"Great." Brad ruffled his nephew's hair. "How about you, sport? Are you planning to try out for a part?"

"Are you kidding? He won't even go onstage," Gracie said. "Although I heard Mrs. Angleman say he might have to this year, if David Myers can't do it because of his suspension." She ate one last mouthful of pancake, stood and carried her plate to the open dishwasher.

Brad frowned. "Suspension?" Melody's son had gotten suspended from school?

"Yeah. Yesterday he punched Michael Thompson at lunchtime," Gracie explained as she put her and Darius's lunch boxes into their backpacks.

"Why?"

"Don't know. They were arguing about something, and the next thing, Michael's crying and David's in the principal's office." Gracie shrugged.

Odd. True, he hadn't seen the Myers twins for almost three years, but they'd always been sweet little boys. Melody and Patrick had been raising them to be well mannered. A school fight leading to a suspension was the last thing he would have expected from either of the boys. Clearly, things weren't going as well for Melody as he'd hoped. And then he'd shown up. No wonder she'd fallen apart the night before. Vulnerability wasn't a trait he'd ever witnessed in her before that.

"Come on, Darius," Gracie said. "The bus is waiting outside."

The little boy jumped up and grabbed his coat from the hook on the door. "We'll see you later?" he asked Brad.

"You bet," Brad said, leaning against the counter. His mind was still on the Myers family. If only there were some way for him to help them. Melody had refused money from him in the past, and after last night, he knew his involvement with her family was still not welcome. He respected and understood that—but still he wished he could do something...

"OKAY, ARE YOU both buckled in?" Melody glanced in the rearview mirror at the twins.

Josh nodded eagerly, a thermos of hot chocolate clenched in his hands. David remained silent, his thermos untouched in the cup holder in the seat in front of him.

Once again, Melody struggled with her decision to do this today. David still hadn't talked to her about the incident at school, despite her attempts to draw it out of him when she'd picked him up from Leigh's after her shift at Play Hard. The moment they'd gotten home, he'd locked himself in his room with his headphones on—the one piece of technology she hadn't taken away—and ignored her. He'd even refused to come out for a snack when Josh had arrived home from school. Most days, with her nonstop schedule, she longed for a shorter shift at the sporting-goods store, but today, at home with a stubborn, angry, uncooperative eight-year-old, she wished she'd stayed at work.

In light of her son's punishment, she would have been hard-pressed to justify this outing. At least she could tell herself Josh hadn't done anything wrong and he deserved to go get a tree, as they always did three weeks before Christmas. And with her unpredictable work schedule, this might have been their only opportunity to do it. So, for now, in an attempt not to ruin one of their favorite holiday traditions, she'd put David's grounding on hold temporarily.

Flicking through the collection of Christmas CDs in the glove box, she held up two of their favorites. "*Chipmunks Christmas* or *Pop Tunes Holiday Hits*?"

"Chipmunks!" Josh said.

David remained silent, looking out the window.

"David, do you have a preference?"

"I don't care," he mumbled.

Melody held on to her patience as she said, "Okay, Chipmunks it is." She opened the case, slid the CD into the player and then backed the van out of their driveway. It was after three. In a couple of hours it would be dark, and she wanted to get the tree set up and eat supper before the boys had to go to bed. She refused to think about her troubles for the next few hours. Especially the one that had kept her tossing and turning the night before—Brad's presence in town. And here she was on her way to his family's farm, heading straight for the place she desperately wanted to avoid. Though, she reasoned, Brad would be much too busy with the filming of the Heartland Country Television special to be anywhere near the tree farm. She hoped.

Twenty minutes later, she pulled into the farm entrance, under the direction of a teenage boy she recognized from Brookhollow Junior High. Dylan Chapman often helped coach the junior boys' hockey team with her brother Ethan. She waved as he directed her to the busy parking lot. Real Christmas trees were a tradition in many Brookhollow homes, and most families put their trees up early in the month, ignoring warnings from the local fire department about the potential hazards of real trees. Freshly cut, a tree could last two months—Mel wasn't worried.

She shut off the van, and then pulled her tan-and-red knitted hat over her wavy chestnut hair and shoved her hands into mismatched gloves. She'd searched the hall closet for a matching pair, but she'd only been able to find a red one and a blue one. Oh, well, they were for warmth. She wasn't trying to make a fashion statement. "Okay, let's go."

Josh was out of the van in an instant, but David lingered, making no move to get out.

Patience.

"Come on, David."

"I'll wait here."

"No. We are doing this as a family, like we do every year," she said, zipping her thermal winter coat higher around her bare neck.

"Oh, yeah? What are we going to do next year?"

Melody frowned. "What do you mean?"

"Never mind." He removed his seat belt and jumped down from the van.

"Don't forget your gloves," she said, reaching into the backseat for them. They always took turns cutting down the tree with the two-handled saw the farm provided, and his hands would hurt holding the cold metal without them.

"I'm fine." He shoved his hands deep into his coat pockets.

Josh, seeming to ignore the tension between his mother and brother, hummed "Jingle Bells" as he slid his hand into hers. They walked toward the path that would lead them to the trees. At the entrance, they met Breanne.

"Hi, Myers family," she said, handing them a saw. "Hot chocolate?" She gestured to a table behind her, where hot chocolate and coffee were steaming in disposable foam cups.

"No, thanks. We brought some along." Melody accepted the saw.

"Do you need any help?" Breanne asked,

cutting a length of string and handing it to Josh.

"I think we can handle it, right, guys?" Melody glanced at David, who was kicking piles of dirty snow with his sneakers. Sneakers? Where were the boots she'd told him to wear? His feet would be freezing in a matter of minutes in those, and she hated to think of the damage the wet snow would do to the only pair of running shoes he owned. She forced herself to take a breath.

"We can carry the tree, Mom. Right, Dave?" Josh asked his brother.

"Whatever."

Who was this kid? "We'll be fine," Melody told Breanne.

The woman looked uneasy as she said, "Okay. Well, as I'm sure you've heard, we have a bit of excitement going on around here. The crew from Heartland Country Television is going to be filming here for the next three days for HCT's Christmas Eve broadcast of 'Home for the Holidays.'" She glanced toward the boys, and then lowering her voice, she added, "Brad's home."

Melody swallowed the lump in her throat as she said, "Yes, I've heard." She'd more than heard—she'd seen. Worse, she'd broken down in his arms. His appearance had made all the hurt and pain she'd struggled to forget resurface, as though Patrick had only died yesterday.

"Well," Breanne continued, "they're just finishing up for today. They're filming on the other side of the lot, so we're asking folks to stay over here for another hour."

"No problem, thanks."

"Have fun," Breanne called as Melody and her boys headed down the trail.

To their right, Melody could see the camera crew and their lighting on the other side of the wall of evergreen trees. Brad's back was to her. She took a moment to study the scene. Dressed in a pair of tight-fitting jeans, a plaid shirt and a thermal vest, his blond hair a gelled mess, he looked as good as ever. His guitar lay in its case near a stool. Melody turned away. *Please, God, do not let him play anything familiar while the boys and I are within earshot.* The light of day was easing the tension of seeing him, but she knew she'd crumble if she heard the music she'd helped to create.

"Hey, I see Brad!" Josh said, excitement in his voice.

David, too, glanced in the direction of the film crew several feet away.

"Can we go say hi?" Josh asked.

The boys had been too young at the time of Patrick's death to fully understand what had happened. All they knew was that the roads had been slippery, it had been snowing, and Brad had lost control of the car. That had been enough for them to know. She often wished it was all *she* knew about the situation. Either way, knowing or not knowing didn't change anything. "No, sweetheart. Brad's busy..." Melody led the boys farther down the trail.

"But I'm sure he'd love to see us, Mom," Josh insisted.

"Yes, he would," said a deep voice behind them. Melody turned to see it belonged to Brad.

MELODY'S MOUTH SET in a thin line, the obvious annoyance in her expression momentarily made Brad wish he'd remained hidden behind the evergreens. But after hearing Josh's voice, he'd had to see the twins. They were his godchildren and he'd missed them. His memories of watching their soccer games and of playing ball hockey with them in the summer both warmed him and made his chest ache. No doubt Melody had stepped into the roles of both parents. Still, it bothered him the boys had not only lost their father, but also the man who should have been there for them during that hard time in their young lives. Yet another source of guilt.

"Hi, guys," he said, tearing his gaze from Melody. He tried to subdue the image that flashed in his mind of their embrace outside the bowling alley the night before.

"Brad!" Josh ran to him, and he bent to accept the little boy's hug. From the corner of his eye, he noticed David was standing firmly near his mother.

Brad held Josh at arm's length and pretended to study him. "David, right?"

"No. Josh." The little boy's frown and pouty lips were too much, and Brad laughed, pulling him in for another hug.

"I know. You two look nothing alike," he said. It was especially true right now. What a difference an expression could make. Smiling Josh with light cheerful eyes and a carefree air was quite a contrast to David with his dark scowl and guarded stance. David had moved closer to Melody and had taken her hand. Not for a second did Brad question who was protecting whom. Understanding David's reluctance, he focused on the one Myers family member who wanted to talk to him. The other two would come around if and when they so chose. He wouldn't force things. He had no right to. Glancing at the saw in Melody's free hand, he asked, "Think you can handle that thing this year?" It felt like a lifetime had passed since he'd last seen them, and yet the three years had gone so quickly.

"No problem," Josh said, taking his hand as he stood. "But you can help us if you want."

"We don't need help," David said.

"Brad is busy," Melody said at the same time.

"No, he isn't. Are you, Brad?" Josh asked, looking hopeful.

Brad hated to disappoint him, but he suspected his tagging along would ruin their family outing. Just being in Brookhollow was already causing Melody heartache, and he refused to intrude on their Christmas family tradition. "Actually, little man, I do have to get back...but I'll see you around?"

"When?"

The kid was relentless. "Um...maybe you could stop by the farm again after school tomorrow. You can help out..." An idea formed in his mind. He looked at Melody. "Mel..."

She stiffened.

"Melody," he corrected. "Maybe David might like to work here tomorrow."

Her cheeks reddened and she shook her head. So did David.

"I just mean," Brad went on, "I heard about David's suspension and I know you work during the day. Troy could use some help with the trimming and snow clearing." Keeping the little boy busy during his suspension sounded like a better idea than letting him do nothing all day at home. "And then Josh could get off the school bus here and you could pick them both up when you're finished work."

Melody hesitated. He knew he was offering a great solution to her problem. "No, thank you. I have things under control."

"Yeah," David grumbled. "And I don't want to work on your stupid farm, anyway."

Melody looked at her son and swallowed hard. "You know what? Maybe it *is* a good idea."

"What?" David let go of her hand and spun to face her. "I don't wanna!"

"Well, that's too bad. I have to work, and if you aren't going to be in school, you have to work, too." Her voice had just the faintest hint of gratitude as she said, "Thank you, Brad. Let Troy know to expect David tomorrow morning."

"Mom!" David wailed.

"Enough!" she said sharply.

"I'm going back to the car," David said, dashing off toward the parking lot.

Damn, Brad thought. He hadn't meant to put a damper on their tradition. He watched as the boy struggled with the handle on the van for a minute, gave up and then slunk down to sit on the snowbank. "Sorry. I shouldn't have interfered."

"No. It's okay. It's a good idea." She stared at her son in the distance as she said, "David's mood has nothing to do with you."

Brad wasn't sure that was entirely accurate, but he could tell there was more going on with the Myers family than he knew.

CHAPTER FIVE

"YOU HONESTLY EXPECT me to get on that thing?" Bridget stood staring at the snowmobile as if Brad had just suggested she climb onto a crocodile's back.

"Yes." Brad moved farther forward on the seat to make room for her. "Come on."

Dressed in an oversize white winter coat she'd borrowed from Brad's mother, the television host shifted from one foot to the other on the crunchy snow. "I'm a city girl. I'm not so sure snowmobiling is my thing."

He was quite certain it was not her thing, but he'd seen the same doubtful look on many faces in the past. He knew as soon as they started down the trail and she relaxed a little, knowing she was perfectly safe with him driving, she'd really enjoy it. He nodded toward the edge of the trail several feet away where the Heartland Country Television camera crew had set up its equipment. "The crew has a bet going that you'll chicken out. You don't want to prove them right, do you?"

She shrugged. "I'm okay with that."

He laughed. "Look, this thing is perfectly safe, and I'll go slowly." At least at first…

"I don't know." Despite the warm coat, she shivered in the chilly early-morning air. A light layer of snow covered her dark hair as it rested on the coat's fur-trimmed hood.

"My six-year-old nephew can drive this thing by himself," Brad said. Not that anyone would be crazy enough to allow Darius on the powerful machine alone, but when he was just a toddler the little boy had ridden with Brad—it was one of the many things he missed now that he lived in Nashville.

"Okay, now I feel like a wimp."

"Good. Hop on." He patted the seat behind him.

"Fine, but if I hate it, you have to promise to let me off," she said. She held his shoulders as she climbed on before wrapping her arms in a death clench around his waist.

An hour later, *she* was driving and he was struggling to hold on to her as they flew down the snowy trails. He tapped her shoulder and motioned for her to slow down as they approached the final trail leading out of the woods and into the park by Main Street.

She slowed the snowmobile and headed to the side of the trail where he'd indicated she should stop. Then she turned to face him. "Why are we stopping?"

He laughed. "City girl, huh?"

"Don't tell anyone," she said with a smile. She looked around them. "Hey, isn't that Main Street?"

"Yes, we took the back paths through the woods. The crew is parked just on the other side on the street." He climbed off the back of the snowmobile and took her hand to help her off. "I thought I'd take you to Joey's Diner for one of their famous milk shakes."

"Ice cream? No." She shook her head, and then tucked her chin inside the warmth of the coat. "Hot chocolate, definitely."

"You'll change your mind," he said, leading the way onto Main Street.

"So, you lived here your entire life?" Bridget asked as they walked. Brad waved to the camera crew, who started following behind them, filming several angle shots of the quiet street with its holiday storefront displays.

He nodded. "Yes—up until three years ago."

"When you first signed the record deal with Propel in New York?"

"Yes." And lost his closest friend. The best day of his life had also been the worst, and he couldn't think of one event without thinking of the other. In interviews, he avoided talking about those first few months after the accident, months when he'd gone through the motions of everyday life in a foggy haze. He'd been incapable of feeling any joy about the record contract, as it had already cost him too much. More than once in those months he'd considered walking away from music, but his therapist had forced him to see past his guilt and anguish. She'd said turning away from a potentially successful future wouldn't bring Patrick back, and if anything, it would dishonor his friend's memory. And so he'd stuck it out, but only just barely.

"Brad," Bridget said, waving a hand in his face.

"Sorry," he said. "I space out sometimes. What did you say?"

"Where did you go?" she asked with a laugh as they stopped in front of Joey's Diner. The red-and-blue-striped overhang and the smell of bacon and eggs wafting through the door brought back another set of memories, ones of better times.

"Nowhere," he said. "Let's eat."

He held the door open for her and followed her inside. The interior of the diner remained unchanged since Brad had last been there. The booths lining the wall, the six bar stools at the counter and the old jukebox in the corner near the window gave him a comforting sense of familiarity. Things rarely changed in Brookhollow. People may have gotten older, and younger generations may have moved away, but the iconic structures and family-owned businesses endured.

Tina Miller, the diner's co-owner, came through the swinging door of the kitchen. Tina and Joey Miller had owned the diner for over twenty years and all of his sisters had worked there as waitresses at one time or another. He'd reaped the benefits, as they'd brought him milk shakes or pie after their shifts. Tina was also his friend Luke's aunt.

Tina smiled when she saw them. "Brad!"

"Hi, pretty lady," he said.

Tina set a fresh pot of coffee on the counter and gave him a hug. "Wow…I was just saying to Luke last week how we needed to get you home for a visit soon." She let him go and turned to Bridget and the film crew. "Hello."

Brad made the introductions. Tina's eyes widened as she shook Bridget's hand. "Such a pleasure to meet you! You're even prettier in person than you are on television."

Bridget glanced down at her bulky coat and the big fur-trimmed boots she'd borrowed from Breanne and laughed. "Thank you!"

During the exchange, Brad scanned the diner. He stared at the corner booth where he, Patrick and Melody used to sit until long past midnight writing and rewriting lyrics. Tina would never kick them out—she'd loved it when Patrick had brought along his guitar and they'd sung her their newest songs.

"I was this guy's first official fan," Tina was saying.

"Yes, she was," Brad said. Luke's aunt had always believed in him. The entire Dawson family had been like a second family to him growing up. He'd been lucky to have their unwavering support, and it appeared he still had it. Knowing that some people in town didn't judge him for his past mistakes lifted a big weight from him.

"I also got his first autograph," Tina said, pointing to the receipt she'd forced him and Patrick to sign for her years ago, before they'd even come close to fame. It was taped to the cash register.

The sight of Patrick's signature nearly did Brad in. It had been the one and only time Patrick had signed an autograph for a fan, while Brad had gone on to sign thousands. Not for the first time, he wondered about fate. Why had he survived and not his friend? For months, he'd wished he'd been the one to die in the accident, so crushing was the force of his guilt. He'd had no one depending on him, while his friend had had a wife and children. Melody's words from the night before echoed in his mind. She couldn't forgive him. He understood that, because he couldn't forgive himself, either.

"So how's he doing?" Brad asked his brother-in-law later that day.

Across the spruce tree lot, David was replacing the burnt-out bulbs in a set of white twinkling lights along the fence.

"Great," Troy said, setting his trimmer aside and drinking from his thermos. He wiped his forehead with the back of his work glove. "He may not have wanted to be here, but he's certainly a hard worker."

"Has he said much?" Brad had hoped the boy would mention the incident at school or give some indication as to why he was so angry.

"Not really. He's kept to himself most of the day." Troy resumed his work.

Brad picked up another box of bulbs and headed across the lot. "Hey, man, how's it going?"

David glanced at him. He threw an old bulb into the garbage bin at the edge of the fence and shrugged. Getting the boy to talk wasn't going to be easy, but Brad would accept the challenge. Anything he could do to help the Myers family would be worth the effort.

Brad unscrewed a bulb at the opposite end

of the fence and replaced it with a new one. "Troy says you've been a great help around here today."

David remained silent.

Brad tried another tactic. "Working on a farm is great exercise," he said. The boy was active, so the physical aspect had to appeal to him at least.

"I've been changing lightbulbs most of the day."

Wow, tough kid. At least he was talking. Brad said, "Having some time alone to think must be nice, though, huh?"

David resumed his work, but he surprised Brad with a nod. "Yeah, I guess so. I like being alone sometimes."

Progress. "Got a lot on your mind these days?" It seemed like a ridiculous thing to ask an eight year old. The only thing on his mind should have been what he was going to ask Santa for. But David certainly appeared to have the weight of the world on his shoulders.

The boy shrugged. Opening another box of bulbs, he started on the other side of the fence across from Brad.

Brad waited. The boy looked as though he

wanted to talk. The expression on his young face quickly changed from sadness to anger, then back again. Brad sympathized with David's internal struggle. His own emotions had gone from one extreme to the other since he had gotten home.

Finally David spoke. "This time of year sucks."

"Oh?"

"Yeah. I mean, who cares about trees and decorations and gifts, anyway?"

Brad sensed that the boy did. "Well, there's more to the holidays than that stuff. The part of the holidays I always enjoyed most was being with my friends and family."

"If that's true, how come you haven't been home for Christmas for three years?"

Brad hesitated. How could he explain? The truth always served him well, and since David had opened up to him, he owed him an honest answer. "I thought coming home after the accident would make things tougher on the people I care about—you and Josh and your mom…your grandparents." So far, he'd been fortunate enough not to run into Patrick's parents in town. They'd made their feelings about him clear the day of Patrick's funeral—neither of them had acknowledged his presence at the grave site.

"Tougher on us or tougher on you?"

Wow, Brad thought. Hadn't expected that from the eight year old. As much as he wanted to believe he'd stayed away for the sake of everyone he cared about, he knew it had largely been a matter of self-preservation. Nightmares of the accident still persisted, anxiety attacks still plagued him whenever he heard the familiar sound of Patrick's guitar on the tracks they'd laid down for the first CD.

"Both," he said at last. "And I've really missed you guys."

The little boy gripped a light with his bare hand and the thin glass shattered. "Ow!"

Dropping his own set of lights, Brad ran over to David. "You okay? Why aren't you wearing gloves?"

"They didn't fit. They were just slowing me down."

Troy was right that the kid was a hard worker. But safety came first. He took David's hand. "You still need to wear them. Let me see."

The boy pulled away from him. "I'm fine."

Just then, a yellow school bus pulled up alongside the lot. The door opened and Josh bounded out, and then hurried toward them.

"I'm here and ready to work," he announced, dropping his backpack and putting his hat on his head.

"Great!" Brad said. "You can take over with those lights." He nodded toward David, who was still holding his hand, a few drops of blood falling onto the white snow at his feet. "David, why don't you go inside and take care of your hand? Josh and I can finish up here and meet you inside for hot chocolate."

"Whatever," David mumbled as he headed across the lot toward the house.

When he was out of earshot, Brad turned to Josh, who had picked up the discarded work gloves from the ground. Josh was busying himself with the lights. "Your brother's quite a grinch this year, huh?" He hoped his tone sounded light. He didn't want Josh to feel torn between maintaining his loyalty to his brother and giving Brad the information he sought.

"Yeah, he's just being stupid and ruining Christmas for Mom," Josh said. He struggled to fasten the new lightbulb in place with his oversize gloves.

"Any idea what that fight at school was about?"

Josh shrugged and reached for another light. "Michael and David fight all the time."

"Maybe, but obviously this was more serious than usual." Brad opened a new set of lights and handed the box to Josh.

"Michael lied and it made David angry."

"What did he lie about?"

Josh bit his lip.

Brad pressed on. "It must have been something really awful for David to react that way. I know your brother would never hit someone over nothing, especially not one of his friends."

Josh stopped working and cast a nervous glance toward the house. "Look, if I tell you, you can't tell him you know, okay?" he whispered. "You promise?"

"Your secret is safe with me," Brad replied, moving closer.

"Michael said we were going to be homeless soon." Josh twisted a light between his thumb and forefinger, a worried frown on his face. Clearly Michael's statement had affected Josh, too.

Brad stopped. "What? Why would he say something ridiculous like that?"

"He said he heard it from his dad."

His dad? What would Jeff Thompson know about the Myers family? "I don't get it. How would he know something like that?"

"Mr. Thompson works at the bank. Michael heard his dad say Mom doesn't make enough money..."

The mortgage. Brad clenched his fists at his sides and tightened his jaw. What was Jeff doing telling his son about the Myerses' financial situation? Small town or not, there had to be confidentiality laws. If the man had been standing in front of him right then, Brad would've...

"I told David that was ridiculous," Josh said. "Mom works three jobs, so she has lots of money."

Brad softened. Both boys were just trying to protect their mother. "What did David say?"

"He said I was too young to understand." Josh rolled his eyes. "Six minutes older and he thinks he knows everything."

"Well, don't worry, okay? I'm sure Michael misheard what his father said." He hoped. The thought of Melody losing the house was too much to contemplate. He placed an arm around Josh's shoulder and turned him toward the house. "Come on, buddy. Let's go inside and see how David is."

MELODY TURNED HER minivan into the driveway of the Monroe farmhouse just before dinnertime. But as she backed up the familiar-looking driveway, she noticed something unusual. Either she was more exhausted than she thought, or Brad had changed the family mailbox. Instead of the usual wooden one that had always stood at the end of the driveway, there was a shiny red metal one with *Jackson* written on the side. What a guy. Clearly the past three years had done nothing to change him. He was still only thinking about himself and his career.

When he'd first suggested David work on the tree farm during his suspension, she'd wanted nothing more than to say no. But she hadn't wanted to abuse Leigh's good nature by taking too much advantage of her free babysitting, so she'd felt she had no other option. The boys' reaction to Brad had unnerved her. Josh, sweet Josh, so open and loving, and David, even more shut down than before. Of course the boys didn't know the circumstances surrounding the accident, but she knew they sensed she blamed Brad. They didn't bring him up often, but over the years she'd heard them talking about him, especially when that first CD was released. She knew she missed him. She hated that, despite everything, so did she. Or perhaps more accurately, she missed the way things had once been. He'd robbed them all of so much, including the opportunity to have him in their lives.

She parked in the driveway, then grabbed her mismatched gloves from the passenger seat and jumped down from the van. The smell of wood smoke from the indoor fireplace reached her nostrils, and the fumes escaping the chimney were illuminated by hundreds of colorful lights. Melody stood there for a moment, enjoying the peace and tranquillity of the property. How many Christmas Eves had been spent at the Monroe farm for the family's annual holiday party? For years it had been a tradition, one she rarely allowed herself to recall. The memories of the laughter and fun were too much. Now once the boys went to sleep on Christmas Eve, she played Santa by herself and then fell asleep alone on the sofa watching old black-and-white holiday movies. She'd never admit to anyone how lonely she felt this time of year.

"You going in?" A voice nearby her made her jump.

"Oh, Troy, I didn't see you," she said, climbing the front steps to the door.

He was sitting on the porch swing, a steaming mug of coffee in his hands. "It's a zoo in there. I needed a break," he said.

"Sorry," Melody said. "I meant to pick the boys up sooner." Her shift at Play Hard was supposed to have been over by four, but they'd asked her to stay an extra hour and there had been no way she could have refused overtime. Not now.

"It's not the boys. They can stay as long as they want. They were a great help on the farm today. You're raising them right, Mel."

The compliment couldn't have come at a better time. "Thank you."

"No. I was referring to the camera crew."

"They're still here?" She glanced around and spotted the van from Heartland Country Television parked on one side of the house. She refused to acknowledge the small pang of envy she experienced. She'd watched their Christmas Eve special every year growing up, dreaming someday... But not today, not like this. She glanced at the Play Hard Sports smock sticking out below her thermal coat, the mismatched gloves, the running shoes. She wasn't going in there. "Um, do you think you could let the boys know I'm here?"

"Melody! Hi." The front door opened and Breanne stepped outside.

Crap. "Hi, Bre. I'm just here to get the boys. Could you...?"

"No way. You can't leave without saying hi to mom. She's been baking all day. She has some cookies and cakes for you." Brad's sister waved her inside.

If it were possible to die from mortification, Melody was about to find out. As she entered the house and seven heads turned to stare at her, she almost wished it were. "Hi," she said, scanning the room quickly. Brad,

Breanne and five people she didn't know. No kids. "I'll be out of your way in a minute," she said. "Just came to collect my kids."

"No worries. We were just finishing up," Brad said, jumping up from his armchair near the fireplace. The microphone cord hidden below his shirt got caught, and as he moved, it lifted the edge of the light blue fabric, exposing severely scarred flesh underneath.

Melody gaped. The realization that he, too, had almost died in the crash shook her. After the accident, she'd seen Brad at the hospital, where she'd received the news about Patrick. He'd been hooked up to monitors, bandages covering over 80 percent of his body. At the time she hadn't thought she'd survive her own pain over losing her husband. She'd been angry at Brad, so angry she hadn't been able to see how close to death he'd been himself. Well, she was seeing it now. She averted her eyes.

He unhooked the mic from the back of his snug jeans and motioned to the woman on his right. "Melody, this is Bridget Marilyn, host of Heartland Country Television."

Bridget stood and extended a hand. "Nice

to meet you. Those boys of yours are quite the charmers," she said.

Melody swallowed hard. Bridget Marilyn was even more beautiful and sophisticated in person than she was on television. In a baby-blue cashmere V-neck sweater and tight leather pants tucked into black-and-gray riding boots, she was camera-ready. Her perfect hair fell in a light wave around her shoulders and her makeup was flawless.

Melody quickly pulled off her gloves to accept the woman's handshake. Mismatched gloves. She was wearing mismatched gloves on the day she was meeting a host from one of her favorite television stations. "Thank you." Uncomfortably, she scanned the room again. "So where are they?" she asked Brad.

"Just in the kitchen with Mom," he said.

"Great, thanks. Nice to meet all of you." Rushing down the hallway, Melody let out a deep breath. There was no way she was going back through the living room. She hoped the entryway off the back deck was cleared of snow. Otherwise she and the boys would be crawling out the kitchen window.

The sound of laughing in the kitchen made her pause before she reached the entryway. Josh's laughter…but also David's. Relief flowed through her. She stood unmoving, her eyes closed, enjoying a sound she hadn't heard much the past few weeks. She only wished she was part of it. Afraid to destroy their fun with her presence, she leaned against the wall in the hallway. She wished things could be different. She wished she had more time to spend with them, doing fun things. Everyone else had the opportunity to enjoy her children, while she struggled every day just to afford to keep a roof over their heads. And now even that was—

"You okay?"

Brad, of course. Her eyes opened. She wished he wouldn't keep catching her in these moments. But since he had, there was no point in her making an excuse. "I'm fine. I just didn't want to rush in. They sound like they're having a great time with your mom." She spoke softly.

Brad kept his voice down, too. "They can stay for a while longer." He moved toward her. She wanted to back away, but had no room to maneuver.

"No, I have to work at the bar tonight. Have to pick up the babysitter…" She stopped. If she started with her long *I have to...* list, they'd be there all evening. "We should go."

"I can bring them home to the babysitter later. In fact, I told Gracie and Darius I'd take them to see the new Disney movie tonight. I'd love to take Josh and David, as well."

All she'd heard over the past few weeks was how much the boys wanted to see that movie, but she'd yet to find the time or the money to take them. She felt like a terrible mother. Strangers were making her children happy. She mentally calculated the cash in her wallet... Not enough. "No, not tonight." They would hate her if they heard her say no. Somehow she'd find a way to take them on her next day off.

"Oh, come on," Brad coaxed her. "I heard Josh telling Gracie he's been dying to see it." He touched her arm.

The touch was soft and almost unfelt through the fabric of her coat, but it made her skin hot at the point of contact. "I was planning to take them after my payday next week." The words were tough to say, but she held her head high as she did so. Not everyone had money to waste.

"The boys could pay their own way with the money Troy gave them for working today."

"He paid them? That was unnecessary. David was being punished and Josh was just happy to spend time with—" She stopped. Him. She found herself nodding before she could find her voice. "Okay, they can go." The truth was she feared otherwise they'd never get to see the movie.

Brad smiled and its effect knocked the wind from her lungs. He'd always been a gorgeous man, but at that moment, she couldn't remember ever seeing his eyes so blue or his dimples so deep. His five-o'clock shadow tempted her to reach out and touch his cheek. She didn't like the odd feelings washing over her as they stood there looking at each other in the hallway.

"Great," he said. "Do you want to go tell them it's okay?"

She shook her head. "I don't know if you've noticed, but David's been a little upset with me. He seems to be having a good time right now with his brother and your mom, and I don't want to interfere. Just let them know I'll call later tonight from the bar, okay?"

"Sure." He opened his mouth again but then closed it.

She moved past him. "Thanks," she said as she walked back down the hall, desperate to get out of that narrow space and away from him.

"Mel, if you need anything…" she heard him say to her retreating back.

She kept on going. The simple offer to take her sons to a movie was already more than she wanted to accept from Brad.

CHAPTER SIX

"FORGET IT, ETHAN. David's grounded," Melody said as she laced Josh's hockey skates in the locker room of the arena the following evening.

"But, Mel, I need him," Ethan said. "We're playing Beach Haven tonight. That Jones kid is a monster, and I need a good defenseman." He checked his coaching chart. "Dylan is sick and Marcus isn't ready to go up against an offensive player with that size and speed."

"Save it. I heard all this already from David." She suspected uncle and nephew thought they could tag team her into submission. Wasn't going to happen. Grounded meant no extracurricular activities, as well.

"Yeah, but you're also punishing me. Coach Harris is so darn smug. For once I just want to beat that team—and I can't do it without David."

Melody had watched enough of her son's

games to know it was true. David was incredible on the ice. Both of her sons were gifted athletically, but David's passion for the sport made him outstanding, and while he wasn't the biggest player on the team, he was the fastest and the strongest. The Brookhollow Blades' goalie had an easy job with her son on the defensive line. But that wouldn't apply tonight. She refused to break her no-sports-while-grounded rule. She'd already allowed him to go to the movie the evening before, and she couldn't show any more signs of weakness. Without their father around to play bad cop, she had to assume both roles. Her boys were good kids—most of the time—and she didn't want that to change. David's recent behavior had her questioning whether she was too easy on them already.

"Sorry, Coach. You're on your own this time." She patted her brother on the back as Josh stood and snapped his helmet into place. "You ready?" she asked him.

"Yeah. But, Mom, we really could use David out there."

Melody tapped him on the helmet. "Not

you, too. You know the rules. Pick up the slack out there for your uncle, okay?"

"Sure."

"I don't know why you're being so hard on him, Mel." Ethan lowered his voice as they left the locker room. "Especially when you still don't know why he did it."

Melody swung to face her brother. "Physical violence against a classmate is never acceptable, Ethan. What's wrong with you?" Her brother was the first one to teach the kids he coached the proper way to handle conflict. "If they fight on the ice or the field, they get suspended for a game," she said.

"Yeah, but that's different. Fighting over a game is unnecessary. I'm just saying, David is a good kid and something must have really set him off."

Despite her attempts to make him talk, David had yet to tell Mel the story behind the incident, and Josh had been staying loyal to his brother by staying quiet. "I know, but until I know what happened, what am I supposed to do?"

"Maybe try a softer approach?"

Softer? The word didn't exactly apply to

her. At one time, she'd had a softer side—before the death of her husband, three jobs and financial problems had caused her to build walls around her heart. The thought of her last two encounters with Brad flashed in her mind. She hated that those rare displays of weakness had been in front of him, of all people. Then, remembering the scars on his abdomen, she shuddered. Any day now, he would be leaving town...

"I don't think I can be softer," she told her brother.

"Try," he advised as he opened the gate leading out to the rink.

"Thanks for the pep talk, Coach. Really helpful," she muttered. She climbed the bleacher stairs to where David was sitting, his expression cold. She sat next to him and he immediately stood and moved several feet away.

Softer. Could she be softer on the boys and not have them become scary statistics someday? Would backing down on her own rule make her look weak? Was she getting anywhere with her unyielding approach to discipline?

She walked over to her son. "Go suit up," she said, before she could change her mind.

His eyes lit up, but they held a look of caution as he turned to face her. "For real?"

"On one condition—we talk later." She waited.

He hesitated, but then he nodded. "Okay."

She tried to hide her surprise. She hadn't expected him to agree that easily. "Okay. Go before I change my mind. Your uncle needs you out there." She sat in his vacant seat as he dashed off toward the locker room. At the bottom of the bleachers, he turned and gave her a smile.

Her breath caught in her throat. A smile. Progress. Maybe softer didn't mean weaker, but rather more trusting and understanding. Maybe her son needed that the most.

HOT CHOCOLATE UNTOUCHED in front of them, neither mom nor son made a move to touch the gingerbread cake Beverly Monroe had sent along with them, although it filled the kitchen with a comforting, tempting aroma. Melody checked the clock on the microwave. Six minutes. She could wait all night.

David shifted in the chair across from her and poked at a marshmallow floating in the dark, creamy liquid. He opened his mouth to speak but closed it again.

Melody cleared her throat and refolded the napkin in front of her. She wasn't letting him off the hook. Even if that meant calling the bowling alley to say she would be late for her shift that evening. This was important.

"I didn't mean to hit him," he started.

Oh, thank God. Melody leaned forward and touched his hand where it rested on the handle of his cup. She tried to control her eagerness, so as not to deter him from speaking more. "What happened?"

"He was bragging about the ice fishing trip he's taking with his dad next week... and I said ice fishing was stupid. I mean, who wants to freeze to death out on the ice, fishing through a tiny hole, anyway."

Obviously he did. She nodded. "Right, of course," she said, mentally making a note to ask her father to take the boys ice fishing later that winter.

"Anyway, he said I wouldn't understand because I didn't have a dad to do those things with." His voice sounded sad and angry. He took a sip of his hot chocolate and then wiped the foam from his top lip with the back of his hand.

"And that upset you." Justifiably.

"It did, but really, I'm kind of getting used to not having Dad around," he said with a shrug. "I just told him that if I wanted to go ice fishing, you'd take me."

A lump formed in her throat as she nodded again. "That's right." Scratch asking Grandpa—she was going to take them.

"And that's when he said we were too poor to afford to do those things."

Anger rose in her, but she kept it in check. "We have to be sensible with our money, it's true, but we always find the money to do fun things, right?" Well, usually they did. "And besides, we have fun doing things that cost nothing—sledding, building snow forts and having snowball fights, skating on the frozen pond…"

He nodded slowly. "I know."

"Okay, well, if you didn't hit him for saying we're poor, why did you do it?" She bit her lip as she waited. It must have been really bad.

"He said we are going to be homeless after Christmas," he whispered.

Oh, no. Michael's father must have mentioned the foreclosure. The sad expression on David's face pushed away any anger she felt toward Jeff Thompson and his big mouth. She got up and moved to sit on the floor beside her son's chair, turning him to face her. She hugged him quickly, then broke away to look at him. Her hands on his shoulders, she said, "Look at me."

David's teary eyes met hers.

Her older-by-six-minutes son never cried, and the sight of the tears almost killed her. "We are not going to be homeless."

He glanced back down at his hands, and she lifted his chin to look at her. "I promise." She refused to lie to him. He was far too young to have been burdened with this worry, but he had been, so being honest was the best way to approach it now. "It's true we may have to move. This house is old and when your dad was here, we planned to fix it up together, but now the upkeep is hard.

But I am going to do everything I can to make sure that's a last resort—I don't want to leave our home, either, okay?"

He nodded.

"No matter what, we will have a home and we will be together."

"But you're going to try to let us stay here, right?"

Her heart ached. The house may not have been fancy, but it was their home. The memories within its walls meant a lot to all of them. "Yes, I'll do everything I can to make sure we stay here."

David climbed down from the chair and wrapped his arms around her neck. "I know you will. You've never let us down."

She hugged her son tightly, not letting go until she was sure no trace of fear or anxiety would show on her face when she looked at him. "And I never will."

"HAPPY HOLIDAYS. Greg Harrison's office," Kim, Greg's assistant, answered on the third ring.

Melody knew the woman's voice well, having called her Play Hard boss three times that week already. "Hi, Kim. It's Melody Myers again. Is Greg available?" She paced her bedroom, keeping her voice low.

She expected the woman to sigh, but instead she said kindly, "Hi, Melody. No, he's traveling this week. He still hasn't returned your call?"

"No. And I'm sorry to keep bothering you, but could I leave another message for him?" Opening her closet, she removed a pair of skinny jeans and pulled them on, struggling to tug the stretchy denim over her hips.

"Of course. Same number?"

"Yes, and please tell him it's important."

"I will. Take care, Melody," Kim said before disconnecting.

Melody sighed as she sat down on the edge of her bed. Somehow she had to convince the Play Hard executive to let her retake the management exam early. Otherwise... She didn't even want to think about her other options. She knew her parents would help if she asked them to, but they didn't have the kind of money it would take to pay down the mortgage loan, and they'd only see it as another opportunity to convince her to sell the house and move in with them. She didn't like the idea of giving up her independence and moving out of the home where so many great memories had been made. Her gaze settled on the picture of Patrick and the boys on her bedside table. Patrick was sitting behind the drum set in the garage and Josh and David were pretending to play guitars in front of him. Could she really sell the equipment? Unfortunately, she may not have any other choice.

SHE PULLED INTO THE lot of the Green Gator an hour later. During the busy holiday season, she waitressed part-time at the popular karaoke bar and nightclub. She scanned the crowded gravel lot for a place to park. It was a Wednesday night, so why was this place so full? She couldn't remember T.J., the owner, mentioning a Christmas party being held there that evening. Must have been a last-minute event. She turned the van into the last space in the farthest row from the main door and slid on a patch of icy snow. She had to fight to steady the wheel and keep the vehicle from colliding with the SUV parked in the space beside her. She couldn't put it off any longer. She needed to get the winter tires. At least a crowded bar meant good tip money.

She jumped down from the van and jogged in her heeled leather boots across the slushy parking lot. Her swollen feet ached and the tight leather gripping her calves made her want to cry. The uncomfortable boots were the last thing she wanted to be wearing, but T.J. insisted on a staff dress code. She tugged the door open and halted. There was standing room only, and in fact people were spilling into the entryway. If either of her firefighter brothers had seen this place, they would have had a fit. The posted maximum occupancy for the place was two hundred. She estimated at least four hundred people were crammed inside. "Excuse me," she said, moving past the crowd and making her way to a frazzled-looking T.J. behind the bar.

"What's going on?" she asked as she hung her coat behind the kitchen door.

He nodded toward the stage.

She turned. *Oh, you've got to be kidding me.* Brad and the Heartland Country Television crew had set up their filming equipment near the blocked-off stage area in the corner of the dimly lit bar. His back was to her, and she took the opportunity to glare at his cowboy hat, low-riding jeans and tight white T-shirt, which stretched across his broad shoulders.

Country music blasted out of the speakers above them. Since when did they play country music in here? They played rock music, other than the occasional karaoke request for something different. She hated that everywhere she turned she was being faced with Brad and his success.

"When was this arranged?" she asked, taking a bottle of tequila from the wall and filling several shot glasses T.J. had lined up in front of him on the bar. The flirty firefighter Mark Adams smiled at her as he waited patiently for the drinks. Sure, he was smiling now, but that would soon change once one of the local authorities discovered the mess of people in there that evening.

"They called two hours ago and said they left a message last week. I don't remember getting it." T.J. shook his head.

"How did everyone find out so fast?" she

asked. Turning to Mark, she said, "Eight-fifty."

"Thanks, Mel." He handed her a ten and headed back to his table in the corner.

"Apparently Brad's publicist tweeted the info an hour ago," T.J. said, pouring a glass of wine and sliding it across the bar to Lindsay Harper.

"Well, if Ethan or Jim..." Melody started, and then stopped. Several feet away Jim was sitting in a booth along the far wall with his girlfriend, Jill, and several of their friends. "Okay, let me rephrase that. If *Ethan* sees this crowd, he'll slap you with a fine." Her older brother, Jim, may have taken his role at the fire station lightly, but Ethan would never have allowed this crowd to remain.

"I said it was okay for one evening," Mayor Parsons said, to her right.

Melody turned, her eyes wide. "Really?" The mayor of Brookhollow was okay with this crazy fire hazard? And he was *here*? The mayor and his wife had never stepped foot inside the Green Gator before. In fact, they made few appearances at any of the local establishments, other than the Fireside

Grill, the only five-star dining spot in town. They preferred the country club in Newark to the Brookhollow night scene.

"Yeah. This promotion will be great for tourism. We have a local star," the older man said.

Perfect. Next they would be erecting a Home of Brad Jackson sign near the Welcome to Brookhollow one at the town limits. She looked past the mayor and watched as Brad sat on a stool tuning his guitar. The camera crew was testing various lighting rigs and backdrops and the already too-beautiful Bridget Marilyn was applying pale lipstick to her mouth. People were gathering as close to the staging area as was possible, and Melody could almost swear a group of girls were creating a puddle on the floor from all their openmouthed drooling. All of this fuss for Brad. To her, he would always be the same old farm boy who'd crashed on their couch too many times. He was nothing special to her.

THE CROWD INSIDE the Green Gator lingered long after Brad had finished his set and the camera crew had retired to the Brookhollow Inn. Stretching his legs out under the table in the corner booth, Brad suppressed a yawn before downing the contents of his soda. He was exhausted, but he was still so charged with the adrenaline he experienced every time he performed live, he knew there was no point in his calling it a night. It was well past midnight, but sleep would elude him for hours yet.

Across from him, Bridget scanned the bar, which was finally starting to clear out. "Wow, you certainly have a lot of friends and supporters around here. I think they were standing out on the deck with the front door propped open toward the end there," she said, toying with the stem of her wineglass. She'd kicked off her high heels and tucked her legs under her. After the cameras had quit rolling, she'd tied her hair back in a loose, messy ponytail and had washed the excess makeup from her pretty face. She almost looked like she belonged at the local watering hole. Almost.

Brad did have a lot of friends and supporters in town. A lot more than he had suspected. As his gaze fell on Melody, cleaning up behind the bar, he couldn't help but wish he had just one more. "Yeah."

Bridget followed his gaze and leaned forward in the booth. "Let me guess. You broke her heart?"

The truth of the statement was a punch to the gut. "Um…" He hesitated, unsure if he was ever "off the record" with the reporter. "Not in the way you're implying."

"Go on," she encouraged, getting out of the booth on her side and joining him on his. The subtle smell of her perfume reached his nose and he wondered if there was anything about this woman that wasn't perfect. Maybe her unquenchable thirst for information. He'd noticed her perceptive eyes taking in everything and everyone. It was slightly unnerving. A man could never be truly comfortable with a woman like Bridget. *Shame,* he thought.

He turned to face her eager expression, still unsure of how much to reveal. "That's Melody Myers, the woman you met last night—David and Josh's mom."

Her eyes widened. "That's the same woman?"

"Yes." He took a gulp of his soda before adding, "She's also Patrick Myers's widow."

"Your former guitar player?"

"Actually I was *his* former lead singer. It was Patrick who started this crazy ride for all of us. The songs on the first album were all written by him and Mel."

"She writes music?"

"She's an amazing songwriter. And an even better singer." He saw that Melody was now putting on her winter coat.

"Well, why isn't *she* in Nashville? She's certainly beautiful enough." Bridget eyed her with interest.

Melody turned and both looked away quickly. *Well,* Brad thought, *that wasn't obvious, not one bit.* He let out a breath. "She should be." All his success should be hers, as well. She deserved it more—she'd worked just as hard for it, if not harder. And he'd taken it from her. He owed her so much, yet she'd accept nothing from anyone, and certainly not from him. If only she'd let him help her in some way. Maybe it would alleviate his guilt a little.

"Bridget, excuse me for a second," he said, moving past her out of the booth. He was scheduled to leave Brookhollow the following day. This was his last chance to try.

Melody was headed for the front door. Dodging several girls who were looking for autographs, he said, "Sure, just give me a minute." If he missed this opportunity to talk to Melody, he wasn't sure when or if he'd get another. He'd have to *make* an opportunity and, well, he wasn't sure he was brave enough to do that. She hadn't exactly been looking at him with the adoring eyes of a fan all evening. In fact, the bar had been so busy he doubted she'd even glanced his way at all. He wasn't sure which bothered him more—being hated or being invisible. Her cell phone rang as she neared the exit and she paused to answer it. He hung back.

"Hi, Bailey," he heard her say. "Yes…I know, I've just been really busy. I'll bring the van in tomorrow morning before I go to work, I promise…Okay, thanks, Bailey." She disconnected the call and stepped outside.

He followed her. "Melody, wait."

She stopped and turned slowly. She checked her watch. "I have to get home, Brad."

"Just give me one sec."

"That's all you get." She wrapped her arms around her body and continued toward her van, her head down against the blowing snow. "Talk while I clear the windshield, then I'm out of here." She struggled with the driver's-side door, finally pulled it open and retrieved a snow scraper from inside.

"Here, let me," he said, reaching for it.

"I got it."

This wasn't going to be easy. Melody had always had pride and a strong streak of independence. She'd married Patrick against her parents' wishes, and he knew she'd made a choice back then to never admit to anyone that she and Patrick couldn't make it on their own. But even when Patrick was so unjustly snatched from her, she hadn't changed. He suspected the Myerses, as well as her own parents, must have offered financial support to her, which she no doubt had refused. At least they better have. Neither set of parents had approved of their child's choice of spouse, so maybe their help hadn't been as forthcoming as Brad assumed. He pushed the thought away before it brought him to anger. He had to get to his point and he had to do it fast.

Following Melody to the front of the van, he started, "Well, Bridget and I were just talking…"

"Yeah, I noticed." Her voice held an edge.

Not a great start. He tried again. "I had an idea that I think could benefit us both."

"Not interested," she said as she lifted the windshield wipers to clear the snow from underneath them.

"You haven't even heard it." Man, had she always been this stubborn? *No, probably just since you killed her husband,* the relentless voice of guilt said in his head.

"Honestly, Brad, I don't even want to. Look, just because I let you take the boys to a movie last night doesn't mean I forgive you. It means I was trying to get back into David's good books." She'd moved on to the rear window.

Two side windows to go and she was out of there. He knew she wouldn't afford him any more time than that. He had to talk quickly. "Okay, here's the thing. I'm not asking you to forgive me. I just need you to help me write a hit song."

She stopped and stared at him. "You have to be out of your mind. Why on earth would I do that?"

"Because you need money," he said flatly. It didn't get any plainer or realer than that.

Her eyes narrowed. "I'm fine. We're fine. Everything was fine until you showed up here as if you owned the town." She swung the scraper wildly and he ducked to avoid getting it in the side of the head.

"Fine? Really? That's not exactly the word that comes to mind when I think about your situation, Mel." If the cold hard truth would wake her up, then so be it. He had nothing to lose at this point.

"What do you know about it? You're back in Brookhollow for three days and all of a sudden you know something about my life? You know nothing." Opening the back door, she tossed the snow scraper inside and slammed the door shut.

"I know you're losing the house."

She swung around to face him so quickly she lost her footing on the icy patch where she'd parked. She gripped the side of the van to balance herself, and then without missing a beat, she stalked toward him. "How do you know that?"

"Josh told me." He didn't want to get the little guy in trouble, but Melody had to open her eyes. She may have been tough, but there were some quagmires even she couldn't climb out of on her own.

"What are you? A freaking child whisperer?" She stared at him in disbelief.

"Look, I don't know why children trust me. Maybe it's because I listen."

"*I* listen. The nerve of you to imply…"

Brad held out a hand. "That's not what I meant." He took a deep breath and raked a hand through his snow-covered hair. "Melody, I can help."

"Here's the thing, Brad," she said, climbing into the van and jamming the key in the ignition. "My family and I don't want your help. We aren't interested in being your ticket to fame and fortune—once again. But, then, I guess you're using your own family for that now." She reached for the door to slam it shut, but he grabbed it.

"What's that supposed to mean?"

"This show, all of this local promotion crap, all you care about is yourself and your career. I bet you're not even planning to spend the holidays with your family. And I bet you've never once considered helping out at the tree farm, giving Troy a break during the busiest month of the year, instead of just showing up and making more work for them." She knocked his arm away from her door. "Now, move out of the way or I'll back out over you."

CHAPTER SEVEN

MELODY PULLED INTO the lot of Bailey's Place early the next day. With its new signage and recently renovated bays, no one would believe the forty-five-year-old auto-repair shop had almost burned to the ground three months before. Brookhollow didn't see many fires, something her family, given its two firefighting brothers, was especially grateful for. Luckily no one had gotten hurt and the rebuild gave her brother the perfect excuse to insist that his fiancée install a new sprinkler system in the building for additional safety. He'd been recommending it for years.

A bell chimed as she entered, and she waved at Bailey, who was visible through the window of the door leading to the back bay. Her future sister-in-law held up a finger indicating she'd just be a moment, and Melody collapsed onto the padded leather stool in front of the counter.

"Van problems?"

Melody swung around to face Brad, who was sitting on the edge of the waiting area couch, coffee in hand and that day's copy of the *Brookhollow View* open on the seat beside him. Of all the places in town to see him. What business could he possibly have at the mechanic shop? "What are you doing here?" She whipped her hat off her head and smoothed her long waves, painfully aware she wasn't wearing any makeup and the hem of her Play Hard uniform was sticking out beneath her coat as usual.

"Well, seeing as how you gave me three seconds to talk last night and then you did most of the talking, I thought I'd try again."

"So you're stalking me now?"

He shrugged. "I heard you say you were bringing the van in this morning. I thought maybe I'd be safer once you were no longer able to run me over."

She winced. She knew her words had been harsh the night before, at the time she'd meant them and now she couldn't take them back. His sudden appearance in town had had a disturbingly negative effect on her. Of course, she never would have hit him with her minivan...or most likely not...though she *had* been furious. "I'm really not interested in hearing anything you have to say, Brad."

Bailey pushed through the swinging door. "Hi, Mel," she said.

"Hi, Bailey. Thanks for taking in the van so quickly." She checked her watch. "I'm late—do you think we could head out now?" Bailey had offered to drive her to work in the tow truck and it was true she was running late, but the other reason for her hurry was now standing to her right, staring at her. What was he looking at?

Bailey's eyes widened as she glanced at Brad, who was now on his feet. "He said he was driving you to work."

He what? Melody's eyes narrowed as she glared at him. "No, he's not."

"Nick's gone with the tow truck and he didn't leave his own car keys. I'm so sorry. Let me radio him to see how far away he is."

Damn it. Couldn't anything just go smoothly for once? Was that too much to ask? She fought the panic creeping over her.

Being late for work at the store was bad any time of the year, but it was especially bad in the busy holiday season. Walking out on her exam had put her on thin ice already. She forced a deep breath. This wasn't Bailey's fault. "Okay." She turned to Brad. "Thanks for nothing. Now I'm going to be late for work."

"Not if you let me drive you," Brad said. "Look, I just want a few minutes of your time."

"I'd rather be late."

Brad checked his watch. "It's ten after nine. I'm guessing you were supposed to be there ten minutes ago."

"It's fine." The ride from the shop to Play Hard was thirteen minutes. Thirteen minutes was too long to be alone in a confined space with him...in a car. She wasn't sure which part of that was worse. "Please radio Nick," she said to Bailey.

Bailey picked up the radio and buzzed her cousin. Static filled the line. "Sometimes the weather affects the transmission." She pointed to the blowing snow outside the shop's front window. She tried again.

Melody shifted from one foot to the other and checked the time on her cell, noticing the battery was almost dead. Great. Of course. Her bad luck was almost starting to get comical, if black comedies were your thing. "Bailey, you don't happen to have a portable cell charger in the tow truck, do you?"

"I have one in the rental car," Brad said.

Why was he still here? "I didn't ask you. You can leave."

"I'll wait to see how long Nick will be. Wouldn't want to leave you stranded."

"I can call someone else if I need to…"

The radio buzzed and Nick's voice came over the line. "You looking for me?"

Bailey picked up the receiver and said, "Yes, how far away are you?"

"Twenty minutes…thirty maybe in this weather…"

"Okay, thanks." Bailey set the radio aside. "I'm sorry, Mel."

If she waited, she'd be an hour late. This time of year, the store couldn't afford to be short a cashier. She knew if she called to say she wouldn't be there for another hour, they would get someone else in and she'd lose the shift. "That's fine. I'll phone Dad." With the patrol car he could get her to work even more quickly. She dialed her father's number despite her reluctance to ask for help. This would be the first favor she requested in three years. Her eyes met Brad's as the phone rang and she turned away. Better her father than the man standing next to her. As the phone continued to ring, her desperation rose. *Come on, Dad. The one time I take you up on your offer of help...* She disconnected the call as it went to his voice mail.

"No answer?" Brad asked.

Oh, for the love of God, just leave already. Ignoring him, she said, "Bailey, I'm going to have to bring the van back after work." She took the keys from the counter.

"Melody, Ethan would kill me if he knew you were finally in here to get those bald tires switched and I just let you leave in this weather without fixing them," Bailey said, a note of concern in her voice.

"Especially when it's not necessary," Brad said.

Melody hesitated as she watched the

heavy snowfall. The dark clouds looming overhead didn't look anywhere near empty. If the snow continued throughout the day, the roads would be terrible later for the drive home, and she may not even make it to the shop. *Think about the boys,* a nagging voice inside her said. She couldn't take chances with their safety. "Fine."

"Fine? You'll accept the ride?" Brad asked.

"No. Fine—I'll leave the van. Bailey, could you call me a taxi?"

"Melody, I could have you halfway to work by now…"

"I don't want to drive with you." The exasperation she felt made her voice rise. Bailey busied herself looking for the taxi company's phone number in the old Rolodex on her desk. Why was it so difficult for him to understand he was the last person on earth she wanted to climb into a car with? Especially in bad weather.

Brad removed the keys from his coat pocket and handed them to her. "You can drive."

She stared at the keys. Didn't matter if he

drove or she drove—they'd still both be in his car. But she absolutely had to get to work. Now.

Bailey paused, phone cradled against her shoulder. "Mel, am I calling the taxi?"

"No, I'll go with Brad," Melody muttered, tugging her hat over her hair and taking the keys from him. At least she would be doing the driving. Pushing through the front door, she shivered as the cold wind whipped through her jacket. She scanned the parking lot for the rental.

"The Toyota Corolla," he said.

Opening the driver's side, she tossed her purse into the backseat and climbed in. The interior of the cab was still warm, and she was grateful for that as she slid the key into the ignition and adjusted the mirrors and seat. The country music blaring from the speakers made her wince and she immediately switched to a soft-rock station.

"Not a fan of country music anymore?" Brad asked, sliding into the passenger seat. He'd barely secured his seat belt before she tore out of the parking lot.

"Not really," she said, her eyes fixed

straight ahead. The lines were covered with snow and she was happy to see few other vehicles on the street.

"There are some really great new acts. I toured with Eric Church last year for three months and he was just incredible."

Seriously? He was going to tell her about how great life was on the road? A life she'd wanted for herself at one time? Clearly this decision to drive with him had been a bad one. "I've said I don't want to talk to you. I wouldn't even have accepted the ride if you hadn't messed up my original plans." She flicked the wipers onto high and turned the radio volume up as an old Janis Joplin tune came through the speakers. Nostalgia almost overwhelmed her. She used to love "Piece of My Heart." They'd done a cover of it when she'd performed in the band a lifetime ago. She wanted to turn it off, but she didn't want to make a big deal of the memory train crashing into her. Images of being onstage at local bars, Patrick behind her on guitar, the crowd cheering as she belted out the raw lyrics. Her hand shook slightly and she gripped the steering wheel more tightly.

"I liked your version better," Brad said, staring out the passenger-side window.

Against her better judgment, she took the bait. "Are you kidding me? Janis Joplin was a legend. We were just lucky to perform such a great song."

Brad shifted in his seat and turned the song down a bit. "Exactly. Which is why you should help me write the next album."

"Drop it, Brad." She pulled the car onto the exit for the highway and the vehicle slid in the lane as she accelerated. She took her foot off the gas and braked a little, which made the car jolt. In the van, the brakes needed work, and she wasn't used to the rental's touchy responses. She fought with the wheel to set it straight.

"It's okay. You got it," Brad said, as the vehicle straightened and she accelerated again, more carefully this time. A long moment of silence passed before he spoke again. "All I'm asking is that you think about it."

"There's nothing to think about." She paused. "Look, even if I wanted to, I'm too busy. You see my life—a little too well, in fact—so how do you expect me to write songs for you?" Of course she wouldn't have needed to if she'd simply handed over the ones she and Patrick had written for an album that had never been released. "Write your own songs," she said, even though she knew it would never happen. Up until he'd learned to play a few chords on the guitar to get by in Patrick's absence, he'd just been the insanely handsome lead singer with a voice that melted hearts and weakened knees.

"I've tried," he said. "It's useless."

The news didn't surprise her. He'd once tried to rhyme "my baby's kiss" with "a crazy twist." Lyrics were not his strong point. Still, he didn't have to write his own songs. "You live in Nashville," she said. "I find it hard to believe there's a shortage of songwriters in that city." She refused to let him get to her. In a few hours he would be out of here and her life could go back to the way it had been.

"I get stuff sent to my manager all the time," he admitted, "but none is the chart-topping kind. Those are sent to the stars of the business. I need something great."

"And what makes you think I can give

you something great?" As a matter of fact, she could. She knew just the one. A song called "When Love Finds You." She'd written it herself one evening when Patrick was on the road. She'd wanted to surprise him with it the night he didn't come home. Hell would freeze over before she gave it to Brad.

"Did you know the songs from the first CD that became singles were ones you wrote? 'Moonlight' hit spot five on the country charts within its first week and climbed to the second spot, where it stayed for three weeks... 'Dancing on Love' debuted at number eight—"

"Stop. That's enough," she said, pulling into the lot of Play Hard Sports. He didn't need to add insult to her injury. That success had belonged to her husband, as well. Didn't Brad realize how hard it was for her to hear all this? Putting the car in Park in the fire lane outside the front doors, she reached into the back for her purse.

Brad grabbed her arm as she swung open the car door. "Please, just think about it," he said. "It could solve a lot of problems—for everyone."

Maybe giving him that song would be the answer to her professional problems, but it would also solve his, and she just couldn't bring herself to assist him in any way. "Forget it, Brad. I'm not helping you." She paused before turning back. "And you know what? I do have a great song—you're just never going to get it."

BRAD REPLACED THE gas pump and rubbed his bare hands together for heat as he climbed back into the vehicle. Staring straight ahead through the windshield, he waited for the feeling to return to his numb fingertips. It frustrated him that Melody refused to help him, herself and her family. He needed her. She needed him. Not a position either of them wanted to be in, but one they were in nonetheless. Patrick had mentioned new music they'd been writing for the second CD, so Brad knew there were songs already written, songs that no doubt would be chart-toppers…songs he needed. He couldn't blame her for her lack of enthusiasm over the project. Obviously helping him was the last thing she wanted to do, but the money would save her home, help her raise her children. It wasn't like her to let her anger and pride cripple her abilities to care for the twins.

His boarding pass for his flight out of town sat on the passenger seat next to him while Melody's words from the night before echoed in his mind. *Not even planning to spend the holidays with your family...never once considered helping out at the tree farm...* She was right. He had come back to Brookhollow for one reason only—to further his career. He'd never considered staying longer than the time necessary to film the promotional stuff for Heartland Country Television. He leaned back against the seat and sighed. All right, then, it was the right thing to do. He would stay. And the decision had nothing to do with the fact that Melody had just admitted to having the song he needed right here. Nothing at all.

"Hey, honey, what are you doing here?" On June Bishop's face was a look of pleased surprise that quickly turned to one of concern. She ushered Melody inside. "Everything okay?"

"Everything's good," she told her mother, removing her hat and gloves in the warmth of the family home. "I just came by on my way to work to drop off the hockey pads you asked me to pick up for Josh for Christmas."

"Oh, fantastic! Perfect timing, actually."

The smell of pumpkin pie wafted through the air. "It smells great in here," Melody said. "You're baking?" In their home growing up, there had always been fresh, homemade baked goods and bread. She'd never even tasted a store-bought cookie until she'd moved in with Patrick.

"Not really. Just heating one of the pumpkin pies I've had frozen since Thanksgiving. Do you want a slice?" Her mother led the way to the kitchen, where she filled the coffeemaker's reservoir with water and set it to brew.

"No, thanks. Coffee would be great, though." She sat down at the table and noted the mess in her mother's kitchen. Seven different rolls of wrapping paper and every color ribbon and bow imaginable littered the island in the center of the kitchen. Rolls of tape, scissors and gift tags lay on the chair across from her, and across the tabletop were dozens of presents still to be wrapped. Her mother rushed to hide one in the pantry. "You can't see that one," she said with a smile.

"You didn't need to get me anything, Mom," Melody said, setting the hockey pads down among the still-to-be-wrapped gifts.

"Sure, I did. You may be an adult now, but you're still my daughter." Reaching for her purse, she retrieved several bills and handed them to Melody. "Thanks again for getting those—saves me a trip. How's the new position going?"

Melody lowered her eyes and shifted in her seat. She may have been an adult, but it was still hard to reveal disappointing news to her mom. Growing up, whenever they did something wrong, her parents never said they were angry, just disappointed, which was much worse. How many times would she have preferred a smack on the bottom to the we-thought-we-taught-you-better speech? "Um…"

"What's wrong?" Her mother sat down across the table from her.

"I didn't finish the management exam last week."

"Why not?"

"Because of David's suspension."

Her mother's eyes widened.

"Dad didn't tell you?"

"No! How does he know?"

"He pulled me over for speeding on the way to the school."

Her mother rested her forehead against the palm of her hand. "Tell me this story gets better somewhere."

"I wish I could," Melody said, but she still hadn't heard from Greg Harrison regarding taking the exam again early. It didn't look promising, and she wasn't sure how to tell her mother about the foreclosure notice.

June stood, poured them each a cup of coffee and went back to her place at the table. "I've got the feeling I'll need coffee for this."

Melody took a sip of hers before beginning. "They say I can take the management exam again in three months."

"I'm sure you're not accepting that as the final word."

"No, I've been calling Greg Harrison every day. I'm hoping he'll make an exception."

"Remind him he stole your brother's girlfriend. That might work."

"As if I hadn't already thought of that," Melody said with a laugh. "Though, really, we should be thanking him for that." Greg's stealing Emily Parsons from Ethan had paved the way for Bailey to act on her feelings for him.

Her mother laid a comforting hand on hers. "Speaking of Bailey and Ethan, they were here last night. She told us about the fiasco at the garage yesterday morning with Brad. She was so sorry she'd been unable to drive you to work."

Melody's smile faded. "Yeah, well, that was Brad's fault. He...wanted to get my attention."

"Why?"

"He's trying to convince me to hand over some of the old music. He's looking for a hit song."

She waited for her mother's reaction, feeling again like a nineteen-year-old who was telling her parents she'd decided not to go to college the fall after high school. That she planned to pursue a career in music instead. It had taken weeks to build up the courage to reveal to her parents she'd never mailed the college application forms. She'd known even at such a young age that college wasn't the right path for her, and that the path she wanted to follow was unsteady and unreliable. Her parents' initial disappointment had been what she'd expected.

"I'm not going to give him the song, of course," she added.

Her mother studied her for a long moment.

"Mom?"

Her mother took a sip of her coffee before saying, "Why not?"

Huh? "You think I should help Brad Monroe?"

"I—"

"The guy responsible for Patrick's death?"

"Well, I just—"

"The guy who hasn't had the decency to come back here for three years and who now has suddenly returned, forcing his family to go along with a promotional stunt?" Her mother couldn't be serious. "Why on earth would I ever help him?"

"Can I talk now?" June asked.

"Sorry, yes. Go ahead."

"Because I think it's about time." She emptied half a packet of sweetener into her coffee.

"About time for what?" Was her mother suggesting it was time to move on? Forgive Brad for the accident?

"It's time you woke up and started dreaming again," June said with a soft smile.

"What?" Was she hearing her mother correctly?

"Melody, for three years you haven't stopped long enough to take a breath. Working three jobs to support the twins, never asking for help, doing everything on your own. And while your father and I couldn't be more proud of you for taking care of your responsibilities, it's been so disheartening to see you move away from your dreams."

"But you guys weren't exactly thrilled when I married Patrick and started pursuing a life in music."

"No, we weren't thrilled when you married Patrick and you helped *him* pursue a life in music. You haven't made music for yourself in a long time."

"I still wouldn't really be doing it for me. I mean Brad will get to record the song…" A song that meant everything to her. She shook her head.

Her mother smiled. "Don't forget royalties, honey."

"They do help," she muttered. Over the years, the royalties from the first album had helped supplement her income from her jobs.

"And you don't honestly think he'll stop at one song, do you?" her mother continued. "And neither will you. It would be a step in the right direction, Mel."

She bit her lip, contemplating her mother's words. "I don't think any direction Brad Monroe is going would be the right one."

Her mother shrugged. "Just ask yourself this—is preventing Brad from getting what he wants satisfying, when you're also preventing yourself from getting what *you've* always wanted?"

"Hey, man, I didn't expect to see you. I thought you were leaving yesterday," Luke said as he and Victoria approached the entrance of the tree farm.

That had been the plan. "So did I, but I decided to stick around until after the holidays to help Troy out around here." He felt guilty that it hadn't been his idea. He'd almost forgotten how busy this time of year was for his family. They hired several high school kids to help, but the majority of the workload rested on Troy and Breanne.

"I'm sure he appreciates that."

"Actually, I'm surprised to see you here. Don't you usually go into the woods and cut down your own tree?" Brad knew his buddy had no problem buying one from the farm, but cutting their own had been a tradition between Luke and his best friend Jim, Melody's brother, for years.

Victoria panted slightly as she moved toward them, the trek from the truck seeming to have drained her energy. She looked pale...or slightly green. "Yeah, I vetoed that trip this year."

"Too dangerous," Luke said, rolling his eyes.

Ah, married life, Brad thought. "Okay,

well, I'll leave you two to find your perfect tree…"

The sound of Victoria vomiting in the bushes behind them made him cringe.

Luke rushed to her. "You okay?"

She looked embarrassed as she straightened up and wiped her mouth. "Sorry, Brad. Must be the seafood I had for lunch."

Sure. "No worries. Happens all the time. Why don't you head inside to freshen up? Mom's in there." He nodded toward the house.

"I think I will, thanks," she said, heading for the house.

"Seafood, huh?" Brad asked Luke with a raised eyebrow.

"Must be," he said, but his proud smile gave everything away. "Anyway, since you're sticking around, you should join us for a game of pickup hockey on the lake behind the house sometime this week."

Brad nodded. Exercise might be a good idea, since he was now planning to stick around. "Yeah, sure. I'll dig out my old equipment."

Three hours later, he'd yet to find his

hockey gear in the family's storage space in the garage. Going inside, he called out to his mother. "Mom!"

"In the kitchen," she said, over the clanging of metal bowls and pans.

"Where's my old hockey gear?" he asked, entering and reaching for a gingerbread cookie from the tray on the counter. He dropped it and shook his hand. "Ow, hot."

"They just came out of the oven. You mean the hockey equipment we bought you when you were twelve? The equipment you used twice before deciding hockey wasn't your thing?"

"Yes."

"We donated it to Legends Sporting Goods before it closed years ago."

"What? Why?"

"Oh, let me think. Firstly, you would never fit into those pads anymore, and secondly, you haven't been home so you haven't had a chance to tell me what old stuff you want to keep." She paused. "Actually, now that you're here..."

Great. He shouldn't have asked.

Another two hours later, after sorting

through all of his old items in the garage and rearranging his mother's holiday decorations as he'd promised, he slipped out unnoticed before she could add more items to the ever-growing to-do list she'd started for him. Moments later he pulled his rental into the Play Hard lot and jogged to the front of the store.

This location was bigger than the one in Nashville and he wasn't surprised to see how busy it was. Luke might have fought against the store in the beginning, hoping to preserve Legends as a town landmark, but even he couldn't deny the benefits of the new store. Heading straight to the hockey section, he selected pads and a new stick, and then proceeded to the busy checkout.

A friendly young woman repeated her spiel to him when it was his turn. "Happy Holidays from Play Hard Sports. Did you find everything okay?"

All but one thing. "Is Melody working today?" He scanned the store.

"You just missed her. She took off an hour early. Said she wanted to bring her boys to see Santa before the mall closes today."

"Santa, right. Thanks," he said, handing over his credit card and checking his watch. He knew exactly where he was going next.

"YOU'RE STILL HERE. Impressive. Did you not notice the to-do list posted on the fridge?" his sister Breanne said when she came home later that day.

"Yeah, Mom must think I'm staying for a month." Brad still hadn't made up his mind about just how long he *would* be in town. He had nothing on his touring schedule until mid-January, except for a New Year's Eve performance in Times Square, and he was scheduled to record in the studio the day after Christmas. But for now, he really had no reason to rush back. Melody's cutting inquiry as to why he was home had definitely affected him. His excuse that he had stayed away for the sake of everyone in town was wearing thin. He couldn't run from the past anymore.

"Are you staying for Christmas?" Breanne asked, lowering her voice as they headed toward the kitchen.

"I'm not sure yet." He didn't see why not,

but he didn't want to get the kids' hopes up only to disappoint them if his plans had to change for some reason. He would stay at least until Christmas Eve, after which Troy wouldn't need him anymore.

He followed her into the kitchen, where the kids were doing homework at the table. Darius's face lit up. "Uncle Brad!" He jumped up from his chair and ran to hug him.

"That never gets old," Brad said, hugging him back. "Hey, guys, I have a surprise for you."

"What?" they asked in unison.

"Yeah, what?" His sister seemed curious, as well.

"I thought we could go see Santa at the mall tonight." It was a tradition they'd had when he lived in Brookhollow. His sister hated the long lines at Santa's Village in the mall and the crowds frustrated her. He knew she'd have finished her shopping in November. But he didn't mind the hustle and bustle of the season. Brookhollow was usually so quiet and relaxed that he enjoyed watching people frantically shopping for everything on their Christmas lists while festive music played overhead. Seeing how excited the kids were to meet the man of the season was the biggest perk.

"No, thanks," Gracie said.

He did a double take. "What? What do you mean, no, thanks? We used to go every year before I moved to Nashville."

"Darius, plug your ears," Gracie said.

"I'm not a kid, Gracie. I know the secret about Santa, too."

Brad shot a look at his sister.

"Don't look at me like that," Breanne said, pulling Brad out into the hall, away from the kids. "We had to tell them. Last year Gracie put a three-hundred-dollar Barbie convertible on her secret list to Santa and cried all day when she didn't get it. We can't afford that stuff."

"Why didn't you tell me?" He wasn't making millions off his music, but he could certainly have afforded an extravagant Christmas present.

"Why? So you could continue being the cool, rich uncle who never visits?"

That struck a chord. "I'm here now. I'm

staying for Christmas." He hung his head. "It's overdue and I'm sorry."

His sister stepped forward and hugged him. "Yes, it's about time."

He couldn't change the past, so maybe he had to start focusing on the future.

THIS TIME OF YEAR, the Brookview Square Mall bustled with holiday shoppers. David and Josh sang along to "Rudolph the Red-Nosed Reindeer" as they made their way to the North Pole Santa Village set up in the center of the mall, near the food court.

A line of children, all dressed in their Sunday best, wrapped around the outside of Santa's hut. Melody bit her lip as she glanced at her boys in their school uniforms of gray dress pants and navy sweaters over white shirts. "Sorry, guys, I hadn't thought of bringing you home to change your school clothes first."

"Doesn't matter," David assured her, waving to a kid from his class farther up in the line.

"There you guys are!" a loud voice said behind her.

Turning, she saw Brad, who was holding Darius's hand. "Huh?" She hadn't been meeting them there. Annoyance washed over her at the sight of him. Hadn't he been on his way to the airport the day before?

"We saved your place in line," he said to the twins, nodding toward the front of the line, where Gracie, in a red velvet dress, wore a look of annoyance that matched Melody's.

"That's okay, Brad. We'll get in the back of the line," Melody whispered. Waiting three hours to see Santa would be better than waiting in line with him.

"Trust me, it's fine." He took Josh's extended hand and led the way.

"Brad," Melody hissed. He continued on, ignoring her. "Josh." The little boy just shrugged.

"Win some, lose some, hey?" David asked as he, too, followed Brad.

"Sorry," she mumbled to the crowd as they made their way beside Gracie. When they stopped, Melody turned to Brad. "I thought you were leaving."

"Well, I thought about what you said and decided you were right."

She frowned. She had absolutely no memory of telling Brad to stay in Brookhollow. She'd hoped her harsh words a few nights before would have been enough to send him on his way. "*I* said something?"

"Yeah, you said the only reason I was here was to use my family to further my career."

Okay, she remembered saying that.

"So I'm staying to help out at the farm and to spend Christmas with my folks."

Fantastic. She shouldn't have opened her big mouth.

"And I was also hoping to convince you to sell me that song you mentioned."

There it was. The real reason he was staying. "You'd be wasting your time to even try." She'd poured all of her heart into "When Love Finds You." It was special and deeply personal. Patrick had never even gotten the chance to hear it. She'd be damned if Brad would.

"It's our turn, Mom," David said, nudging her forward as the line moved.

"Okay, let Gracie and Darius go first, since they did let us cut in line." She held her eager son back.

"It's fine, Ms. Melody," Gracie said, pushing the boys ahead. "We really didn't even want to see Santa. Uncle Brad insisted we had to...tonight. I was planning to watch *How The Grinch Stole Christmas*." She folded her arms across her chest.

"Why did you decide to come?" she asked Gracie. She noticed Brad shaking his head behind the little girl's shoulder. She gestured for him to stop.

"He paid us. And we're supposed to ask you to join us for hot chocolate after, too."

Melody raised an eyebrow as she turned her attention to Brad. "Not using your family, huh?"

"You kids are never going to get to sleep tonight," Melody said an hour later.

The twins and Gracie and Darius sat in the corner booth at Joey's across from Melody and Brad, their hot chocolate mugs overflowing with whipped cream and chocolate sprinkles, a candy cane draped over the edge of the cup. Ice cream sundaes sat melting in bowls on the table, and only the crumbs remained of the chocolate chip cookies he'd treated them all to.

"I don't know about the kids, but I'm certainly jacked up," Brad said. He pushed his pie away but then reached for one more bite. It was Christmas, after all.

"That's because that's your third piece of pie," Melody said. Her voice lacked the edge it usually held when she spoke to him, and when she turned in her seat to meet his eyes, he felt an overwhelming urge to just stare at her. She'd always been one of the most beautiful women he'd ever met. Her talent and love of music had made her even more intriguing, as had her fantastic capacities as a mother. Despite their hardships since Patrick's death, her little family was close. The boys were well mannered and thoughtful. He just hoped she would work to fulfill her own dream of making music again.

After Gracie had sold him out, he'd never expected Melody to agree to have hot chocolate with them, but she'd surprised him. Did he dare hope she was softening a little? In a mere twenty-four hours, she'd gone from threatening him bodily harm to sitting at the same table with him at the diner. It was progress. Of course, the other kids had left her little choice.

"Mom, doesn't this remind you of the night David broke his arm sledding in the park and we all came here for hot chocolate after his arm was set?" Josh said. "The only person we're missing is Dad."

David stared at his cup and even Gracie and Darius were quiet.

Yes, they were missing Patrick. As much as life went on, he wondered if it would ever feel the same without his friend. He knew Melody must wonder about that every day.

"It does, sweetheart," Melody said with a soft smile at her son. She turned to Brad. "I also remember it was Brad who carried your father to the van after he passed out at the sight of David's arm twisted the wrong way."

Brad laughed. The injured little boy had been more concerned about his father than the pain in his arm. "My favorite Joey's memories are still of us coming after your soccer games in the summer. Nothing beats Tina's chocolate malts. Speaking of which..." He glanced around for the waitress.

"Seriously? Where are you going to put it?" Melody glanced at his stomach, which had started to bulge slightly over his jeans in the week he'd been in town.

"I'll find room. Once I get back to Nashville, who knows when I'll get a chance to have one again?" He waved at Tina as the front door of the diner opened. *Great.* He lowered his eyes to his hot chocolate.

"Grandma and Grandpa!" Josh's squeal of delight made Melody turn. All the color drained from her face. A look of panic flitted across her dark eyes before a forced smile appeared on her lips.

"Delores and Dan, hi," she said, as Patrick's parents approached the table.

Brad's mouth was dry and all the sweets he'd just consumed threatened to come back up. Staying in town longer than he'd planned had basically guaranteed a run-in with the Myerses, but this was the last way he'd wanted it to happen. No doubt the friendly looking reunion would be unsettling to Patrick's parents.

Pain, anger and confusion showed in Delores's eyes as she glanced between him and

Melody. Only anger burned in Dan's. So Brad avoided both.

"Hi, everyone." The woman's voice was tight, and Brad flinched, unsure what to do. Should he say something? Should he leave? He desperately wanted to escape the situation, but he reminded himself he was here to face the mistakes of his past. Avoidance was no longer an option.

"Grandma, we saw Santa at the mall—look!" Josh said, extending the photo of him and his brother on Santa's lap.

"What a great picture," Delores said, her eyes resting on the photo in her visibly shaking hand before passing it to her husband, who stood silently behind her.

Dan Myers had been a corporate law attorney for over forty years. He'd retired early five years before, after Patrick had made it perfectly clear the business suit and high-powered career was never going to be his path. He'd then sold his firm, which he'd been hoping to pass along to his son. In the two years before his death, Patrick hadn't spoken more than ten words to his father—or rather, Dan had forced distance between them. The man no doubt held his own torturous guilt over that decision.

"Can you guess which one I am, Grandpa?" Josh continued, standing in the booth to peer over his grandfather's shoulder.

Dan looked at the Christmas photo and shook his head quickly before handing it back to the little boy. "You both look great."

A long silence followed as Josh slid back into his seat next to his brother. The tension at the booth made it difficult to breathe. *This is my fault,* Brad thought. The Myerses would surely have shown more interest in their grandsons had he not been there. He wished someone would just yell at him or slap him—anything to interrupt the heavy silence.

"Are you and Grandpa coming to the school Christmas concert this year?" Josh asked hopefully.

"Of course, sweetheart," Delores said. "Your mom sent us the information last week."

"Uncle Brad is staying in town for Christmas. He'll be at the concert, too," Gracie said, popping a whipped cream—covered cherry into her mouth.

Delores nodded. "That's great."

Brad knew what she was thinking because he was thinking it, too. Another unfortunate opportunity for them to see each other. Another opportunity for him to ruin their family time with his mere presence. But he needed to be there for Gracie.

"Have a seat, Grandma," Josh said, shifting over in the booth and patting the seat next to him.

"Oh…um…"

"You're welcome to join us," Melody said, shooting Brad a look.

That's right. He was the outsider. The unwelcome one.

Dan's eyes widened as his wife hesitated. "We have to go," he said finally.

"Sorry, boys. Another time, okay?" Delores said.

Brad stood up. He wasn't running away—he was just giving the family some space. "Please stay and visit. I'm the one who should leave. Gracie and Darius, whenever you're ready, I'll be outside."

"MOM, WHY DID Brad leave the diner to-night?" Josh asked as she turned off the boys' bedroom light a few hours later.

Because he was lucky enough to escape that uneasy situation. Melody turned the bedroom light back on and approached the bunk beds, where both boys were still wide-eyed even though it was two hours past their normal bedtime. Not surprising, given the amount of sugar they'd consumed that evening. She sat on the floor next to Josh's bed and said, "He just needed some air, and your grandparents are still..." What? Hurt, angry, unforgiving? She could say the same things about herself. "Um..."

"Mad?" David supplied, tossing a base-ball up in the air and catching it. He lay on his back staring up at the ceiling.

Definitely. "I think so..."

"Why?" Josh asked, propping himself up on his elbows on his pillow.

"It's complicated, boys." Were they old enough to understand this? She didn't think so, but she'd explain it the best way she could. "You boys know the accident that night was sort of Brad's fault..."

The boys nodded. David stopped playing with the ball and turned to look at her.

"Well, Grandma and Grandpa—" and me, she didn't add "—are still having a hard time forgiving Brad."

"Are they mad at us, too?" Josh asked.

"No! Why would you think that?"

"Grandpa just doesn't talk to us very much," David said.

"Yeah, and Grandma always looks sad when she sees us," Josh added.

"Of course they're not mad at you. They love you. How could they not? You guys are awesome." She ruffled Josh's hair and reached for David's hand, which was draped over the side of the bed. "It's just hard on them. They see a lot of your dad in you guys, and they miss him." She knew that was true. They may not have understood their son or agreed with his choices, but they'd loved him. She knew her resentment toward Brad could never compare to theirs. She'd lost a husband, but they'd lost a child. "Anyway, you both need to sleep. Big day tomorrow—parts are being assigned for the school Christmas play." She kissed both of their foreheads and headed toward the door.

"Mom?"

"Yeah, Josh?"

"I'm glad *we're* able to forgive Brad."

Her heart fell. Was she able to forgive him? Would she ever be able to? "Good night, guys."

CHAPTER EIGHT

"THIS IS ONLY three lines. You can totally do this." Brad eyed Gracie's script for the Christmas concert play—it was the same one he'd performed over twenty years before. The wrinkled pages of the twenty-five-page script had been laminated in recent years to prolong its use. Maybe it was time for someone to write a new one. He'd heard about a new bestselling author in Brookhollow. The school should ask him.

"Yeah, three lines is nothing," Darius said.

Gracie swung to face her younger brother, eyebrows arched. "*You* don't even talk!"

He shrugged, unfazed. "If I did, I could do three lines."

Brad hid a laugh. He gave a gentle nudge to the little boy sitting on the kitchen counter. "Get down before Grandma sees you up there."

He took a gingerbread man from the snowman-shaped cookie tin before hopping down from the counter.

"No way. Not before dinner," Brad said, taking the cookie and popping it into his own mouth. "Okay, let's try it. I'll play the shepherd, you play your part." He swallowed the cookie and read from the sheet. "'My wife and I have traveled far, dear innkeeper. Please tell me you have room for us.'"

Darius nodded his approval. "Not bad."

"Thanks, man. Okay, Gracie, your line."

"I don't know, Uncle Brad. This is embarrassing."

"It's just us here. Come on. I'll start again." He repeated the line and waited.

Gracie hesitated but then said, "'I'm sorry, because of the snowstorm, we are full tonight.'"

"See? Not hard at all." He cleared his throat. "'But my wife is with child. I beg of you—you must have somewhere we can sleep.'"

"'We do have a stable I could offer you. It's not much, but it's warm and dry.'"

"'We'll take it, good sir. Thank you.'"

"'Come with me,'" Gracie said, a look of

relief on her face at having finished saying her lines.

"Awesome! See, I told you—there's nothing to it." Brad smiled. He opened the cookie tin and took another gingerbread man. On the upstairs bathroom scale that morning, Brad had learned he'd gained an extra ten pounds in the past week. He wasn't worried. If you gain the weight quickly, you can lose it quickly. At least that was what he was choosing to believe. "Anyway, you'll do fine, so quit worrying," he told his niece.

"It's different when it's just us," she said. "I just know that once I'm up onstage, I'm going to freeze." The little girl frowned and tucked her script back into her backpack.

"Remember what I told you. Find one person who is smiling and focus on them until you feel comfortable. It really does work, Gracie. I do it at every show."

"Will you be there? Will you be my smiling face?" she asked.

Brad didn't hesitate. "Wouldn't miss it."

The kitchen door opened and Breanne entered, holding the children's photos with Santa. "Um, Brad, as cute as these children are, they're not my children."

He frowned, taking the photos from her. Josh and David's smiling faces stared back at him. "We must have gotten the photos mixed up."

She laughed. "I'll get Gracie to take these to school. No doubt Melody will notice soon enough that she's framing pictures of my two." She reached for the photos, but Brad held tight to them.

"That's okay," he said. "I'll make the switch."

Breanne eyed him with suspicion. "Kids, go upstairs and wash your hands before dinner," she said.

Brad stood up.

"Not you," she said.

She blocked his way and shooed the kids out of the kitchen. "What's going on?" she asked him when they were gone.

"Nothing."

"Nothing? Really? Since when you do purposely want to see Melody Myers?"

"I saw her last night and things were… fine." He avoided his sister's eyes as he reached into the snowman cookie jar for another gingerbread cookie.

She slapped his hand. "You're getting fat."

She leaned against the counter with her arms crossed in front of her. "What are you doing, Brad? Is Mel the reason you're still here?" She looked disappointed.

"No, it's not like that." He hesitated. "She has a song I want." The last thing he needed was for his sister to think he had feelings for Melody.

"So, it's exactly like that. Brad, don't you think you've forfeited any right to ask that woman for anything?"

"Yes, but she needs this, too." He refused to tell his sister or anyone else about Melody's dire financial situation. "Music is her passion and she's wasting her talent."

"You're doing this for *her*?" His sister's look of disbelief annoyed him.

"Is it really that hard to believe I would want to help her?"

"All I'm saying is, Mel has struggled the last three years to get things back on track and make a life for those kids. The last thing she needs is for you to complicate that life."

"That's not my intention."

"Yeah, well, sometimes even good intentions go wrong."

CHAPTER NINE

"Oh, come on," Melody said. Her key refused to turn in the rusted padlock on the door of her shed. Josh never seemed to have any trouble with it. Maybe that was a sign. Or maybe the metal lock was just old.

She felt ill about the choice she was about to make. But what else *could* she do? Another unreturned message to Greg Harrison that week had confirmed her suspicion—the man was avoiding her, and at this point, she didn't think she wanted to hear his answer, anyway.

Her key finally turned, and a rough push later, the shed door gave way. Entering the insulated space, Melody reached for the light switch along the wall. When the room lit up, her breath caught in her throat. The shed was exactly the same. Somehow she'd expected things to look different...feel different. They didn't. Patrick's guitars still hung on the wall on her right—two acoustic ones and an electric one she'd given him as a wedding present. Their electronic keyboard was set up on the left, and a drum set was sitting in the center of the room next to two microphone stands. Binders of CDs lined a bookshelf along the wall under the window, and the music books Josh was learning to play from were scattered across a coffee table.

On either side of the table were two old plush chairs she and Patrick had moved out there for their writing sessions. Evenings, once the boys were asleep, they used to spend hours writing melodies and lyrics. Patrick could play every instrument in the room—his talent had amazed her. It was one of the things that had attracted her to him most. One of the things she longed for most.

"Man, I've missed this place." Brad's voice behind her made her jump.

She swung around to face him. "What are you doing here?"

"I knocked out front, but there was no answer. I noticed the door was open back here."

"Okay, so what are you doing here?" She knew going along with the events of the evening before had been a mistake. She hadn't intended to give Brad the impression they could be friends. Having him think he could show up at her home unannounced, as he used to, certainly hadn't been her plan.

"I wanted to bring you these." He handed her the boys' Santa photos.

"But I have these."

"No, you have pictures of Gracie and Darius."

She clenched her jaw. "Another one of your manipulations?"

He held his hands up and shook his head. "I swear I had nothing to do with this one. Simple mix-up."

She wasn't sure she believed him, but she tucked the photos into her coat pocket and nodded. "Okay, well, thank you. I'll get the others for you." She took a step outside, pushing him out with her, but he stood firm.

"Wait. Can I? Please?" He gestured inside the shed.

Damn it. The last thing she wanted was to be in that shed with him. "No."

"Just for a minute? I just…I miss all of this," he murmured.

God, how she wished he'd never come

back. Why had she gotten friendly with him the evening before? She sighed. She would regret this. "Fine." If he wanted to go in there, she'd let him, but she'd wait outside, or in the house. "I'll go get the pictures, and then you have to leave."

He nodded, not looking at her. Instead, he stood there taking in the space the way she had just moments before he had intruded.

She made her way into the house through the front door and picked up the bag from North Pole Santa Village on her counter. Sure enough, the photos she had were of Gracie and Darius. She waited another minute before heading back toward the shed.

At the doorway, she saw Brad approach the electric guitar, and her lips tightened as he reached out to pick it up. She looked away, refusing to watch him hold something so dear to her. This had been a bad idea. A second later, the sound of the guitar made her flinch. That was enough. "Here are the photos," she said, stepping inside.

Brad quickly replaced the guitar. "Sorry, Mel." He shoved his hands deep into his jean pockets.

She shook her head. "It's just a guitar." That was the attitude she needed to have if she planned to sell any of it.

"I'm surprised you still have all of this."

"It belonged to Patrick." Except her microphone, which she'd been coming in to get when Brad had interrupted. It was the one piece of equipment that was hers. The piece that would break her heart to sell. But she had no choice.

"Do the boys come out here?"

"Josh does. He's trying to teach himself to play." Why was Brad still there? "Here are the photos."

"Look, I know you said you wouldn't consider it, but since I'm here, can I at least hear some of the new stuff you two were working on?"

He was relentless. "If I find the CD for you, will you leave my shed after you're done listening to it?"

"Yes."

"Fine." Crossing the room quickly, she opened a CD case and flipped to the back where the new songs were—all of them except the one she'd written. She handed the CD to him and left the shed.

"You don't want to listen?" he asked.

"I've heard them."

AFTER SLIDING THE disc into the CD player, Brad removed his coat and sat on the edge of one of the chairs. A few bars into the intro, a feeling of nostalgia hit him. He remembered this first one. It was a song Melody and Patrick had written about the twins. When Brad had heard it years ago, it hadn't held much meaning for him, a bachelor without kids of his own. Now he longed to know what it felt like to be exhausted after an all-nighter with a sick child or to come home to a family after a long tour. Patrick had had the best of both worlds.

Brad leaned back in the chair and closed his eyes as the next song started. Melody's voice filled the space around him. Man, he loved her voice. Her talent rivaled that of any female vocalist on country-music radio. If only she'd give it another shot.

He listened to the next track, and the next one, each song warming his heart and tearing it apart. Patrick and Melody had been the real talent, not him. He'd always known that. He'd always been happy just to be along for the ride. Good-looking front men were a dime a dozen, but Pat and Mel had been special. Performing the songs they'd written had always made him feel like a fraud. He didn't even come close to having their natural gifts, yet there he was, climbing his way to stardom. It wasn't right.

But no matter how much guilt or self-loathing he experienced building his career on his friend's platform, he couldn't walk away from the industry. His therapist was right. Patrick wouldn't have wanted that.

The shed door opened. Brad had no idea how long he'd been sitting there. "Hey, I have to go pick up the boys."

He stood and reached for his coat.

"You don't have to leave just yet," she said, "but if you could lock up…"

He'd already spent enough time in the shed. He knew the song he needed was one she'd never give up. He slid his arms into his jacket and met her at the door. "It's okay, I'm done."

She hesitated before asking, "Did you… um…find anything?"

"No, but it triggered some great memories, so thank you."

Her eyes met his and she nodded. "What happened to your eyes?"

"My publicist," Brad said.

"Colored contacts?"

"Yeah. She said my different-colored eyes didn't fit with my new look." He ran a hand through his highlighted hair—another idea of Roxanne's.

"I liked them just fine," Melody said, clamping her lips together.

"Thank you. Me, too. But you gotta know Roxanne."

"I don't think I want to. This is the same woman who changed your last name, right?"

"Yes, that's the one."

She glanced at her watch as he joined her outside. She looked like she had something to say, but she remained quiet as she shut the door and fastened the lock.

"What?" he asked.

She hesitated. "Why did you let her make all these changes?"

Brad rubbed his forehead. How many times had he asked himself that very question? "Because when it comes down to it, I want success, Mel. For years, Patrick and I did the local bar scene. We toured all over the state, playing in dingy taverns. We recorded CDs and mailed them out—you know how hard we worked. You did, too," he said. "We all wanted this." They had all wanted to live that dream—being onstage performing to sold-out crowds, hearing their songs on the radio, seeing their names on the top of the charts. But now that it was only happening for one of them, those measures of success felt bittersweet.

"Well, you're there, Brad," she said, quietly.

"Not quite," he said, leaning forward and studying her. "And what about you? Isn't there a small part of you that still wants this?"

"Music isn't my dream anymore," she said, looking away.

"You're so full of it."

"I have the boys, work… I've moved on."

Brad bent to look into her eyes. "If that's true, why do you still have all of this?" He gestured at the equipment. "You could have sold all that stuff years ago, but you kept it."

"It was a part of Patrick."

"It's also a part of you." He shook his head. "The truth is, Mel, I just never understood why you took a step back from performing. You were the most talented of the three of us."

"No way. And besides, I had the boys…"

"So did Patrick. All I'm saying is, other music couples make it work—Tim and Faith…"

"Do you hear yourself? You just compared Patrick and me to country music's hottest duo."

"Why couldn't it have been you two? Why didn't you at least try?"

She checked her watch. "I have to go pick up the boys and the babysitter."

"Let me watch the boys for you tonight," he said, following her across the snowy backyard. He wouldn't be in town for long, and who knew when he'd get the chance to spend time with them again.

"No."

"You're turning me down just like that? Not even going to consider it?"

"Nope." She reached for the door handle of her minivan, but his hand on hers stopped her.

"Please, Mel. You said Josh wanted to learn to play guitar, so let me teach him."

The boys' father used to play circles around Brad, but unfortunately they were stuck with him now.

Her expression got cloudy. "I don't know if that's a good idea. It might be hard on Josh."

He nodded. "Okay, well, maybe ask him. At least give him the chance to say no himself."

She sighed. "Fine." She removed his hand from hers and opened the door.

A moment later, he watched her drive out of the cul-de-sac. Shoving his hands into his coat pockets, he sat on the front step and waited.

"THAT'S IT, you got it," Brad said to Josh later that evening as the boy played his father's guitar.

It shouldn't have surprised her that Josh would have jumped at the opportunity to hang out with Brad and learn music from him, yet his excitement had unnerved her a little. Was her little boy that starved for male attention? His uncles did their best to be around and be positive male role models, but Josh's connection to Brad seemed unique. Melody could hear them in the living room now, and it took all her concentration to keep straightening her hair in the bathroom mirror.

"Now just strum." She heard Brad demonstrate the G chord on his guitar and wait for Josh to do the same.

The rich sound filled the air, followed by Josh's excited, "I did it!"

"That actually sounded good," David said from his perch in front of the TV.

Unplugging the flat iron and checking her reflection one last time, she left the bathroom and made her way to the living room.

"Okay, let's try a C chord," Brad said as she entered.

Brad helped Josh rearrange his tiny fingers. The boy struggled to reach the fifth string with his pinky.

"It's a tough one. I remember having trouble with this one, too, when your dad was teaching me to play." Brad positioned the little boy's finger on the fret.

That got David's attention again. "Our dad taught you?"

"Yeah. I couldn't play a note, and your dad said if I was going to be the front man

I had to at least learn the basic chords for the slower ballads."

"I think I remember watching you guys practice," Josh said.

"You did all the time," Melody said, checking the time on the clock on the mantel above the fireplace. She had a few minutes before she had to leave, so she took a seat on the couch. Something about the relaxed, cozy environment in her home that evening made her long to stay there with them. "You would sit out here with your plastic guitar and pretend to play along for hours," she told Josh.

"That's right," Brad said. "And if you keep practicing, someday you'll be as good as your dad was."

Josh beamed. "That would be awesome. Dad was the best!"

The room grew silent for a long, excruciating moment. Time to go. Melody stood up. "Okay, well, I'm heading out." She plucked her winter coat from the back of the armchair and kissed both boys on the forehead, aware of Brad's eyes on her.

"Where's mine?" he asked, teasingly.

She turned to face him with a puzzled

look. Was he flirting with her? She stared at him, uncertain how to respond.

"I was kidding," he said.

"Of course." Melody headed for the hallway. "Don't let them stay up past eight-thirty," she called. She grabbed her keys from the key rack near the door and went outside.

Twelve minutes later, as she entered the bowling alley, her mind was still on Brad's request for a kiss. Heather waved in greeting.

"Hi, Heather," she said distractedly, hanging her coat behind the kitchen door. Brad couldn't have been serious about wanting a kiss, could he? No, he'd said he was kidding. So then why was it bothering her? Actually, what was truly bothering her was that it had sounded tempting. Just seeing him with Josh… She frowned. Maybe letting him babysit the boys had been a bad idea. He was obviously getting too comfortable with her family again.

"You okay?" Heather asked.

"Yeah, I'm fine." She was both desperate and scared to hear what Heather would think of the situation. Her friend would give it to her straight. She just wasn't sure she could handle it right now. Her own doubts about whether she'd made the right choice that evening were bad enough.

"You look a little spaced-out." Heather studied her.

"It's been a crazy few days."

"Did you hear back from Greg Harrison?"

"No, and I'm starting to think I need to accept the fact that I have to wait to retake the exam."

A customer approached the bar. "Hey, John, what can I get you?" Melody asked, putting her conversation on hold.

Heather tapped her red-and-green acrylic nails against the bar as she waited, shooting John an annoyed look as he scanned the holiday-inspired drinks menu.

"Um…how's the candy-cane martini?" he asked, running a hand over his thick white beard. He played Santa at the local mall for good reason—with his real beard and round belly, he looked the part, even without the red suit.

Heather sighed.

"It's minty?" Melody said. She hadn't actually tried any of the new concoctions.

"Huh, maybe not. What's in the elf cock-tail?"

"You won't like it. Here's your usual," Heather said, sliding a Bud Light toward him and grabbing the ten-dollar bill from his hand.

"Hey, you just cut your tip in half," John said, a frown wrinkling his forehead.

"Who said you were getting your change?" Heather turned her attention to Melody. "Continue with your story."

Melody moved Heather away from the register. Taking out a five-dollar bill, she extended it to John. "Sorry, John. Heather's from New York." She winked. "That's what they're like."

John took it and stuffed it into the tip jar before rejoining his group—several men playing poker in a corner booth.

"You have to be nicer," Melody said, still shaking her head. "You're never going to make tips that way."

"Not sure I care." Heather leaned against the bar. "So what are you going to do about the house?"

"I've decided to sell some of the musical equipment."

"What? Are you sure you want to do that? I thought Josh used it."

"Oh, I wouldn't sell Patrick's guitars, but the drum set maybe…" And her microphone.

"But that would mean you really are done with music." Heather looked disappointed.

"I've been done with music for a long time." Why had that been easier for her to accept than for everyone else? "Like I told Brad today, I have to focus on the boys now."

"Brad Monroe? You spoke to him?"

Melody cringed. "He's babysitting the boys tonight." She waited for Heather's lecture.

"Why would you let him do that?"

Good question. "He decided to stick around to spend the holidays with his family…and he is the boys' godfather. He offered to teach Josh how to play the guitar." She bit her lower lip. This didn't feel right. "I made a mistake, didn't I?"

"All I'm going to say is, be careful. Don't let him get too close. This man could hurt you."

"Okay," Melody said, as reassuringly as she could. She suspected she had already let him get too close.

"THANK GOD YOU'RE HERE. Let's go," Luke said as he opened the door to his home the next afternoon. He softly closed the door behind him and picked up his skates and hockey sticks from the deck.

Brad accepted a stick but nodded toward the SUV parked in the driveway next to his rental. "Hey, isn't that your mom's vehicle? Shouldn't I go in and say hi?" Surely, they knew he was there. He didn't want to be rude. Luke's parents had been like a second, slightly less crazy family to him growing up. His friend only had two annoying sisters, which had been much better than his five. And Luke's father had given him a part-time job stocking shelves at the family pharmacy when he was a teenager. They had always shown kindness to Brad.

"No," Luke said, shaking his head as he zipped his jacket and bent to tie his boots.

"Why not?"

"First of all, Kayla is in there and unless you want her falling all over you…"

"I don't know. I hear she's grown up to be quite a looker," Brad teased his friend. A stern look from Luke made him add quickly,

"Kidding, man. Just kidding." Sisters were off-limits. Always.

"Hey, buddy, I'm just trying to do you a favor. Mom is in there, too, and tomorrow night is the holiday bachelor auction at the community hall. If you go in there, you won't be leaving without a number."

"They still do that?" Brad shook his head. Not much changed in the small town. The bachelor auction annually raised money for the local medical clinic. He'd participated every year before moving to Nashville and he'd been one of the few men who'd enjoyed it—he was comfortable onstage, and he'd never been one to turn down a date with a pretty lady. Hmm, maybe he should participate. He wondered if Melody would be attending. Would she bid on him? A date with his best friend's widow. A shiver ran through him at that thought. She was about as off-limits as Luke's sister. What the hell was he thinking? His joke about the kiss the night before had been bad enough.

"Yes. And believe me, the only single women around here with unlimited cash flow seem to be Mrs. Norris and Lindsay Harper."

Brad laughed. "Fine, I won't go in."

He'd barely heard the front door creak before he was pushed straight into the hedges at the side of the house. What the...?

Luke's eyes widened and he placed a finger to his lips as his mother stepped onto the front porch.

Brad ducked lower.

"I thought I heard Brad out here," Mrs. Dawson said, looking around.

"Oh, yeah. He headed down to the lake already."

"And left you to carry his hockey gear?" She pointed to the hockey bag at Luke's feet.

"Ah, you know, since the accident he's kind of weak and stuff..."

Brad glared at his buddy over the hedge. Weak? He'd kick Luke Dawson's butt any day. Probably today if he kept up the trash talk.

"Oh, okay...well, Victoria is wondering about the paint color for the you-know-what." The woman's voice lowered.

Brad's suspicions had been right. His friend and his new wife were expecting. Well, they were smart to try to keep things to themselves, but they were crazy if they thought they were doing so successfully.

"I'll be right in," Luke said.

Mrs. Dawson went back inside and Brad came out of hiding. "Jeez, man. Weak?"

"I did it to save you. Trust me, the women at that auction are crazy. Anyway, I have to go help Victoria. I'll meet you down at the lake. Steve and the boys are already there setting up the nets." Luke bounded up the porch steps and waved him away.

"Sure. I'll carry your stuff. Prove I'm not weak."

Following the path to the lake's edge, Brad trudged through the deep, heavy snow. He shifted the hockey bags on his shoulder, wishing his leg didn't ache so much. Without the weekly physiotherapy sessions, the pain in his right shin was intense. The cold, damp weather wasn't helping. But as he drew closer, the sound of the crowd at the lake helped to distract him from the pain.

A large section of the frozen lake had been cleared of snow and a hockey net had been placed about twenty feet from the shore. Luke's nephew Steve was positioned as goalie in one net, and in the center, Melody, David, Josh and Melody's brothers Jim and Ethan were fighting for control of the puck. Brad hesitated before going farther. He hoped the Bishops wouldn't mind him being there. The family looked to be having such a great time, he didn't want to destroy the mood. Melody's smile lit up her face, and her dark hair whipped across her cheek as she skated toward the net and shot the puck. It sailed in past the teenager with ease. Impressive.

He set the equipment down on the shore and waved as David spotted him. "Hey, Brad, come on. Uncle Ethan and I could use some help. Those guys are kicking our butt." He gestured toward his mom and brother.

"Hey, I'm not used to the uneven surface," Ethan grumbled as the group made their way closer to shore to wait for Brad to lace up.

"Good excuse as any, I guess," Melody said.

Brad lowered himself to the ground and tugged off a boot, fighting his nerves. Luke hadn't mentioned that the family would be there, and while he was happy for the opportunity to spend more time with David and Josh, he suspected that Ethan and Jim wouldn't be pleased to see him. Still, he was ready to accept whatever they had to say. He deserved whatever was coming, no matter how bad.

Jim hung back, his expression tough to read, but Ethan's dark look was easy enough. "Monroe," he said tightly.

"Hey, Ethan."

Ethan scanned the trail behind him. "Where's your entourage?"

"I assume you mean the Heartland Country Television crew? They left last week. We're done filming."

"So why are you still here?"

"Ethan," Melody interjected with a quick glance at the boys.

Brad shifted on the cold ground and abandoned his skates. Maybe he should go. He obviously wasn't welcome here.

"He's teaching me to play guitar!" Josh chimed in excitedly.

"He's what?" Ethan turned his attention to Mel.

She looked uncomfortable, but she nodded.

Ethan's cell rang in the pocket of the coat

he'd discarded on the snowbank. He hesitated a moment before skating to the side to answer it. A second later, he was saying to Jim, "Come on! We're needed at the station. Sorry to cut out so early, guys." He dropped to the snowbank to untie his skates. Looking up at Melody, he asked, "You going to be okay?"

"Of course."

"Okay..." Turning to Brad, he said, "Watch yourself around my family."

MELODY STUDIED BRAD as he stood, skates on, hockey stick in hand. Dressed in a pair of navy ski pants and a formfitting, blue, down-filled jacket, he looked ready for the slopes of Vermont. He was far too well dressed for a game of shinny hockey in Brookhollow—and far too handsome. She felt her cheeks burn at the thought and quickly glanced away. Her brother's unfriendly warning had been a bit much, but she couldn't expect them to welcome Brad with open arms. In fact, she would have been hurt if they had.

Steve tossed out the puck and the game began again. They played two-on-two, with one goalie for each team. But with Brad's unsteadiness on the ice, she scored a goal for Josh's and her team.

"Where did you learn to play this well?" Brad asked, skating up next to her. He was slightly out of breath.

Melody brushed her hair away from her face. "I grew up with two hockey-crazed brothers and now I have twin boys of my own—what choice did I have but to learn to kick butt?"

"Well, I grew up only with sisters, so go easy on me, okay?" He winced, and Melody slowed her pace a little.

"Your leg bothering you?" She'd noticed him favoring it while playing, and she had also been aware of his slight limp when he'd walked into town. It seemed to have gotten a little worse every day since he'd been there.

"It's not too bad."

"Liar. Your limp has been getting worse," she said.

"It'll be fine once I resume my physio sessions back in Nashville," he said, positioning himself in front of her to battle for the puck.

That's right, she thought. He had a life in Nashville and therapy sessions he was missing in order to be here. Had what she'd said to him about using his family really affected him? Or was he just here in hopes of getting her song? She was so distracted she missed the puck drop and Brad snagged it away with ease, skating toward Steve in net and softly sending the puck past him, earning him high fives from his teammate.

Josh skated to the edge of the rink and collapsed in the snowbank. "I'm done."

"David, are you ready to go, too? Or do you want to play longer?" Melody asked.

"Can we stay?" David asked.

Melody glanced at Brad. "How are you holding up?"

"Great. Besides, I just tied the score, so we can't leave yet. When Luke gets here we can play two-on-two again," he suggested.

"Don't hold your breath," she said with a laugh. "Every time the poor guy tries to leave the house, his mother and Vic drag him back for something." She took her position across from Brad, set her stick on the ice and nodded for David to drop the puck. "Ready."

"Think you can take me and Brad all by yourself?" her son challenged.

"Without a doubt," Melody answered. "Drop it." Her eyes locked with Brad's and the amused look on his handsome face made her breath catch in her chest. As the puck hit the ice, she stumbled a bit, missing the opportunity to steal it.

Brad skated around her and passed the puck to David. "Without a doubt, huh?" he whispered as he whizzed toward the net. "Over here, I'm open," he said.

Not for long. Skating hard, Melody advanced to him as the puck sailed across the bumpy ice toward their sticks. Not slowing down, she collided with Brad and captured the puck.

"Whoa," was all she heard before Brad crashed to the ice. The sound of his head bouncing off the cold surface made her wince.

She dropped her stick and quickly knelt beside him. "You okay?" she asked, as his eyes shut and his head dropped to the side.

Apparently not.

THE COLD WETNESS seeping through his sweater beneath the edge of his jacket at his waist felt almost real this time. Brad waited for the familiar sequence of events to play out in the dream. Any second now he'd experience a shot of pain in his...head?

"Brad! Can you hear me?"

Melody? What was she doing in this dream? Feeling two soft, warm hands cup his face, he allowed his eyes to flutter open and expected to see an overcast sky and big white snowflakes falling. Instead, he was staring into a pair of beautiful dark eyes. Long, dark strands of hair hung against his exposed neck and the smell of gingerbread lingered in the air. His eyes closed again, and a slight wave of nausea overtook him.

"Brad!"

The voice calling his name sounded far away, but it was just loud enough to create an echo in his ears. One that made his head throb. "Shh," he whispered.

The voice softened, lowered and drew nearer to his ear. A warm cheek touched his cold one. "Brad, open your eyes," the voice urged.

He did, and despite the double vision, he smiled up at the two Melodys hovering above him. "You smell like cookies."

"What?"

"Gingerbread—" he sniffed the air "—and maybe a hint of cinnamon."

"Okay, you must have a concussion. Stay still. I'll go get Luke."

"No! Don't leave." He gripped her arm as another wave of nausea washed over him. With his other hand, he felt the uneven ice near his leg and his hockey stick. Clearly he was on his back on the lake, but he hadn't a clue how he'd gotten there. "What happened?" he asked, attempting to sit up. *Whoa, bad idea.* He lay back down and three smaller faces appeared above him. Okay, the twins were really messing with his vision.

"Mom bodychecked you to get the puck," Josh said.

At least he thought it was Josh.

"I did not," Melody protested. "It was an accident."

"No way," Steve insisted. "It was totally a direct hit…and an illegal one. Brad didn't even have the puck."

"You took me out of the game?" Despite the throbbing in the back of his head, her competitive nature made him laugh.

"I didn't mean to," Melody mumbled. "Can you sit up?" she asked.

"Maybe." He tried, but when he did his surroundings spun out of control. "Maybe not. You know what? I'm okay here. I'll just sleep it off."

"You can't sleep. You could have a concussion. We should get you to the clinic."

"What's going on?" Luke asked, joining the group.

"He fell," Melody said.

"Mom pushed him," David said.

Luke looked at Melody in surprise. "But I thought you two were…communicating."

From the ground, Brad tried to swipe at Luke's leg. "Shh, don't tell her I said that. We're making…progress…" The mumbling protest died on his lips as everything started to go black again. His eyes were too heavy to hold open, but the voices continued around him. He must still have been conscious.

"He needs to go to the clinic. Can you help me get him back to the van?" Melody asked Luke.

"Sure. Where did you park?"

"Just in the cul-de-sac outside your house,"

Melody said. They hoisted Brad up and off the ice.

"Here, I got him," Luke said, supporting his weight. "You should go bring the van to the street on the other side of that snowbank," he said, gesturing across the lake.

"Why?"

"He can't go near the house. Mom keeps looking out the kitchen window, checking for him. If she sees him, he's as good as Bachelor Number One for the auction tomorrow night."

That snapped Brad to attention and he jerked his head. *Ow!* He reached up and winced as his hand touched the goose egg on the back of his head. "Even injured?"

"Knowing Mom, she'd use it as a selling point."

CHAPTER TEN

"FOLLOW THE LIGHT with just your eyes," Dr. Carson said, holding her tiny flashlight in front of Brad's face twenty minutes later.

Brad perched on the edge of the examination table at the walk-in clinic and did as he had been instructed. The waiting room had been almost full of patients hoping to be seen by Dr. Carson, but they'd all insisted Brad go ahead of them, as he had been struggling to remain conscious.

"Good." The doctor set the light back into the pocket of her lab coat and gently touched the back of his head, then applied pressure to both sides. He winced when her fingers found the lump. "Wow, that's a doozy. How did it happen?"

"Playing hockey on the lake behind the old Kingston home—my friends Luke and Vic's house," Brad said. He couldn't give her any more detail than that. All he knew was that one moment he had been waiting to accept the puck and the next he had been opening his eyes to a gorgeous pair of dark ones.

"Rough game," the doctor said, taking his temperature. The thermometer beeped with its reading. "Just a low-grade fever—nothing to worry about. Your vision and hearing are fine. Are you still dizzy?"

"Not so much anymore," he said. He'd battled dizzy spells on the fast drive to the clinic in the front seat of Melody's van, as she'd constantly warned him not to sleep. Thankfully, since arriving at the clinic, the dizziness had eased off.

"Well, you're going to have a headache, and you should stay awake for at least four or five hours. But other than that, I think you're fine. If the dizzy spells or waves of nausea return, please come back here right away."

"Will do," Brad said, climbing down slowly from the table. The back of his head ached. "Any idea how long this pounding on my skull will last?"

"Normally just a few hours. I'll write you a prescription for some painkillers. Just give me a minute." Dr. Carson left the room.

Brad wrapped his scarf around his neck and sat down to put his winter boots back on. The simple motion of leaning forward made him slightly queasy. He rested his head against the wall. A baby photo fell onto his lap, and picking it up, he turned to stick it back onto the pegboard. There he saw several photos of his godsons. Born three weeks early at a little less than six pounds each, they had been the cutest babies he'd ever seen. He suspected he remembered that night as well as, if not better than, Melody did.

The band had been playing a gig in Beach Haven, in a tiny dive bar with about ten people scattered throughout. They had been in the middle of the third song in their set of eight when Patrick's cell phone ringing had caused their amplifiers to make the most god-awful screeching sound. And no matter how loudly the club manager yelled that they'd never play a gig in New Jersey again, they'd taken off, speeding down the highway as quickly as the slick November roads would allow. Patrick had been so nervous, talking on the phone to his panicked wife, promising her he would make it in time.

Brad had been determined to get Mel's husband to her side before she gave birth. He'd gotten a speeding ticket, but he'd delivered his best friend to the clinic in time for the birth of his children. Everything had worked out—that night.

The office door opened and the doctor reentered. "Here you are," she said, handing him the prescription for the painkillers. "Take no more than two tonight."

"Thank you."

"Oh, and maybe try not to annoy Melody Myers any more on this visit, huh?" she added with a smile.

"Trust me, this was nothing. Last week she threatened to run me over with her van."

"SO, SHOULD I DRIVE you back to Luke's for your rental car?" Melody asked as Brad climbed into the passenger side of the minivan. While he'd been in the clinic, she'd dropped the boys back home with the babysitter and changed for her evening shift at the Green Gator.

"Um…no, I shouldn't drive while I'm on these prescription painkillers," he said, putting on his seat belt.

"Back to the tree lot, then?" She turned the van out onto the street.

Brad eyed her. "You changed." He turned and glanced into the backseat. "Where are the boys?"

"I drove them back to my place. I have to work at the Gator tonight. So, home?"

He hesitated. "How busy will it be there tonight?"

"At your house?" How would she know? She suspected the farm might be a little busy...

"At the Gator."

"Oh, completely dead," she said. The nasty weather and driving conditions tended to keep families at home this time of year. "Maybe a couple of staff parties..." She glanced at him. "But surely your head hurts too much for even the slightest noise."

"Have you been to my house this time of year?" He laughed. "Ow." He rubbed the back of his head.

He had a point. "Okay, the Green Gator it is."

He sniffed the air and scanned the van. Giving her a puzzled look, he leaned closer and smelled her hair.

"What are you doing, weirdo?" she asked, moving away from him. She hadn't had time to shower. The last thing she wanted was him sniffing her.

"I smell gingerbread cookies again," he said.

"I don't know..." Then she realized. Her new holiday-scented lotion. "Oh, it's my body lotion. It's ginger spice."

"That delicious smell is coming from your skin?" he asked, intrigued.

Melody swallowed hard and ignored the comment. After a few minutes, she parked the van in the lot of the Green Gator. "Here we are." She cut the engine, opened her door and jumped down. Never before had she been so grateful for the freezing winter air—now it cooled her warm, crimson cheeks. He thought she smelled delicious. She wished she could define the feeling coursing through her. It was odd, different... not totally unwelcome...which of course made it completely unwelcome. *It's Brad Monroe. Get ahold of yourself.*

Inside the bar, only two tables were occupied. "Looks like you have your choice of seats." She gestured to the empty booths along the wall and the vacant tables near the karaoke stage.

"I'll sit at the bar," he said.

Of course he would. Lifting the gate, she went behind the bar. "Hey T.J.," she said. He already had his coat and hat on.

"I think you can handle this crowd tonight." T.J. handed her the keys to the place. "I'm heading out."

In recent months, he often left her to lock up on their slower nights. She preferred to be alone at the end of the shift, but tonight Brad would be there, and the thought of being in an empty bar with him later that evening made her heart race. She said, "Yeah, I got it. Drive safe." She tied her black bar apron over her tight jeans and red V-neck shirt. She grabbed a dish towel and emptied the dishwasher. "Do you want something to drink?" she asked Brad.

He removed his coat and draped it over the back of the bar stool. "Water to take another one of these horse pills would be great. The first one doesn't seem to be doing much." He opened the bottle and shook one into his hand.

She poured him a glass of water and slid

it across the bar. She filled a bowl with peanuts and placed it between them on the counter. Neither of them had eaten yet, and her stomach was rumbling.

"Hey, Mel, can you flick the light switch?" Kyle Johnson, the local DJ and karaoke host, called to her from the staging area, where he was set up for the evening.

"Sure," she said, hitting the switch for the multicolor floor lighting around the small stage.

"You mean he's still going to set up when there's no one here?" Brad said, swallowing the pill and draining the contents of the glass.

"Afraid so, and it looks like *they* will be this evening's entertainment," Melody said, nodding in the direction of a booth in the corner where four twentysomething girls were huddled over the song-selection book, writing their requests on tiny slips of paper. The ever-growing pile on the table in front of them made her cringe. She'd seen several of them in here before—not one could sing a note. "I may need a few of those myself." She gestured toward the bottle of prescription painkillers still sitting on the bar in front of Brad.

A girl took the stage a moment later and began singing Taylor Swift's "Love Story." Brad turned to Melody with a look of horror. "How do you stand it?" he asked, resting his elbow on the bar and casually covering his ear closest to the stage with his fist.

Melody laughed as she made a pot of coffee. They were going to need it. It was going to be a long night. "On busy nights, it's not that bad. I can usually tune them out as I work."

The girl failed to hit a high note and Brad winced. "Taylor would die if she heard her song being tortured like that."

Melody raised an eyebrow.

"Sorry, I'm name-dropping again."

He was, but she couldn't help but fall for it as she leaned on the counter across from him and reached for a handful of peanuts. "You've met Taylor Swift?"

"Just once at a charity event last summer. Sweet girl."

"David is in love with her. He doesn't think anyone knows, but I saw her songs on the MP3 player his grandparents gave to him for his birthday."

"I have her autograph on a shirt from the event. I'll send it to David when I get back to Nashville."

"Wow, he'd love that, thank you." She knew her son would cherish the item—secretly, of course.

"So, do you ever sing, Mel?" Brad nodded toward the stage as the girl finished her song to the applause of her friends.

"Sometimes…when it's slow." She usually enjoyed evenings like this at the bar. As the crowds dwindled late in the evening, she often found herself onstage, singing to the bar's empty walls, as Kyle took extended smoke breaks outside. Sometimes she'd even let herself imagine what it would be like if she'd followed her dream of going to Nashville years before. Where would she be now? How would her life have changed? Would she have made it?

"Now would be a good time," he said, rubbing the back of his head. The next girl onstage singing "Hit Me with Your Best Shot" was no better than her friend had been.

"I don't think so." The idea of singing in

front of him made her uneasy. She wasn't sure why it made her uneasy all of a sudden, but it did.

"Oh, come on—you owe me for the concussion."

"Well, you shouldn't have been on the ice if you can't play with the big boys," she said, ignoring the voice in her head that was warning her not to flirt.

Brad leaned forward on the bar, placing his hands on her arms to hold her in place. "Rematch anytime, anywhere. I'll even let you pick the game."

She prayed the dim lighting in the bar hid the deepening color on her exposed neck and chest. Agreeing to play any game with him would be more than stupid—it would be dangerous.

A loud shriek made her jump and she backed away from Brad. As one of the girls approached the bar, she was both grateful for and annoyed at the interruption. "Looks like someone finally recognized you," she muttered, turning to the coffeepot. She needed caffeine and something to occupy her hands. From the corner of her eye, she watched the pretty redhead flirt with Brad, a scene she'd witnessed a hundred times before. So why was it bothering her this time?

"I just love your new single 'In the Morning,'" the girl was saying. A hand to her chest, she hummed several bars.

Hopefully it doesn't sound exactly like that, Melody mused.

"I feel like you're singing the words right to me…" the girl continued to gush.

Oh, come on, Melody thought. That was exactly what country music was supposed to do. The genre was made of songs that people could relate to, about real love, real heartache…

"Yeah, that's a great song," Brad said when the girl stopped for breath. "It's not one of mine, though."

Oh, my God.

The karaoke singer frowned. "You sure?"

This was too much. Melody laughed, and then covered it with a cough.

"Definitely would have remembered recording it," Brad said.

"Well, whatever. Sing for us." The girl grabbed his arm.

"Oh, no, I'm just here hanging out with Mel."

The girl swung her eyes to Melody, apparently noticing her for the first time. The jealousy in her eyes took Melody aback. "She won't mind, right?"

"He's all yours," Melody said, a tight smile on her lips. She meant it—the girl could have him. *She* certainly wasn't interested...

"See?" Turning back to Brad, the redhead plastered a flirty smile on her face.

"Really, I'm not here to perform..."

"Come on, Brad. Just sing for the girl."

He shot Melody a look, and then reluctantly said, "Fine. What do you want to hear?"

"'Hey Girl' by Billy Currington."

Brad's face fell, and Melody turned quickly to hide another laugh. Not even one of his own songs. Talk about a blow to the ego. She felt badly for him—almost.

"Okay, Billy Currington it is," Brad said. "Why don't you go put the request in?"

Melody watched as the young girl rushed back to her table to fill out the song request sheet for Brad.

"Do not laugh," he said, pointing a finger at Melody.

She held her hands up. "I'm sorry, but that was almost painful to watch."

"Now do you see why I need your help? The only songs people want to hear me sing aren't even mine."

"WHERE DO THESE GO?" Brad removed several shot glasses from the dishwasher a long six hours later.

"You really don't have to help," Melody said. She was sweeping the wooden bar floor in front of the karaoke stage. "Besides, you're concussed, remember?"

"Not too concussed to help you out. The painkiller's working," he said, locating a spot on the glass shelf behind him for the tiny glasses. "But you know what would make this more fun?"

"Forget it," she said.

"You don't even know what I was going to say."

"You were going to ask me to sing again."

"Okay, maybe you do." He emptied the remaining beer glasses. "Come on, Mel. Just one song. I did a couple." The group of girls had been relentless with their requests of him, but given his concussion, he'd only consented to two. None of the songs they'd requested had been his, anyway, which had been a drag. But he was dying to get Melody up onstage. He wanted to see if she still had the spark, the vibrancy she used to exude onstage. He suspected she did. More than that, he wanted to see her passion—he knew it was still there.

"No."

Crossing the bar, he wrestled the broom from her. "There's no one in here. What are you afraid of?"

"I'm not afraid," she said, bending to unplug the artificial Christmas tree near the stage. "I just don't want to sing."

He stopped sweeping. "That's not the Melody I remember. The one I remember didn't want to do anything but sing."

"That was a long time ago."

He moved toward her, setting the broom in the corner of the wall next to the bar. "Not that long ago. Besides, I don't think it's something that goes away."

"Brad, just drop it, okay? I'm begging you."

"One song and I'll leave you alone."

"One song and you'll *never* leave me alone." She grabbed the broom again and handed it to him. "Get back to work."

CHAPTER ELEVEN

THE NEXT MORNING, Melody pulled the van over to the side of Main Street near the only traffic light in Brookhollow. Leaving the vehicle running, she jumped down and approached the fire truck parked in the lane. Her brother Jim was dusting heavy snow from the lights and Ethan was controlling the ladder from inside the vehicle. Her younger brother had discovered he had a fear of heights at that year's FireFit challenge competition. Now he preferred to pull his captain's rank card whenever possible and make the others do anything that required climbing. He rolled down the window as she approached. "Hey, sis. What's up?"

"Hey, does Bailey have a dress I could borrow?" she asked, unable to conceal the desperation in her voice. She couldn't believe she hadn't thought of this before now, but then again, her life had been falling apart around her in recent months. After she had dropped Brad off and driven home the night before, she'd received a message confirming her performance at the annual Mayor's Christmas Gala. The party was that evening, and Melody was in panic mode.

"Have you met my fiancée?" Ethan gave her a look suggesting she was crazy.

"Crap." He was right. It had been a long shot. Her brother's fiancée was more comfortable in her work coveralls than in anything remotely feminine. Melody had been shocked when she'd agreed to be in Victoria and Luke's wedding party three months before. She wondered how the town mechanic would enjoy wearing a wedding dress.

"Why do you ask?"

When she told him, Ethan shuddered at the mention of his almost father-in-law, Mayor Parsons. Despite having dated the mayor's daughter for ten years, he'd never really gotten along with her family, and luckily Emily had moved to Miami, leaving Ethan to discover true love with Bailey. "Why on earth would you even consider going to that?" he asked his sister. "Pretentious cocktail parties are not exactly your idea of a good time."

"They hired me to sing." She wished she could have refused, but she needed the money.

"Done!" Jim called out to Ethan, who lowered the ladder slowly. "Hey, Mel. What brings you by?" He shook the snow from his jacket.

"I was hoping Ethan could help me with a dress for tonight," she said.

Jim looked back and forth between them. "Something you two aren't telling me?"

Melody rolled her eyes. "I meant a dress of Bailey's."

Jim laughed. "Seriously? *Ethan* would have a dress before Bailey. What do you need it for?"

"The Mayor's Christmas Gala tonight."

Jim made a face. "That sucks. Are you sure it's a dress you need and not a stick up your…"

"Hey! The Parsonses aren't that bad, Jim." Though he came to the family's defense, Ethan's protest still sounded weak.

"I'm glad you two think this is funny," Melody said. "Anyway, I better go look elsewhere for a dress."

"Jill might have something," Jim offered. "I could check with her." He'd climbed into the truck and was leaning around Ethan to talk to her through the open window.

"Yeah, right." Jim's girlfriend, Jill, was a personal trainer and a health fanatic. Anything Jill owned would be too small for Melody.

"What size are you?"

"As if I'd tell you that." How Jim even had a girlfriend was beyond her. He clearly did not understand women.

"Fine. If you change your mind, give her a call. She has a closet full of stuff that still has tags on it," he said.

"Okay, thanks," she said. But she doubted asking Jill would be an option.

Ten minutes later, she parked her van in front of the only formal clothing store in Brookhollow, Daisies and Dukes. She rushed inside and went straight to the counter.

The owner, Lily, looked up with a smile. "Happy holidays, Mel. What can I do for you?"

"I need a fancy dress. I don't care what color, just something in a size four..." She cleared her throat. "Size six..."

The store owner looked at her as if she were crazy.

"Okay, fine. Size eight." She'd gained weight since having the boys...and her hips had seemed to expand another inch each year.

"No, honey, it's not that. I just don't have anything left. Tonight is Mayor Parsons's—"

"I know. That's what I need it for." Nothing left? How was that possible? How many women in Brookhollow were going to this event, anyway? Why had she left this until the last minute? She frantically scoured the rack of dresses lining the wall. "What about those?"

"Those are prom dresses."

That explained the hideous pastel colors. "You have nothing? You're sure?"

The store owner shook her head apologetically. "I had two returns, but one has a tear..."

"Where?" Maybe she could work with that. She wasn't much of a seamstress, but Victoria's mom was the best seamstress in Brookhollow, and maybe she would be able to make it wearable.

"Right on the shoulder. It won't work, Mel."

"The other?" She remained hopeful. She needed a dress.

Lily reached behind her and picked up a navy-and-white eyesore. Melody tried to hide her distaste for the garment. Her seventy-year-old grandmother wouldn't wear that. "Who returned it?" Better question: Who bought it in the first place?

"Mrs. Norris."

"Ginger?" The seventy-four-year-old woman owned the bakery on Main Street. "Why did she return it?"

"Said it made her look old." Lily hid a smile.

"So that's it?"

"Sorry, Mel. I won't have any new stock until January. My designers are all taking a few weeks off over the holidays."

Melody eyed the navy-and-white fabric. Maybe she could dress it up with a great pair of shoes?

When she suggested as much to Lily, the shopkeeper shook her head. "Forget it, Melody. I am not selling you this dress. Sorry, honey. I wish I could have been more help."

"It's my fault for waiting until the last minute. Thanks, anyway, Lily." She exited the store and phoned Jill. Somehow or other she would have to squeeze her body into something hanging in her future sister-in-law's closet.

"Hi, Melody," a friendly voice said after the third ring.

"Hey, Jill. Can I come raid your closet?"

"MAYOR PARSONS, don't tell me you've waited this long to get your tree," Brad said as the older man approached. In a tan overcoat and dark brown dress shoes, the mayor stepped carefully across the packed snow and ice. Not exactly tree-hunting clothes, Brad thought. He suspected the man had come straight from his office.

The mayor nodded and removed his leather gloves. "I'm afraid so… And our annual holiday party is this evening, so I'm desperate."

Brad lowered his voice and nodded toward his brother-in-law and nephew, who were helping the Mason family secure their tree to the top of their SUV. "Don't let Troy hear you say that—the price may go up."

The mayor shrugged. "Well, I'm at his mercy. Show me what you got left," he said. He followed Brad through the trail of trees behind him.

"Were you looking for a spruce or a pine tree?" Brad asked for what seemed like the hundredth time that day. The family farm was as busy as it had always been, and he marveled at his sister's and brother-in-law's ability to take care of things mostly on their own. He was happy to be able to help them this season.

"Pine, I think." He paused. "Lillian's going to kill me if I get this wrong…"

Brad waited.

"Ah, she'll probably be too busy with the last-minute party preparations to notice," he said with a laugh. "Let's just go with a pine."

"Okay, over this way…"

Twenty minutes and fifteen untied, examined and retied trees later, Brad secured the chosen tree to Mayor Parsons's SUV. "Okay, you're all set."

The man reached for his wallet. "Great. You quite possibly just saved me from the doghouse. How much do I owe you?"

"Forty-five."

"Here you are. Thank you and Merry Christmas!" The older man extended a hand and Brad accepted it.

"Same to you." Brad slid his hands back into his work gloves and scanned the long line of customers waiting by the gate. His sister Breanne handed out saws to the groups interested in cutting down their own trees, but the line for the precut ones was growing by the minute. It was going to be a busy afternoon. Thank God he'd gotten a decent sleep the night before, and no longer even had a headache.

He watched as the mayor carefully made his way to his driver's-side door, and then hesitated before opening it. "Hey, Brad, what're you doing tonight?" he asked.

Damn. Brad realized he should have moved on to the next customer right away. The last thing he wanted to do was attend the mayor's stuffy holiday party. He searched his mind for a good excuse. "Um…I think the kids' Christmas concert is tonight."

"That's tomorrow," the mayor said.

"Right."

"So you're free, then?"

Unfortunately. "Looks that way." After

a long day working on the tree lot, the last thing he wanted to do was get dressed up to go to the most pretentious party in Brookhollow that season. In Nashville he attended high society events and for the most part always felt uncomfortable. A country boy at heart, he preferred jeans and a T-shirt to a tuxedo.

"Well, I know it's not the formal invite my wife sent out to her hundreds of friends three months ago, but please accept my invitation. We would love to have you. Heck, if we'd known you were sticking around, we'd have canceled the band..."

"You've hired live entertainment?" While the mayor and his family lived in the small town, they entertained like big-city politicians. Their four-thousand-square-foot home at the edge of the town park was extravagant and out of place in the quaint, picturesque town. And most of their party guests would be from out of town. Few locals made the guest list.

"Yes," he confirmed. "A fantastic jazz band from Boston...and Melody Myers has agreed to grace us with her lovely voice."

"Melody will be performing?" Brad had

assumed when she'd given up singing, she'd given it up completely. Apparently she still performed at local events. Interesting. She could claim to have left music behind all she wanted, but the fact that she still performed, given the opportunity, revealed otherwise. He mentally tucked away that tidbit to use the next time they argued over her future in music.

"It took a lot of convincing, but yes," the mayor said. "So we can expect to see you tonight?"

Definitely. He'd never pass up an opportunity to hear Melody sing and then use it to try to convince her to reconsider his offer. "What time should I be there?"

"MAY I TAKE your coat?" A man dressed in a tuxedo asked as Brad entered the large foyer of the Parsonses' home that evening. The home was phenomenal and impressive, decorated tastefully with red and white poinsettias on the tabletops. Large thick boughs of holly and white lights had been draped over the railing of the spiral staircase that led to the large open area upstairs. There he could see the party guests dressed in their finest.

He could hear the jazz band's saxophon-ist playing "I'll Be Home for Christmas." The song held meaning for him this year. He removed his overcoat and handed it to the woman working the coat check in the foyer. "Thank you."

"Champagne?" A pretty waitress in a red velvet dress asked as he readjusted his bow tie and buttoned his tuxedo jacket. He'd been lucky that the men's clothing store in the mall also rented wedding attire. This time of year, he'd been able to rent the tuxedo without any trouble. Anything other than the formal wear would have been unacceptable at that evening's function.

Tempting. "No, thank you." He headed up the stairs.

Darlene Dawson spotted him first and wagged a finger in mock annoyance as she approached. "You missed my bachelor auc-tion last night."

"As handsome as the men are around here, they're not exactly my type," he said. He hugged Luke's mother.

"You know that's not what I meant, young man," she said, kissing his cheek. "Great to see you."

"The pleasure is mine. You look beautiful as usual," he said, twirling her around and letting out an appreciative whistle. Luke's mother didn't look a day over forty, with her long blond hair showing no gray and her incredible, well-maintained shape. She looked stunning in a red-sequined gown.

"Watch it, Brad," Frank Dawson said as he approached and wrapped an arm around his wife's waist. The pharmacist in town kept himself healthy and youthful, too, and looked like a slightly older version of his son. Victoria and Luke's new addition would certainly come from good genes.

"Merry Christmas, Frank," Brad said, extending a hand to the man. Brad scanned the room. "Great crowd." He estimated that there were close to 150 in the open-concept dining and living area where the invitees had all congregated.

"This holiday party is well attended every year. We started preparations in August," Darlene whispered.

As the head of the social committee in Brookhollow, Darlene Dawson was the best event-planner in town. Brad was searching the room for one guest in particular. "Have you seen Melody yet?"

Darlene's eyes widened. "No, but she *will* be here…"

"It's okay. We've…" He had no idea what he'd been about to say. Then out of the corner of his eye, he noticed her coming up the staircase behind them. Champagne glass in one hand, off-white fabric of the long, flowing gown she wore in the other, she looked beautiful. Sleeveless and high-collared, the dress was elegant and conservative, yet the soft fabric hugged her curves, giving more than a hint of the shapely body underneath. Her diamond bracelet and matching earrings reflected the crystal snowflakes hanging from the ceiling and created a glistening effect all around her as she moved. "Excuse me," he told the Dawsons, without as much as a glance toward them. He couldn't tear his eyes from her.

"Enjoy your evening, son," he barely heard called after him as he approached Melody at the top of the staircase.

She gave a nervous smile when she saw him. Man, she was gorgeous. Every day, not just that evening—although the dress she wore tonight commanded the attention of everyone in the room. He shook his head. He had to get a grip. He was not allowed to ogle Patrick Myers's widow.

"Hi," she said.

"You are stunning." Ogling and simply stating the obvious were two different things, he told himself.

"It's not even my dress," she said through a small laugh. "I borrowed it from Jill."

He didn't fail to notice the slight shaking of her hand as she raised her champagne glass to her lips, which were painted hollyberry red. "Trust me, it's not the dress that has everyone staring."

Her cheeks turned the color of her lips and she glanced away. Noticing the crowd, she said, "Look at all these people!"

"Oh, it's nothing. Just two hundred of the state's finest."

"That's not helping," she swiped at him and he caught her hand. He tucked it into the crook of his arm as he moved to stand next to her.

"Oh, come on. Look at them. So uptight...so boring. You have nothing to worry about." He couldn't resist the temptation to lean closer to her. Just as he'd expected—gingerbread. Never again would he be able to associate that smell with anything but Melody's skin.

"You're sniffing me again," she said, moving away slightly.

"Try not to smell so good. Maybe then I'll stop," he said, his eyes meeting hers squarely. Man, what was wrong with him? Flirting with Melody would only result in bodily injury—as it should.

Instead, she surprised him by saying, "One green, one blue."

"I ran out of colored contacts."

"This is better," she said. "This is the guy I know."

He swallowed hard. What was happening here? She hadn't slapped him, she hadn't walked away. And she'd flirted back. That was almost more unsettling.

"Melody! We were starting to think you'd changed your mind," Lillian Parsons's shrill voice cut the air between them.

Melody took a quick step away from Brad. Turning to Lillian, she said, "Oh, only every three minutes."

"Nonsense. You will be fabulous."

To Brad's ears, it almost sounded like a command.

"And you look amazing. Where on earth did you find that dress?" The woman did not try to conceal the look of envy in her eyes.

Melody opened her mouth, but Brad cut in. "It's from a new up-and-coming designer in New York," he lied. "Boretchelli." The made-up name slid off his tongue and earned him a frown from Melody.

"Boretchelli," Lillian repeated. "I have to remember that name. Okay, darling, the band is ready for you."

"Is there somewhere I can warm up for a few minutes?"

Lillian checked the nonexistent watch on her slender wrist. "Sure, take ten. Down the hall to your left. The sitting room is quiet and no one will bother you there."

"Thank you," Melody said as Lillian moved to join her husband, who was talking to the Miller family. "Why did you lie to her?" she hissed at Brad.

Brad shrugged. "Couldn't help myself."

"Well, try to behave," she said.

"And die of boredom? Forget it."

"I don't have time to babysit you. I have to go warm up. I'll...see you later?"

She'd better believe she would. He didn't want to part with her now. "Definitely," he said, and then caught her hand as she turned away. Her soft skin made him want to pull her closer. "Want some advice?"

She raised an eyebrow. "Don't do it?"

"It's too late for that. Find a smiling face in the crowd to look at until you get comfortable." Moving closer, he whispered against her cheek, "Try mine. I won't let you down."

"I was the one who taught you that," she said over her shoulder as she walked away.

In the room down the hall, Melody fought to calm her racing pulse. She'd been nervous enough before arriving. Just the thought of performing in front of this wealthy crowd made her uneasy. Weddings and funerals were different. At those she just had to perform one song, and the attendees were usually distracted, wrapped up as they were in feelings of joy or grief. Tonight she had to perform five songs with the jazz band, which people would be paying attention to. And then of course Brad would be there.

Had she imagined the moment that had just transpired between them? Things were getting ridiculous—first his joke about the kiss, then his company at the Green Gator. Now she was even flirting back.

She sipped her room-temperature water, glancing over the sheet music for her set and humming the melodies softly.

A man in a tuxedo entered the den. "They're ready for you, Ms. Myers," he announced.

Wow, Lillian really had meant ten minutes. "Okay." Straightening her dress over her hips, she followed him back to the main party area. The band had stopped playing and Lillian Parsons was standing on the raised platform stage they'd constructed for social events such as this one.

"We are pleased to announce our special guest vocalist of the evening—Melody Myers," she said.

As she gripped her lucky microphone, Mel was grateful she hadn't sold it yet. She carefully crossed the stage in Jill's strappy silver heels and took her place near the smiling saxophone player. "Hi," she whispered, setting her score sheets on the podium. She knew the familiar Christmas songs by heart, but sometimes nerves could take over. It was comforting to have the sheet music nearby.

"Hi. I'm Dexter...this is Mike and Armando..." the saxophonist introduced the other members of the band, one on piano, the other on flute.

"Nice to meet you all. Start with 'I'll Be Home for Christmas'?" she asked and got a series of nods.

She turned and positioned herself near the front of the stage as the sound of the intro began on the piano behind her. She swallowed the lump in her throat and scanned the crowd. Where was he? As nervous as his being there made her, she knew he was probably the only one in the crowd who could put her at ease. The sound of a small cough to her left caught her attention, and her eyes met his. He was leaning against the bar, his jacket unbuttoned. His eyes were on her, a wide, knee-weakening smile on his face. Okay, maybe looking at him wasn't such a great idea, she thought as she started to sing. Still, she kept her eyes on him for the first two bars before she felt her shoulders relax to the gentle sound of the saxophone next to her. She proceeded to take in the rest of the captivated room. She couldn't deny it. She loved to perform.

BRAD WATCHED AS Melody made her way through the swarm of people complimenting her on her performance a half hour later. Still perched near the bar where he'd marveled at her goose-bump-inducing delivery of "Silent Night," he waited, not wanting to take her away from the praise she so deserved, yet desperate to offer his own. The woman had incredible talent. Her voice was like silk and her stage presence was by far the best he'd ever seen. If only she believed in herself. Her eyes sparkled as she approached him. He knew the rush of adrenaline coursing through her now—he felt it every time he performed. It was intoxicating and addictive.

"Hi."

"Hi, yourself," he said, handing her a glass of champagne. "Wonderful performance." He wished he could add something the others hadn't. Taking her hand, he said, "You absolutely glow up there."

She took a sip of the champagne, her hand trembling slightly. "I'm still shaking."

"Adrenaline, not nerves, right?"

"Yeah," she said with a wistful sigh, climbing onto the empty bar stool next to him.

"I love that feeling—the rush, the excitement, the thrill of doing what you love." Somehow he had to make her see, she could have this. She deserved it.

"You're relentless," she said.

"Maybe." As the band resumed, he asked, "Care to dance?" All of a sudden, he had an irresistible urge to be closer to her. The faint scent of her ginger-spice body lotion lingered in the air and he longed to breathe her in. Tomorrow, he would put to rest these unexplainable feelings, but right now, the temptation was too strong.

"I don't know. It's getting late."

"Come on, you can't leave yet. You're a star. Enjoy it." He took her glass and set it on the bar before helping her down from the stool.

"Okay," she agreed. She followed him to the middle of the dance floor, where couples were moving in time to the slow music.

Brad kept his smile in place under the scrutinizing looks they received. His grip tightened on Melody's hand as he felt her shrink back momentarily. Turning, he gripped her other hand, drawing her into the space between them before she could escape. Placing a hand firmly on her exposed lower back, he began to step to the music, forcing her to follow him. A nagging voice told him this wasn't a good idea, but he ignored it.

Her eyes were on his chest as she whispered, "People are staring at us..."

"They're not staring at us, they're staring at me. I'm a celebrity—it happens all the time." His voice was light and teasing. He placed a hand under her chin and tipped her face up to look at him.

She cocked her head to the side.

"It's fine," he said. "Relax. We're just two friends dancing." He wished it were that simple. But the history they shared already made this so much more. He *wished* the only feeling he was experiencing was a friendly one.

"Are we?" Melody searched his face.

He prayed he could conceal how he was really starting to feel about her. He pretended not to understand. "Dancing? Sure, sort of. I mean, not as well as…"

"That's not what I meant. Are we friends, Brad?"

He grew serious as he pulled her closer and buried his face in her hair. God, that delicious smell was going to be the death of him. "I hope so," he whispered.

MELODY STARED AT her reflection in the bathroom mirror as she reapplied her lipstick moments later. What was she doing? Dancing with Brad in front of all of these people? Even more disturbing was how the dance had made her feel. The euphoric sensation of performing had paled in comparison to the pleasure she'd gotten from being held in Brad's strong arms. Her busy, stressful, work-filled life never allowed for moments of pure enjoyment such as the ones she'd experienced that evening. She felt a little like Cinderella in her borrowed dress, enjoying borrowed time. By midnight, it would all be over.

She wouldn't prolong the inevitable. She had to leave. She needed to distance herself from all of this, especially from Brad, before everything got too far out of hand. She hoped it wasn't already too late.

"Leaving so early, Ms. Myers?" the coat-check girl asked.

"Yes."

"Oh, I was hoping you'd sing again tonight—your voice is so beautiful," she said wistfully.

"Thank you," Melody said as she accepted her coat.

"Do you need us to call a taxi for you?" the girl asked.

Shoot, that was right. She didn't have her van with her. The last thing she'd wanted was to arrive at the mayor's elegant home in her run-down vehicle. She'd come in a cab.

"Yes, please," Brad said from behind her as he handed the girl his ticket for his coat.

The girl's expression turned to one of awe as she rushed to retrieve his coat. "Yes, Mr. Monroe...uh...Jackson."

"Monroe," Brad said. He turned to Melody. "Leaving without saying goodbye?" he asked.

"It's getting late," she replied. "I have to get home to the boys, but you shouldn't leave." Them leaving the party together wouldn't look any better than their dancing together. And the idea of sharing a cab with him really didn't appeal to her. She just needed to get away from him, away from the unwelcome emotions she was experiencing when in his presence.

"After you leave, there won't be anyone here I want to talk to."

"You really should stay," Melody said again as he took her coat and held it open for her. As she slid her arms through, he lifted her hair over the collar and his hands grazed the sides of her neck, causing a shiver to ripple down her spine. They definitely shouldn't spend any more time together, especially not alone.

"Nope, I'm leaving." Brad put on his own overcoat and wrapped his scarf around his neck. He reached into his pocket and pulled out his gloves. They made their way to the door, where they could already see a taxi parked outside. "Do you have gloves?" he asked.

She shook her head.

"Wear these," he said.

"I'm fine."

"Stop being stubborn." He took her right

hand and pulled the large glove over it, and then proceeded to do the other. "I'm sorry if I made things awkward."

She'd have liked to blame him. Over the years it had gotten easy to do so. But tonight had been her fault as much as it had been his. She'd enjoyed dancing with him. Enjoyed how it had felt to be looked at the way he'd looked at her. Enjoyed the feel of his arms around her. And she had no right to enjoy any of that. "That's not why I'm leaving."

His gaze locked with hers. "Isn't it?"

As the cab pulled up, she turned away. She opened the door and climbed into the backseat, and then moved all the way to the other side as he climbed in behind her.

"Where are you folks headed?" the driver asked, glancing at them through the rearview mirror.

Melody started to give him her address, but Brad interrupted her.

"I have an idea." Leaning forward, he said to the driver, "Would you please take us to Main Street?" He opened his wallet and handed the driver a bill.

It must have been a big one, as the driver

smiled at them in the rearview mirror. "You got it."

"No, Brad. I have to get home…" The point of leaving the party had been to end her time with him. Get out of this dress and back to her real life. "Besides, everything is closed on Main Street. It's almost ten o'clock."

"Not everything is closed. Trust me."

She couldn't. And worse, she couldn't trust herself. "Should I?" she asked, her gaze locked with his in the dim lighting of the cab.

His only response was a smile.

CHAPTER TWELVE

BRAD EXTENDED A hand to Melody from within a horse-drawn sleigh at the entrance of the park on Main Street ten minutes later. "Come on," he said. She hesitated.

"No." She cast a glance around them. The street was quiet. As she'd said in the taxi, all the stores on Main Street had closed hours before, and now the only lights coming from the buildings were from the lit holiday displays in their windows.

"No one is around…except James here." He nodded to the man holding the reins, who was waiting to complete the last ride of the evening. The old man had operated the local horse stables for many years, and while his kids had taken over the business, he still insisted on driving the sleigh during the holidays. At eighty-two, his eyesight was less than ideal, and Brad suspected the horses navigated the sleigh, not the driver.

Melody shivered and danced from one strappy heel to the other on the slushy sidewalk. She rubbed her arms for warmth. "This isn't a good idea."

"There's a heated blanket in here," he said.

"Okay," Melody said finally, accepting his hand and climbing into the sleigh. Sitting across from him, she quickly draped the blanket around her and pulled it up to her neck. "That's better."

"Are you at least going to share it?" Brad asked, joining her on the other side and forcing her to slide over.

"Only if I have to," Melody grumbled, lifting the edge of the blanket for him.

"You're right. This is much better." Brad extended an arm around her shoulders. He felt her stiffen just a little, but he didn't move his arm. They were friends...or at least they used to be. This was another step in trying to recover some of what had been lost, and nothing more, he told himself.

Lies. All lies.

The sleigh began to move and as they drew closer to the illuminated park gates, she spoke. "So what's it like?"

"What's what like?"

"Being famous." She shifted in the seat and turned to face him.

"You're going to hate my answer." For as long as he could remember, performing had been the only thing he'd ever wanted to do—fame and fortune had come second to his desire to be onstage. And in truth, it was lonely. He had a handful of friends in Nashville, but between touring and trying to find new songs to record, the only people he consistently had time for were music-industry professionals and his physiotherapist. He knew his answer wouldn't be what she was expecting.

She took a deep breath. "The jealousy might kill me, but I'd like to hear about it."

"It's really not that great. I mean, don't get me wrong, performing is a high like no other—as you know—but it doesn't last long. When I'm on tour, I'm onstage for about five hours a week. The rest of the time I'm just doing a lot of work. And if I'm being totally honest, it's also lonely." She stared at him in disbelief.

"I know I must be coming across as a total jerk right now. Poor me and my problems."

"A little bit. I guess I just don't understand

how it's possible to be lonely when you have so many adoring fans." She glanced at the scenery passing by the sleigh but could not focus on it. "Our definitions of lonely must be very different."

"Well, at the end of the day, there's no one waiting for me at home. My friends have moved on to have families of their own, and the distance from my family makes staying in touch a little tough. I've been watching Gracie and Darius grow up through Facebook photos."

"Do you want a family of your own?" She sounded surprised.

He could understand her reaction. He'd always been content to play the field, to date a different woman in each city his band played. He was the guy who was never going to settle down—at least that's the impression he'd given everyone around him. In truth, he'd wanted what his friends had. "Always have," he said softly. "I probably shouldn't say this, but I was always jealous of you and Patrick."

Her eyes widened. "You were?"

"Of course. You two were solid. The love and support you gave each other was amazing, and to a guy like me, floating from one casual relationship to another, it was enviable."

"But you seemed to enjoy being a player—there was no shortage of beautiful women on your arm."

"There was never anyone special. Never anyone I wanted to make a life with. I always told Patrick he was the luckiest man on earth."

Her mouth fell open in shock.

"Sorry, I shouldn't have said that. I just made things weird again, didn't I?" He frowned.

"No," she said, but her cheeks had turned crimson and she was avoiding his eyes.

Quickly, he changed the subject. "So, this job at Play Hard—it's what you want?"

"It pays the bills. And once I retake the management exam and hopefully get a promotion, I'm planning to give up my shifts at the bowling alley and the Green Gator. Spend more time with the boys."

He knew firsthand that retail or food-industry jobs constituted the majority of employment opportunities in the small town, and he knew she was choosing the best of the options available to her. He just wished Brookhollow could offer her better options. "And you really won't consider writing music again?"

"The royalties from the music definitely help, but I need consistent work, Brad, and at the end of the day, there's no time to do both. I have the boys to care for. Their dreams come first now."

Brad leaned closer to her. "It could be consistent work. Before, when you were writing all the time, you could write a song a day."

"Not anymore," she said, but he caught the glimmer of hope and interest in her dark eyes before she looked away.

"Come to Nashville. Stay with me and give it a try." He'd thought about it for all of fourteen seconds, but he knew instantly it was the right thing to suggest. In Nashville, he could introduce her to people, get her into a recording studio. Before long she would be writing music for stars and, heck, she might even get back into performing.

Unfortunately, she was staring at him as though he'd suggested she move to the moon. "Wow, that concussion was more serious than I'd thought."

But he knew her too well to be deterred. Given a worry- and guilt-free way of taking him up on his offer, she would have jumped at the opportunity. He'd seen the way she'd looked performing that evening. She couldn't deny that her passion for singing had never faded. "What's holding you back?"

"Brad, haven't you been listening to anything I've said? We have a life here in Brookhollow, the boys and I. We have a home..." She paused and he saw her swallow hard before continuing. "The boys love their friends and their school, their sports..."

He jumped in. "Exactly, think of the sports. The opportunities for the boys in sports alone in Nashville would be worth it. And they'd make new friends." She couldn't honestly believe the boys would be offered the same opportunities living in sleepy Brookhollow that they would living in a large city.

She shook her head. "The answer is no."

"I don't think you're really taking the time to see the benefits, Mel."

"Do you ever give up?"

"No, because I think it would be a great thing for all of you."

She shook her head.

"I understand that as a mother," he went on, "you're putting the boys first, their needs first, but flash forward ten years. What makes you think the boys will stay in Brookhollow? I mean, David's natural athletic ability could take him anywhere, and Josh really does have a talent for guitar."

She smiled.

He sensed he'd scored a point. "The boys move on with their lives, and where does that leave you? Alone in Brookhollow, a shell of a woman who used to have big ambitions and the talent to see them through, if she'd only had the courage to try."

She stared wide-eyed at him for a long moment. Then clearing her throat, she said, "Okay, maybe you're right. Maybe someday I'll regret not taking a chance on a life of my own, but once you become a parent your own happiness takes a backseat to what's right for your kids." Her voice was firm. "Now, please just drop it, okay?"

She turned her attention to the scenery

around them as the sleigh passed the colorful light displays and ice sculptures lining the path. Only the sound of the horses' hooves on the crunchy snow and the bells jingling around their necks could be heard. White flakes continued to fall from the dark night sky onto her long eyelashes and the tip of her tiny nose. Unable to resist, he reached out and wiped one away. "Okay, but I'm just going to say that my door is always open to you and the boys...for anything at all." His hand softly caressed her cheek.

"Thank you."

Her hand came up to cover his. His mouth went dry. Was this the right thing? Did he care? It felt nice...wonderful, even... Reaching out with his other hand, he gently turned her to face him. He swallowed hard as her eyes met his. "You are so beautiful, Mel. Not just your incredible smile and captivating eyes, but your heart and your strength and your talent." He lowered his forehead to hers. "And this week...seeing you again, being with the boys, just reminds me of how much I miss this...how much I miss you." When he'd returned to Brookhollow, he'd expected heartache and guilt to be the only emotions he struggled with.

"Brad, I…" Her eyes flitted to his lips, then down to their entwined fingers on her lap above the blanket. "I shouldn't be feeling this way. Not now, and certainly not about you."

"Why not now? Why not about me?" He knew the answers to both, but at that moment he was choosing to ignore the voice in his head. "It's been almost three years, Mel. It's okay to be happy, and if I make you happy, what's wrong with that?"

"Our history…you were Pat's best friend, the boys' godfather…"

"Exactly. I've always loved you and your children. Who knows your past better and would cherish your future more?" He wasn't sure where the words were coming from— all he knew was that he meant each and every one of them. He loved her. He was falling *in* love with her. And there was only one way to find out if she felt the same. Raising her chin once more, he lowered his mouth to hers and kissed her gently, tenderly.

He pulled back slightly so his gaze locked

with hers and he waited for her to move away. She didn't.

He kissed her again. Her breath was warm against his mouth. She should have been stopping him. He should have been stopping himself. "Mel…" he murmured against her lips, begging her to do what he wasn't strong enough to do.

Instead, she returned the kiss, her lips soft, inviting…and so off-limits. But at that moment he didn't care. His mind raced with all the reasons he should have pulled away, but he ignored them all. Instead, he cupped the back of her head, holding her firmly in place as his heartbeat echoed loudly in his ears. He moved closer and slid his fingers down the length of her exposed neck. He felt her shiver. Sliding his arms beneath the blanket, he drew her closer, never wanting the moment to end.

BUT IT DID. Pushing against his chest, Melody broke away from him, frantically tossing the blanket aside as if the fabric were to blame for what had just happened between them. A shaky hand flew to her lips as she got to her feet. "Oh, my God." What had she just done? Had she completely lost her mind? She wanted to slap him, but how could she? He may have started the kiss, but she'd returned it, however briefly. He'd given her every opportunity to prevent it and she hadn't.

"Mel," he said, a pained look on his handsome face. "Come back. Sit down."

"You shouldn't be standing in the sleigh," the driver said, glancing back at them.

She shouldn't have been doing a lot of things—dancing with Brad, riding on this sleigh and most of all kissing him. Panic made her heart race as she lowered herself onto the cold, snow-covered seat across from him, shivering outside the warmth of the heated blanket.

"Here," he said, laying the blanket across her lap.

She had to get out of here. She looked around. They were in the middle of the park at night. She'd been crazy to go along with this. Turning to the driver, she said, "Could you turn us around, please?" Her stomach was in knots and she thought she might throw up. She'd just kissed the man responsible for her husband's death. The man responsible for taking so much from her family.

"Sorry, Melody, the trail isn't wide enough. The ending is about another half mile," James said.

A half mile at this leisurely pace was too far. "Okay, stop. I'm getting out."

The driver stopped and shook his head. "That's not a great idea in those shoes."

"She's not getting out," Brad said. "Keep going, please." He reached for her hands on her lap.

"Don't."

"I'm sorry. I don't know what I was thinking."

She took slow, deep breaths in an effort to calm her frantic mind and racing pulse. She hadn't kissed anyone in almost three years. Her last kiss had been with Patrick, next to Brad's car in their driveway, right before the two men had headed into the city for the meeting with Propel Records. In three years, she hadn't had any desire to date, and now here she was kissing the last man on earth she should have been kissing. Whatever was happening between them had to stop. Did he really think this was okay? Did he honestly believe something could happen between them? Her breath got caught in her throat as a thought struck her.

"Oh, my God," she said. "This is all about that song, isn't it?" Brad always got what he wanted, and he rarely cared about the people standing in the way of getting it. She was crazy to have thought that this kiss, this evening, had been anything more than a ploy for him to get his wish. She had once again become a means to an end, and that should have given her a sense of relief. It didn't.

"No."

"Then what was it?"

"I'm falling in love with you, Mel," he said quietly.

That was much worse. "I don't want your love. I don't want to see you anymore, Brad. Please stay away from me and the kids."

He forced her hands into his and held tight when she tried to pull away. "I can't do that, and I know you don't really want me to."

"Nothing can happen between us, Brad. We both know that. What happened tonight can't ever happen again. I don't even know what it was that happened. I can't possibly have feelings for you. Not good ones, anyway."

"Melody." His voice sounded pained.

"Brad, I was married to Patrick. You were his best friend. The accident happened and we both lost him, and now we can't just pick up where we left off and forget all about him. If he were still here, this wouldn't be happening."

"But he's not here."

She swallowed the lump in her throat and attempted to pull her hands away once more.

He refused to let her go. "He's not here... and life—"

"Goes on?" she finished, her head snapping up and her eyes blazing. *How dare he?* "Maybe for you, Brad. I mean, you took off as soon as you could and never looked back. You're only here now to help further your career."

"That's not fair. I did what I had to do. The Myerses all but ran me out of town while I was still in a wheelchair and you certainly weren't sad to see me leave. And, you know what, I miss my friend. Unlike you, I have to wake up every morning with the knowledge and guilt that I'm the reason he's not here. I'm the reason you and the boys are suffering and struggling to make ends meet, and I'm the reason the Myerses were robbed of their only son, a man who had talent I could only ever dream of having. So if from where you're standing it looks like I've moved on, well, maybe that's because life hasn't allowed me to stay in the past. I knew my best friend almost as well as you did, and I believe Patrick wouldn't have expected or wanted us to." He stopped at the sight of the tears rolling down her face. "Mel, look at me...please."

She couldn't. She didn't dare look at the man who shared so much of her passion and pain, the last man on earth she should be having feelings for.

After a long, fraught silence, he released her hands. "Fine. If you truly don't want me, I'll leave you alone."

"That's all I've ever asked of you, Brad," she said.

ALONE IN HIS cab minutes later—Melody had insisted on taking her own cab home—Brad rested his head against the backseat. What a mess. Not only had he experienced something amazing for one brief moment, only to have reality shatter the temporary illusion, but now he knew there was no way to convince Melody to give him and a career in music another chance. He didn't regret kissing her. It had been the first honest moment he'd had in three years. He knew she'd felt it, too, and it was a fear of being vulnerable that had caused her to pull away, he was certain. Hell, normally it would have been reason enough for *him* to have pulled away. As if he didn't have enough reasons to feel guilty or angry with himself. He ran a hand through his snow-dampened hair, and as they passed her cul-de-sac, he couldn't stop himself from glancing toward her house, where he saw her going in the front door.

He sighed. In three years, none of the women he'd dated had stirred any real emotion in him, any desire to settle down. No kiss had affected him the way this one had. And there was nothing he could do about it, besides accept that it would never happen again.

He watched her front door close and the hall light turn on. Then something else caught his eye.

"Hey, can you pull into this cul-de-sac?" he asked the driver, keeping his eye on Melody's house as the driver did a U-turn. As they drew closer, Brad's suspicions were confirmed. There was someone standing in the bushes outside the house.

Before the cab came to a full stop, Brad had opened the door and jumped out. Then he ran toward the house and grabbed the stranger's shoulder. "Who are you?"

"Hey, let go!" the stranger said, shaking his shoulder free of Brad's hold.

Brad cornered him against the railing of the porch. "Let me ask you again—who are you?" He glared at the man. After the evening he'd just had, he would love an excuse to hit the guy.

"Look, I'm nobody, okay? Just a photographer from Newark," the man said quickly, pulling his camera from the pocket of his coat.

"What were you doing taking pictures of this house?" Brad asked.

"I wasn't," the man said.

Brad shook the man's jacket, adrenaline coursing through him.

"Look, I swear I wasn't taking pictures of the house."

Brad grabbed the camera and turned it on. He scrolled back through the digital images. Photos of Lee Brice and Eric Church... Julia Roberts. Paparazzi had followed *him* to Brookhollow? Roxanne had said no one knew about him being there, and certainly no one in his hometown would have set the press on him. Would they have? He remembered telling Bridget Marilyn about his history with Melody. Surely the Heartland Country Television host wouldn't have done something like this. "Who tipped you off?"

"I can't say, man." The guy's shifty eyes looked anxious as he scanned the area for an escape.

Brad tightened his grip on the man's shoulder. "You have less than a second to tell me." This guy had chosen the wrong night to mess with him.

"Roxanne Klein," the guy said finally. "Now let go. I may be a paparazzo, but I can still charge you with assault."

Brad released the fabric and took a step back in the deep snow. "What? My publicist?" Roxanne had told the press he was here after claiming no one would know? Why? It didn't make any sense. And how would this guy know about the Myerses? He'd never told Roxanne about Melody and the boys.

"I don't know who she is, man. I just got a call yesterday. The woman said I'd find you here."

Clearly Bridget must have told her. Nashville was a different world from Brookhollow. He'd learned early on that there were few people he could really trust. This incident had just confirmed that lesson. "What shot were you trying to get just now? Why the Myers family?"

"Come on, man. Just let me go."

"What photo were you paid to get?" Brad asked again, a menacing scowl on his face.

"A picture of you with the woman who lives here—as many as possible." The man moved around Brad. "Can I have my camera back?"

He thought so. "No. Get out of here. You're lucky I'm not calling the police. There's a young girl and children in this house—you could have terrified them." The idea that this guy could have frightened the boys or their babysitter made his blood boil again. Thank God this piece of scum hadn't gotten a shot of any of them.

"I was just doing my job. I need those photos," the guy insisted.

Brad dropped the camera into the snowbank and covered it with the snow at his feet. "Oops. Now get out of here."

"Thanks a lot," the man grumbled as he snatched up his camera and took off.

Moments later, Brad trudged through the slush on Main Street's patterned brick sidewalk, his hands in the gloves Melody had been wearing earlier that evening. They were still warm and smelled faintly of her. It was the only thing calming his frazzled nerves. He couldn't believe Roxanne had stooped so low as to hire paparazzi to harass her own clients. Snow collected on his hair and coat, but he kept walking. It was almost eleven o'clock...ten in Nashville. He took his phone from his coat pocket, and without hesitating, dialed Roxanne's number. This time of year, this time of night, he didn't expect her to answer, but she did on the third ring.

"Hello?"

At least he thought it was her. "Roxanne?"

"Brad?" she sniffed.

He frowned, the unexpected sound causing him to lose his angry momentum. "Are you crying?"

"Of course not!" she snapped.

Ah, there she was. "Okay…" He hesitated when he heard a small sob. Great. Five seconds ago, he was ready to tear into this success-at-any-cost woman and fire her, and now he was at a loss for words. "You sure you're okay?" he asked with a sigh.

"I just got dumped, okay? Two days before Christmas."

Crap. Couldn't her boyfriend have waited until January? Brad could certainly understand his decision, but if he'd made it this far, what was another few days? "Sorry to hear it," he mumbled.

"Do you want to know why?"

Not really. "That's your business…"

"He said I was pushy and overbearing," she said, and he could hear the sound of ice clinking against a glass as she took a sip of something. No doubt her usual, whiskey on the rocks.

The boyfriend's assessment sounded

about right. In fact, those were exactly the words Brad had been planning to use. How was he supposed to say them now? In all the time he'd worked with Roxanne, she'd never once shown any sign of vulnerability or weakness—hadn't shown much emotion at all, really. Now she was falling apart and perhaps slightly drunk, exactly when he needed her to be her feisty self.

He gritted his teeth. The woman had just gotten dumped two days before Christmas, and now he was going to fire her? He forced himself to shake off the feelings of sympathy. This one brief moment of humanity couldn't erase the stunt she'd pulled. "Listen, Roxanne, I'm sorry you're not having a great night." His wasn't exactly going swimmingly, either. "But I called to tell you I don't want you as my publicist anymore."

She was silent on the other end of the line.

He stopped walking and waited.

Nothing. "Roxanne, did you hear me? I mean it. That paparazzi exploit was the last straw."

Still no response.

"Roxanne?"

The sound of muffled snoring was all he heard on the other end of the line.

Seriously? "Roxanne, wake up!" he tried.

The snoring continued.

Fantastic. Even when he wanted to fire her, the woman still got her own way.

"NOT A CHANCE. I refuse to take it," the owner of the pawnshop just outside of town said. He was standing behind the counter the next morning, glaring at Melody.

"You have to, Tom. Unfortunately, I need the money." Melody placed the U 47 microphone on the counter and took a step back. She wished the floor of the shop would open up and swallow her whole. Selling this treasured item did not feel right, and it didn't help that her former high school classmate was refusing to buy it. Three times she'd turned the van around on the way to the shop that morning, but each time the reality of the foreclosure notice had forced her to continue on. Not to mention the fact that she'd yet to buy a single holiday present for anyone, and Christmas was two days away.

"It's never come to this before," he said, admiring the expensive piece of equipment.

"Well, my finances haven't, either. Look, Tom, this isn't easy for me, so would you just take it?" She hated the note of desperation she heard in her own voice. For three years she had resisted doing this, but now she had no choice.

With a sigh, Tom picked up the microphone and examined it. "It's beautiful."

She nodded. It took all her strength not to grab back the microphone and leave the shop. At least she'd gotten the chance to use it one last time at the party the night before. After the baby christening in January, she was going to start declining singing requests around town.

"You're sure about this?"

Not at all. She nodded again, not trusting her voice.

"I can buy it from you and put it aside for three months—you can make payments on it."

She appreciated his kindness, but she knew she'd never be able to afford to buy back the microphone or take a chance on a future in music again. "No. I won't need it."

"Okay. I'll give you four thousand for it," he said.

It had been worth six new, but it was used, and four thousand would keep the bank from foreclosing on the house. For now, anyway. It would give them a Christmas. And buy her some time as she fought to convince the Play Hard executive to allow her to retake the test early. This was the right thing to do. The microphone, though she cherished it, was just an object. No one could take away the important things like her memories, and that's what mattered. "I'll take it," she said.

MELODY SHOVED THE last of her shopping bags into her bedroom closet just as Josh entered the room, shepherd costume on and toothbrush in hand. She quickly shut the closet door. "Wow, you look great."

"What were you doing?" he asked suspiciously, scanning the room.

"None of your beeswax," she said, escorting him back out into the hallway. Ethan and Bailey had agreed to babysit the boys while she completed her Christmas shopping that afternoon. The pain of having to sell the microphone had eased a bit with each new gift she'd bought the boys. She couldn't wait to see the excitement on their little faces two days from now. In a way, Brad was right—life was forcing her to move on, whether she wanted to or not. Her stomach did a small lurch as she thought of Brad. What on earth had they been thinking? They couldn't be together. He was a country star with a touring schedule, and she was a single mom with a life to get on with. Guilt hit her when she realized that for a few moments the night before, she'd forgotten their history. "Where's your brother?" she asked.

"In the bedroom. He won't come out. Says he's not going."

"Why not?"

"His costume," Josh said before continuing to brush his teeth.

Melody gave him a little shove toward the bathroom. "Finish getting ready. I'll go get him." At the bedroom door, she paused and knocked before opening it. "David?"

"Go without me," he called.

"It can't be that bad," she said as she entered, but with one look at her son in the camel costume she knew it was that bad—worse, even. The tight beige leggings clung to her son's thick, tree-trunk legs, and the camel humps barely wrapped around his body. The costume was also too long, which caused the camel's head to hang far too low and obstruct his view. There was no way he could wear that onstage in front of everyone. *Think fast.*

"See, it's awful. I knew it." Folding his arms, David sat on the edge of his bed. "I won't do this."

She glanced at her watch and saw they had twenty minutes to get to the school for a last-minute play rehearsal before the concert.

"Come on, guys," Josh said, entering the room. When he saw his brother in the camel costume, his expression spoke volumes.

Glancing between the boys, she had an idea. "Okay, remember how I told you guys you were never ever allowed to do that twin-swap thing?"

The boys nodded.

"Well, we are throwing that rule out the window. Just for tonight," she was quick to add.

"What do you mean?" Josh looked worried. Clearly, he knew where this was headed.

"You two switch costumes."

"No way!" Josh said.

David eyed his brother's shepherd costume, but he shook his head. "He has lines, and I don't know them."

"They can't be that hard," Melody said, and then she approached Josh. "Honey, you're slightly taller than David, and you're less…" How did she say it without offending either son? "Well, you're leaner than your brother."

"I'm fat?" David frowned.

"No! You're muscular."

"And I'm not?" Now it was Josh's turn to be offended.

"That's not what I'm saying." Not really. "Look, I'm just trying to help. If you switch costumes, no one will notice, and you'll both be more comfortable onstage."

"What's in it for me?" Josh asked.

"Your brother will owe you one," Melody said, pointing a finger at David to silence the protest she expected was forthcoming. "Anyway, it's just a nice thing to do. Bonus points with Santa."

Josh's eyes widened.

Thank God, at eight years old, the boys still believed.

"Okay, I'll do it," Josh said.

"Great. Quick, let's do this swap before I come to my senses."

CHAPTER THIRTEEN

THE ELEMENTARY SCHOOL auditorium had standing room only. As Brad peeked around the curtain backstage, he thought the kids' school concert had drawn almost a bigger crowd than most of his shows did. If he had to guess, he would say 80 percent of the town residents had shown up for that evening's performances. Immediate and extended family members and their friends continued to pour in through the doors.

Gracie appeared behind him, poking her own head through the curtain. Her face paled as she dropped the red velvet fabric and turned to face him. "I can't do this," she wailed in full panic mode.

Brad draped an arm around her shoulders and moved her away from the stage. "Yes, you can. We've gone over the game plan. When you get onstage, what's the first thing you do?" He sat her down on a small plastic chair and knelt in front of her.

"Find you."

"That's right. I'll be in the sixth row, first seat from the middle aisle. And I'll be smiling. What's next?"

"Take a deep breath and start speaking."

"Perfect. Simple, right?"

The little girl didn't look convinced.

Darius came up behind them. "Gracie, Miss Lawlor is looking for you. We have to take our places now."

Gracie's eyes widened in fear.

Pulling her to her feet, Brad said, "You're going to do great. Remember, sixth row."

She nodded, her look of fear replaced by one of determination. "I've got this," she said and Brad released a breath he hadn't realized he'd been holding.

Standing there a moment longer, he watched the Nativity-scene actors walk past him onto the stage and take their assigned positions.

"Hey, Brad," a camel said as he approached.

Brad squinted in the dim lighting and

lifted the edge of the camel mask. "Josh? I thought you were going to be a shepherd."

The little boy giggled. "Josh *is* a shepherd. I'm David."

The actual David appeared behind him in the shepherd's costume. Brad glanced between the two innocent-looking faces before nodding slowly. "Right. My mistake." He wondered if Melody knew about the switch. When the boys were young they were always trying to deceive everyone with their mixed identities, and Melody had enforced a no-switch rule after the dentist had removed one of Josh's teeth instead of David's. The older the boys got, the harder it had become for them to pull off switches—the differences between their bodies and personalities were so pronounced. But in the costumes and from a distance onstage, they were sure to get away with this one.

Taking his seat next to Breanne a moment later, Brad wiped his damp palms on the legs of his jeans. He fanned himself with the evening's performance schedule and bounced his knees.

"Hey, relax," his sister said. "You're not the one up there."

"I know. This is worse. How are you staying so calm?" As the mother, he expected her to be at least a little anxious.

"Oh, Brad, just wait until you have children. You'll learn fast that if you stress over your child's every life experience, you will do nothing *but* stress. She's a kid, she's resilient, and no matter what happens up there tonight, she'll be fine. Besides, I don't have to worry, 'cause you're doing enough worrying for the both of us." She tapped his shoulder.

Forcing his legs to remain still, he scanned the crowded auditorium. Gracie's performance that evening wasn't the only thing he was stressing about. All day, his thoughts had been on Melody. No matter how hard he tried, he couldn't erase the memory of their kiss in the sleigh or how great it had felt to hold her. And how stupid he'd been to allow it all to happen. Any chance of a rekindled friendship with her was now gone, as was any hope he'd had of convincing her to give music another shot.

His gaze drifted over the heads of the spectators as the curtains opened, and fell on Melody. She was sitting on the far left side in the eighth row, with Patrick's parents and her family. Her eyes were forward and her face was lit up in a proud smile as she watched the children onstage. She was so beautiful inside and out that he wanted to stare at her forever. But damn, what gave him the right to feel that way?

As the opening music started, he turned his attention back to the performance. His niece was counting on him and he refused to let her down. As he'd instructed, she immediately located him in the sixth row, and he smiled and sat straighter in his chair. She didn't smile back, and from where he was sitting, he could see her hands clutching the fabric of her costume at her sides.

The play started, and with Gracie's eyes locked on his face, he kept smiling. *Come on, you can do this,* he silently urged her as other kids said their lines. He knew hers were coming next. Then, on cue, she opened her mouth to speak. His fists clenched in eager anticipation, and he held his breath, still smiling.

His smile grew wider as she delivered her lines, even braving a quick glance around the auditorium before settling her attention back on him. When she finished her speaking role, Brad jumped to his feet, clapping and shouting, "Woohoo!" More than a few parents turned to glare at him.

"Brad, sit," his sister hissed. "It's not over."

Still smiling, he sat down. "She did it," he said, giving a thumbs-up to the little girl onstage. She was now looking anywhere but at him, and her cheeks were glowing red. He relaxed against the seat. "I might have embarrassed her," he said.

His sister raised an eyebrow. "You think?"

"So you're one of *those* parents."

Melody paused at the bottom of the stairs outside Brookhollow Elementary moments after her boys' performance in the pageant. As much as she wanted to ignore Brad's voice behind her, she couldn't bring herself to keep walking. Not when every minute inside the auditorium she had looked directly at him, the dull ache in her chest getting worse each time. Twenty-four hours ago, she'd been in his arms, allowing herself to feel something she shouldn't have, and now they were further apart than ever. She turned. "One of what parents?"

Jogging down the icy steps, he said, "The ones who watch their own kids perform and then take off." He paused in front of her. When his eyes met hers, they held a trace of merriment.

She knew his remarks were just an effort to lighten the tension between them, but she said, "Not usually, but tonight I have to get to work." She glanced at her watch. Her shift started in six minutes. Luckily everything in Brookhollow was close by.

"Listen, Mel, I just wanted to apologize again for last night."

She couldn't stop the words that came out next, despite her best efforts. "Which part?" *What does it matter?* her brain screamed. He should be sorry for all of it—they both should. They both owed Patrick so much more respect than what they'd shown the evening before.

He dug his hands into his overcoat pockets and rocked on his heels. "All of it…none of it…"

"So, you're not apologizing?"

He took a step toward her and reached

for her ungloved hand, but she pulled it out of reach. He said, "For hurting you, yes. I can't apologize enough for that. Hurting you seems to be all I've ever done." He cast his eyes down and said, "Unfortunately, it doesn't change the fact that last night was the best night I've had in so long I can't even remember." He raised his eyes and his voice softened. "Mel, I didn't mean for that kiss to happen, but it did and now it's the only thing I can think about…and I can't stand to be feeling this way about you, about us, but I do."

Her spine straightened as she turned away. "I'll make this easy for you. I meant what I said last night—stay away from us. I don't want to see you again." She managed to take two steps toward her minivan before he grabbed her arm and swung her around.

"You can't mean that."

"I do." Anger flared within her as she advanced toward him. "Are you crazy? Don't you realize that the two of us together is… is…" Lost for words, she turned and once again headed toward her van, desperate to get away from him. The urge to dive into his warm arms and stay there forever was far too tempting.

Following her, he finished her thought. "A mistake, a bad idea, possibly the dumbest thing either of us could ever do? Yes, you're right. Us together is all of those things," he said behind her as she fumbled with the door handle of the van. "But can you really just forget last night, that kiss, this connection between us? 'Cause I'm not sure I can," he said softly, shutting the van door again immediately after she'd gotten it open.

Summoning every ounce of strength she had left, she met his gaze. "Yes, I can, because he was your best friend and my husband—honoring his memory is the least we can do. The truth is, Brad," she said, hoping she could pull off the biggest lie of her life, "whenever I look at you, all I see is everything I lost."

BRAD WOKE EARLY the next morning, if the few hours of tossing and turning he'd done all night could be called sleeping. Melody's harsh words the night before had stung, and he hadn't been able to clear his mind of them. He deserved them. All he'd ever done was hurt her and her family. And that had to stop. Even when Patrick was alive, Brad's presence had caused tension between the couple, so why on earth would she ever love him? He couldn't believe he'd even had the nerve to try. Reluctantly pushing himself up from the deflated air mattress, he pulled on his jeans and grabbed a sweatshirt from his open suitcase in the closet. Then he quietly crept downstairs, lured by the smell of coffee brewing.

As he pushed the swinging door to the kitchen, he felt something blocking it on the other side. His sister's voice called quietly through the tiny crack, "Who is it?"

"Brad. What are you doing?"

Breanne moved the chair that had been blocking the doorway, allowed him to enter and replaced the chair. "I'm wrapping presents," she said, returning to her post at the kitchen table, where rolls of wrapping paper, bows, tape and scissors were littered.

"A little last-minute to be wrapping, don'tcha think?" he said. His sister was usually the organized planner who had all her shopping and wrapping done early.

"I bet you haven't even started your shopping yet," she shot back.

Brad poured her a cup of coffee and handed it to her. "You caught me. I'm heading out to shop this morning. Was there anything on the kids' Christmas wish lists that you didn't pick up yet?" he asked. He usually sent the kids money in the form of toy-store gift cards from Nashville, but this year, seeing as he was in town, he wanted his gifts to have a more personal touch.

She pulled a folded piece of Christmas notepaper from her pocket and handed it to him. "I knew you'd ask eventually. Here's a list of the things they mentioned over the past few months. I had trouble finding some of the items locally, so if you're going farther than the Brookview Square Mall, perhaps you could take a look."

"Sure, no problem. I'll go to Newark. They'll have a better selection of the latest toys." He poured coffee into his old Brook-hollow High travel mug and secured the lid.

"So what time does our fake family special air tonight?" she asked. In her teeth she clenched the other end of a ribbon she was holding in her hand and cut off several lengths of it.

He'd left countless voice mails for Bridget, hoping to somehow convince the station to cancel his segment, but having received no return calls, he'd given up. He suspected it was too late to change anything now, anyway. Next year he would hire someone new to do damage control as he attempted to restart his career under his own name. "Nine o'clock," he mumbled. He wouldn't be anywhere near a television at that time that evening.

THE TRAFFIC WAS heavier than usual as Brad drove his rental back to Brookhollow after a successful day of tackling busy malls in Newark. The bumper-to-bumper, slow-moving vehicles were further delayed by the heavy snowfall that had started sometime while he was inside the last shopping center. Turning the wipers on high, he slowed even more as he rounded a corner. Since the accident, he had become cautious, not only when driving but when doing anything. So he found it difficult to understand his complete and utter abandonment of common sense when it came to Melody. He should have known she'd push him away. He was responsible for Patrick's death, and nothing he did now or in the future could ever change that. A part of her, if not all of her, would always hate him. He had to accept that as best as he could and try to move on.

Flicking on the local soft-rock radio station, he tried to shake the memory of their sleigh-ride kiss. Unfortunately, because the first song the station played was Sheryl Crow's version of "Silent Night," it was only replaced with a memory of Melody singing at the mayor's party. Reaching forward, he changed the station to the local Christmas-music-all-the-time station and cringed at the sound of a woman singing "I'll be Home for Christmas." Was there no way to escape his thoughts of Melody? Frustrated, he switched to the country music station, only to hear the final three bars of his current single from the album he'd released the year before— "Forever on My Mind."

"We just heard the latest from Nashville's own Brad Jackson," the announcer said. "That one's currently hitting the country music charts at number twenty, and I'm hoping it makes it to number one. Next on…"

The sound of the announcer's voice faded in the background as Brad pondered the words. The elusive number one. As catchy as the song was, he knew it wasn't going to be a chart-topper. He'd be lucky if it made the top ten. And he didn't even want to think about the stack of songs he had so far for the next album.

Turning onto the exit for Brookhollow moments later, Brad glanced at the stack of gift-wrapped presents on the passenger seat next to him—the gifts he'd bought for the twins and the one for Melody. It was after five already, and she'd mentioned going to her parents' house for dinner that evening to exchange presents. He didn't think they would be home, but pulling onto their cul-de-sac, he saw their van still in the driveway. He hesitated. He'd wanted to just leave the presents on the porch, honoring her wish for him to stay away. He didn't want to make things awkward or ruin their Christmas Eve. But as he passed the house, the front door opened and David and Joshua came rushing out, arms full of presents. They saw him and called his name.

Now he had to stop. In fact, he wanted to—his flight to Nashville was the following afternoon after Christmas dinner with his family, and this would be his last opportunity to say goodbye to the boys…and to Melody. He pulled the car to the curb and grabbed the gifts from the front seat.

As he exited the car, David and Josh ran to greet him with cries of "Merry Christmas Eve!"

"Yeah, tonight's a big night," Brad said, ruffling David's hair and then Josh's.

"Are those for us?" David asked, his wide eyes glued to the stack of presents Brad was carrying.

Melody appeared on the front step and gave David a disapproving look. "Manners," she reminded him.

"Sorry," David said.

Brad offered Melody a smile, which she politely, if reluctantly, returned as she slid her arms into her winter coat. "Yes, these are for you," Brad said, opening the van door for the boys to set their own gifts inside, before handing them his. "Why don't you bring those inside for later. The one on top is for your mom," he whispered.

"Awesome," Josh said excitedly, accepting the stack of gifts and rushing past his mother on the step. "Look what Brad brought us."

"Yes, that was nice of him," Melody said tightly, as the boys ran past her to set their early gifts under the tree. "Hurry. We're late already," she called to them. Then, turning to Brad, she said, "Thank you, but you really shouldn't have."

"Of course I should have—I have three missed Christmases to make up for," he said, choking on the tense, cold air swirling around them. "Sorry, I meant to just leave them on the porch."

"It's fine."

Her tone said it was anything but, yet he couldn't seem to turn and walk away. "Heading to your folks' place?"

"Yeah." She checked her watch. "We were supposed to be there ten minutes ago. Come on, boys!" she called to them.

That was his cue to leave. "Well, I won't keep you," he said as the boys reappeared outside and Melody closed and locked the front door. "I'm leaving tomorrow…" Was it his imagination or did her expression soften just a little? "I just wanted to say bye to… all of you."

"When will you visit again?" Josh asked.

"I'm not sure. I promise it won't be another three years, though. Okay?" Brad bent to hug the little boy. Turning to David, he extended a hand. "Take care of your mom, okay?"

David nodded as he accepted the handshake before he rushed off to the van with his brother. They closed the door, but Brad could feel two pairs of eyes watching him as he approached Melody. "Well…merry Christmas," he said, his mind frantic. Hug her? Kiss her cheek? What goodbye was appropriate for the woman he was in love with, a woman who'd said she never wanted to see him again?

Luckily she made the decision for him by stepping into his arms and hugging him quickly. "Merry Christmas," she whispered.

He breathed in the sweet smell of her hair and hugged her tighter for a long moment. Releasing her was the hardest thing he'd ever done. "Mel…"

She shook her head as she moved past

him. "Tell your family we said Merry Christmas."

"Mel, I love you." He knew saying it was wrong. That it wouldn't change anything. Except possibly make things worse. But if this was the last chance he'd ever get to say it, he would always regret not trying.

She stopped and turned, a look of defeat on her beautiful face. "Brad..."

He stepped forward and touched her cheek. "Shh. I didn't say it to hear it back."

Their eyes locked, and then with her head down against the blowing snow, she rushed to the van, not glancing back at him. Moments later she was gone.

CHAPTER FOURTEEN

"I THINK I'M going to steal," Jim said, sitting across from her at the family's dining room table later that evening. The meal was over and the dishes were cleared. Everyone was too full to move.

Melody quickly covered the gift in front of her with both arms. "Don't you dare. I've seen you eyeballing my gift the entire time," she said.

Instead of the adults exchanging presents, each year the family did a White Elephant Gift Exchange. Everyone brought two mystery gifts, one good and one gag, to place in the center of the table. When it was his or her turn, each person had the option to select a new gift from the pile or steal one of the other players' gifts. Melody had chosen first, an item she believed to be her favorite orange-flavored chocolate, and so far she'd been fortunate enough to keep it. Now her older brother's gaze was locked on the small, square present. She wanted to kick him under the table.

"Hmm…" Jim pretended to think. "Maybe I'll take this one." He slowly reached for a long, round package in the center, and then shook his head. "Nope, I want Mel's." He extended a hand across the table.

"You're an awful brother. You know that, right?" She pouted as she handed him her gift.

"You'll get a chance to steal it back," Bailey reminded her.

"Shh!" Jim said.

"That's right," Melody said. "I get another turn." Sitting back in her chair, she took a sip of her wine and watched as Ethan and Jill selected their gifts from the pile. Seeing the happy couples around the table—her parents, Jim and Jill, and Ethan and Bailey—made it harder to ignore the sense of loneliness she felt this time of year. Whoever said time heals all wounds had obviously never been without their lost spouse in the holiday season. And now, on top of the hollowness she felt inside, she had a crushing sense of guilt. Yes, guilt, at the nagging realization that she longed for a different man to be sitting there that evening. As much as she'd tried to forget them, his parting words echoed in her mind. He loved her. The last man on earth she could ever have a future with loved her. Worse was the knowledge that somehow she'd allowed herself to fall in love with him, too.

An hour later, after reclaiming her chocolate from Jim and then sharing it with him, she said good-night to her family. The boys were getting sleepy, and she still had to play Santa after they'd gone to bed.

"Good night, sis," Ethan said, giving her a hug at the front door. "You're sure you don't want Bailey and me to come over tonight?"

Melody shook her head. This was the couple's first Christmas Eve together. She wasn't about to let her depressed, lonely self interfere with their happiness. "Yeah, I'm sure."

"We really don't mind," Bailey said, wrapping an arm around Ethan's waist.

Melody forced a smile for the couple's sake. "Trust me, I'm fine. I'll be out like a light as soon as the boys go to bed," she lied. She suspected this Christmas Eve would be the toughest one yet. She'd be lucky if she got any sleep at all.

"If you need anything, call us, okay?" Ethan said.

"Not on your life. Go cuddle with your fiancée."

"Merry Christmas, Mel," he said as he closed the door behind them.

Melody made her way to the van, where the boys were already buckled in and half asleep. She knew her family worried about her, especially at this time of year, but she wondered what they would think if they knew that for the first time, it wasn't only Patrick she was missing.

BRAD CARRIED A sleeping Darius up the stairs to his bedroom. Pulling back his superhero comforter, he gently placed the little boy beneath the sheet, being careful not to wake him. The excitement of the evening had wiped the boy out. After kissing his nephew's cheek, Brad yawned and descended the stairs. He wouldn't be awake that much longer himself.

"It's channel forty-six," he heard Breanne say as he approached the living room, where the rest of his family were.

"I thought it was forty-three," his mother argued.

"It doesn't matter. We're not watching it," Brad said as he entered the room. He knew his family couldn't wait to watch the "Home for the Holidays" special, but he cringed at the thought. The fact that he'd asked his family to pretend to be something they weren't now disgusted him. What had he been thinking when he'd let Roxanne take over his life the way she had? Fame or no fame, he was calling the shots in his life and his career from here out.

"You bet we are," his mother said. "I didn't allow strangers to rearrange my furniture for nothing."

"Okay, well, I'm not watching." How could he? "Good night, everyone. See you all in the morning."

"Gracie and Darius both set their alarms for five-thirty, in case they sleep in," Breanne said with a laugh, resting her legs on her husband's lap on the couch. "We told them to wake Uncle Brad first."

He tossed a throw cushion at his sister. "Nice. Thank you." With that, he headed back upstairs.

Lying on his air mattress, he stared at the ceiling in the dark. No matter how hard he tried, he couldn't stop thinking about the family across town that he longed to be spending the evening with. He wanted to be there with Melody on what had to be one of the toughest nights of her year. He wanted to hold her on the couch in front of the fireplace and then in the morning share in the delight of watching the twins, children he would do anything for, open their presents.

The sound of his family talking and laughing downstairs only soured his mood more as he lay there alone, missing the woman he loved. Suddenly he got up, pulled on his jeans and sweater and quietly made his way back downstairs. After putting on his boots, he grabbed his jacket and the keys for the snowmobile and left the house.

A half hour later, he cut the engine of the machine. He'd left the house with no destination in mind...or maybe he had. Either way, here he was. Getting off the snowmobile, he tucked the keys into his pocket and made his way along the snow-cleared stone pathway and through the cemetery gates. He wasn't sure of the exact location of Patrick's grave site, but as he walked, memories from the day of the funeral replayed in his mind, leading him to the small marble plaque that marked his friend's grave. He read the engraving: *Patrick Myers. Forever remembered as a loving husband, father, son and friend.*

His eyes blurred as he thought of everything the plaque didn't say. That his friend had been a talented musician who could have realized his dreams, given the chance. That he had been secretly saving money to take Mel on the honeymoon they'd never had. That he'd stopped for flowers and had been rehearsing his apology for being late before the car had crashed that fateful night. Those heartbreaking facts played on repeat in his mind, along with a million *If onlys.*

Tears froze on his cheeks and he wiped them away. "I'm sorry, man," he murmured, lowering his head.

What felt like hours later, he heard the crunching of snow behind him. He didn't even turn until the person stopped beside him.

Looking up, he saw Dan Myers. His shoulders tensed. "Sorry, sir. I was just leaving."

"Stay," Dan said quietly, and Brad remained where he was.

Silence enveloped them. The only light on them was coming from one of the pole lamps scattered throughout the grounds. At last the older man spoke again.

"There's so much I didn't get to say to him."

Brad had no idea if a response was required, so he just nodded numbly.

Dan went on, "You just never know when you're going to run out of time to say all the things you need to, you know?"

Brad did know. How many times over those first few months had he longed to talk to his friend? Seek redemption and forgiveness? The fact that neither of the men at Patrick's grave would ever receive it now gave them a shared source of anguish and torment. "I'm so sorry you didn't get the chance…" Brad began. His voice broke and he swallowed hard, unable to clear the lump in his throat.

Dan put a hand on Brad's shoulder. The touch broke him completely, and his body shook as the tears started to flow. He'd never be able to make this right, never be able to undo the past and give this man and Melody and the boys the peace they deserved. Coming back here and staying to face his past had been the right thing to do, but it changed nothing. "I'm so sorry," he said again. He'd never be able to say it enough.

AFTER POSITIONING THE last gift under the tree, Melody stood back to admire her work. For the first time in far too long, presents extended into the middle of the room. The boys were going to lose their minds the next morning. The thought made any regret she might have had over selling the microphone disappear.

Draining the contents of her wineglass, she hung their three matching red-and-green wool stockings on the fireplace hooks and tried to ignore the temptation of the television in the corner of the room. She almost wished she hadn't paid the cable bill at the last minute—it would have taken away the agonizing choice she was now forced to make. The clock on the mantel read ten minutes past nine. Maybe Brad's segment was already over. She'd read in the show's listing that Martina McBride was also being featured that evening on the "Home for the Holidays" special. She would hate to miss that.

She turned on the television, and then hurried to the kitchen to refill her glass with wine. She returned just as the show was coming back from a commercial break. She curled her legs under her in a corner of the sofa and reached for the quilt, which she draped over her knees. The Monroe family farm appeared on the screen, and her heart raced as she watched footage from the day she and the boys had picked out their tree. A sense of pride filled her at the sight of the farm and Brad's family on television, even though they were pretending to be a completely different family, or at least a family with a different name. Next, they showed Brad at Joey's Diner, where she and Patrick and Brad used to keep the place open long past closing time, working on their music. When the show reached its final clip of Brad singing in front of the family's Christmas tree, after an on-screen dedication of the episode to Patrick's memory, tears were running freely down her cheeks. She didn't try to stop them.

A moment later, after the song ended and

the segment on Martina McBride began, Melody struggled to clear the lump in her throat. She stood and reached for a tissue from the festive box on the coffee table, and from the corner of her eye, she noticed a gift sticking out from under the chair next to the tree. She wiped her tear-stained cheeks and bent to retrieve it. It was light and beautifully wrapped, and it had her name on the tag. Had the boys gotten her a gift she didn't know about? She couldn't remember a time they'd gone shopping without her, but maybe Bailey and Ethan had taken them.

She contemplated waiting until the morning, but a second later she found herself tearing into the wrapping. On top of the white box from Chantelle's—a high-fashion store she'd only ever dreamed of walking into—were the words "A matching pair. Love, Brad." She knew what was inside before she opened the lid, but a gasp still escaped her lips as she discovered the pale blue cashmere gloves, wrapped in layers of white tissue paper. Removing them from the box, she slid her hands inside the soft, beautiful fabric and brought them to her face. Then, picking up the box, she hugged the message tight to her chest, no longer fighting the feelings for the man she shouldn't love, but did.

She stood and rushed to the closet for her winter coat and boots. Grabbing the keys to the shed, she made her way through the deep snow in her backyard and struggled with the frozen lock. "Come on," she said as she tugged on the rusting metal. The lock gave way, and she flicked the light switch as she entered.

Heading straight for the bookshelf, she retrieved the set of CDs in the black leather folder, flipping through to find one in particular. Ah, there it was. She pulled the CD from the case, tucked it into her pocket, and after locking up the shed, hurried back into the house. In the kitchen, she wrote "For Brad Monroe, track number eight," on the CD label, then put the CD into a Bubble Wrap mailing envelope. She addressed it to Arnie King in Nashville—she still had the manager's information in an old file.

If she couldn't give Brad her heart, she could at least give him her song.

"YOU MISSED THE cue again, Brad," the sound engineer said from the mixing booth, a note of annoyance in his voice. It was two days after Christmas, and Brad was at a popular studio in Nashville laying down tracks for his newest single.

"Sorry, man. Once more and I'll get it." Brad rotated his shoulders and took a sip of the water on the table beside him in the recording booth. Sweat formed on his brow as the prerecorded music track for his upcoming single began to play through his headphones. He hated the confined space of the booth, and the longer he stood in it, the smaller and smaller the space seemed to get. The sound treatment foam blocks seemed to trap him on all sides. But today, it wasn't just the booth that was making him lose focus. His mind kept straying to the day before, when he'd left Brookhollow. It had been tough saying goodbye to his family and the kids, and not getting to see Melody and the boys again was tearing him apart. The farther the jet had gotten from New Jersey, the deeper his frustration and hurt had become.

When the cue came this time, he was ready. *Fake it until you make it,* as Patrick used to say. This CD needed to be released in January, when his tour was set to start—with or without a number-one hit song. Belting the lyrics to the upbeat song about young, exciting love made his chest hurt. His brokenhearted songs fit his mood much better.

As he finished the last verse, his manager, Arnie King, entered the mixing booth. He gave a nod as the music ended, and the man waved him into the room, a wide smile on his face. Arnie had been his manager for years, since back when Patrick was alive, and now had taken Brad's career to a whole new level, securing him a New Year's Eve gig in Times Square, among other high-profile performances.

Removing the headphones, Brad quickly escaped from the vocal booth, grateful for the break. Entering the mixing room, he extended a hand to his manager. "Happy holidays, Arnie."

The man gave him a hug instead.

Weird. In all the time he'd known him, Arnie had never struck him as a hugger.

When he pulled away, Arnie waved a CD in his right hand. "Happy holidays, indeed.

It's a little late, but I'll take a Christmas present anytime," he said.

Brad frowned. "I don't know what you're talking about."

Arnie slapped the sound engineer on the back. "What a joker this guy is. Had me sweating bullets all through the holidays, and then this arrives." Again he showed the CD, one Brad had never seen before.

"Seriously, man, I have no idea what that is." Brad ran a hand through his disheveled hair and sat on the worn leather sofa in the studio. He couldn't wait to finish this recording session and get to his therapy appointment. His leg had been hurting ever since the flight home and he just needed to relax. His Times Square event was only four days away, and he needed to get his head back in the game before then.

"You haven't heard this?" Opening the case, Arnie scanned the studio for a CD player. "All this expensive equipment and no CD player?"

"Give it to me, old man," the sound engineer said, sliding the disc into his computer. "It's called technology."

Brad leaned forward as the sound of the

music filled the room. "Turn it up," he said, standing. He forgot his painful leg as soon as Melody's voice began to sing…

Waiting all alone
In this silent emptiness
This house no longer a home
Without your touch and tenderness
These walls won't let me breathe
Closing in so tight
I just want you here with me
Each and every lonely night

I want to be
All that you see
When love finds you
I want to be
The voice that calls you home
When loneliness surrounds you
And I want to be
All that you need
When love finds you

His mouth was dry and his gaze was transfixed on the computer. This was it. This was exactly what he'd been hoping for. But more than that—it was as if she'd read his mind. A duet. This song was meant to be a duet. As the music faded at the end of the repeated chorus, he turned to Arnie. "When did you get this?"

"It was shipped to my office by overnight courier yesterday from—"

"Melody Myers," Brad supplied. She was giving him the song she'd told him she had. One that obviously meant a lot to her. One she had previously been unwilling to give up.

"So we need to move quickly," Arnie said. "I already have the band lined up to record the tracks separately tomorrow morning, and then we'll need to record the vocals in the afternoon—"

"I want this single to be a duet," Brad interrupted.

The sound engineer nodded. "I was thinking the same thing as I listened."

Arnie shrugged. "Fine. You two are the experts. As long as the track is ready to go in two days. I'll get Lisa to start looking for a female vocalist, though on such short notice, we may not get the best of the best."

Brad already had the best of the best in mind. There was only one female he wanted singing the title track on his CD with him. "I want Melody Myers on this track."

"Patrick's widow?" Arnie frowned. "Look, Brad, I agree that her voice is amazing, but the woman's an unknown. If we can get a bigger up-and-comer..."

"It's Melody or no one." Grabbing his coat, Brad headed for the door. "And if I have to drag her to Nashville kicking and screaming, she's going to do it."

CHAPTER FIFTEEN

"Boys, if I keep tripping over these new things, I'm going to get Santa's elves to come take them back," Melody called down the hallway to the twins. It was two days after Christmas, and the boys were in their bedroom playing their new video game.

"Okay, Mom. As soon as we beat this level, we'll clean up," Josh said.

"You, too, David," she said, a hint of warning in her voice.

"Yes, Mom," he said.

She sighed and shook her head. She'd bet he was so preoccupied with that game that he didn't even know what he was agreeing to.

She heard her cell phone ring. Damn, where was it? She had to follow the sound to find it between the couch cushions in her messy living room. How on earth did it get there? She picked it up and her heart sank.

The Play Hard Sports local store number lit up her display. Of course they would call her in on her only day off that week, apart from Christmas Day. Returns after Christmas sucked. The store was just as busy now as it had been the month leading up to the holidays, but now people were grumpy. Could she afford to not answer it? "Hello?" she said, picking up on the last ring before the call went to voice mail.

"Melody?" A male voice.

"Yes."

"Hi, it's Greg Harrison."

She searched for the television remote control to turn down the cartoons that were blaring on it, but it was likely buried in the mess. She moved into her bedroom instead. "Sorry about that, Greg. My house is a zoo right now."

"With two boys, I can only imagine. Anyway, sorry it's taken me so long to get back to you. I was traveling before Christmas and then Emily went into labor a few weeks earlier than we expected..."

"I hope everything's okay." Emily Parsons might have made a mess of her relationship with Ethan, but she'd known the woman since high school and she cared what happened to her.

"Yes, she's great. The baby's fantastic—he's a boy." Pride was evident in his voice.

"Congratulations, Greg."

"Thank you. Anyway, I just wanted to let you know that I did receive your voice mails and I think I can make an exception for you this time. I'm at the store in Brookhollow today, so if you can get here within the next hour or so, I'll administer the exam myself."

Happiness and relief flowed through her. She'd been prepared to beg T.J. for extra shifts at the club. "Thank you. Yes, I'll be there right away."

"Great. See you soon."

Melody disconnected the call and tossed the phone onto her bed. Opening her closet, she pulled out a pair of jeans and her Play Hard shirt. "Boys, put the game away and get dressed. We have to go. I need to drop you guys off at Grandma's for a few hours."

An hour later, she sat in the lunchroom at the back of the busy store, staring at the exam. The questions were different than they had been on first one, but they covered the same ideas. She worried that over the last month, she might have forgotten some of what she'd studied, but as she turned the pages, her confidence grew. She felt great as she turned to the last section of essay questions. The call from Greg had been a good sign. Things were getting back on track after the tumultuous past few weeks.

"Melody." The voice coming from behind her in the doorway of the lunchroom made her jump.

Brad. Oh, no. She closed her eyes. What was he doing here? She hadn't heard from him or Arnie since she'd sent the song, and she'd tried to push all thoughts of it from her mind.

"Sorry, you can't come in here," Greg said. "Melody's writing an exam."

"Sorry to interrupt," Brad said, standing just outside the doorway. "But this is important."

Melody forced her voice to remain calm as she swung to face him. "So is this, Brad."

"You don't really want this promotion," Brad said, entering the room.

"How do you know what I want?"

"Because I know you. You sent me that CD for a reason."

"Yes. To tell you I'm done with music," she said through gritted teeth. She was being given another chance at her much-needed, much-deserved promotion, and she refused to let anything screw it up this time.

"That's crap and you know it."

"Mel," Greg interrupted, glancing at his watch, "he has to go or I'm going to have to cancel the exam."

"Please trust me," Brad said.

She glanced between the two men, her mind racing. Damn it. Two minutes ago, things had been so clear.

Brad stepped closer to her. "I need you to come with me to Nashville. I need you to record that song with me. *I need you.*"

Her breath caught in her throat. She met Brad's eyes, and the love and affection in them made it impossible to refuse his request. Why couldn't he have just stayed away?

"Mel, are you staying or going?" Greg asked.

Collecting her coat and purse from the back of the chair, she prayed she wasn't about to make the worst decision of her life.

"I'm sorry, Greg. Thank you so much for the opportunity, but I have to go."

"JUST RELAX. THIS is nothing. Just pretend you're onstage at the Green Gator." Brad's soothing words did nothing to ease the fear and panic creeping over Melody as she stood in the vocal booth, headphones positioned over her ears. It was the day after Brad had persuaded her to come to Nashville.

"Right, no problem…except that this isn't the Green Gator and it's not nothing. It's your career." Hyperventilating wouldn't help, but she had no control over the quick little breaths she was taking. How he'd ever succeeded in getting her and the boys on a plane to Nashville the day before, she'd never fully know. She remembered saying no about a thousand times while he ignored her and packed all three of their suitcases for the trip. She also remembered gripping the door handle of her home before he'd physically carried her out of the house and into his rental car.

Brad removed her headphones. "Okay, take a breath."

The feel of his hands softly stroking her bare arms wasn't helping. It just gave her another reason to hyperventilate. "I don't know if I can do this."

"I do. You can."

His confidence in her was astounding. Glancing at the producer in the mixing studio, she knew it was now or never. Never would have been her preference at that moment. But deep within her was a desire to take this chance to realize a dream she'd fought against for three years. Then the door to the studio opened and David and Joshua entered, excitement shining in their eyes. Excitement and something else. Pride.

"Thought you could use a fan club for moral support," Brad said.

Her nerves settled as she waved to her boys. "Thank you," she whispered.

"We all know you can do this. *You* know you can do this." Brad hugged her.

"Okay. I'm ready." Swallowing hard, Melody placed the headphones over her ears again and shut the vocal-booth door. Then, closing her eyes, she forgot everything else as the music filled her head.

FROM THE MIXING STUDIO, Brad listened as Melody's voice provided the harmony on the chorus. Their voices sounded perfect together. Her voice was perfect. She was perfect. And here she was in Nashville. He'd gotten her this far—would she consider staying?

She was smiling widely as she removed the headphones and exited the booth, and it gave Brad a surge of hope. She'd loved it, just as he knew she would. The boys were busy learning what all of the buttons on the mixing equipment did, so he slipped out to meet her in the hallway. "That was fantastic," he said.

"A couple of notes were off," she said, struggling to speak as he hugged her tightly.

"Only *you* noticed, and besides that's what Auto-Tune is for." He reluctantly pulled back but still kept his arms draped around her waist. "So?"

"So what?"

"It was awesome, right?"

She sighed, but the gleam in her eye betrayed her. "Yes, it was awesome. Thank you for this, Brad." Her voice was soft when her gaze met his.

He kissed her forehead, letting his lips linger on her skin. She smelled good, and felt even better. It wasn't until he had his arms around her that he realized how much he'd missed her. He had no answers about the future, but he'd do anything he could to make sure she was a part of his. "Thank *you*. Arnie's on the phone already to the local radio station. He says he'll have the song played in the region within a week."

"Wow."

"He's pretty amazing." He paused and gently traced a hand along her cheek. "Speaking of amazing," he said, lowering his voice.

"Mom!" David and Josh came running out into the hallway. Melody took a step away from Brad and knelt to hug the boys.

"You were awesome!" Josh said.

"Yeah, Mom, that was pretty cool," David said.

Brad knew no matter how much success or praise Melody received from family, friends and fans after the song was released, none would matter more to her than the pride on her sons' faces at that moment. "Let me just say goodbye to Arnie and then we can get out of here," Brad said. "Go celebrate." There was a restaurant nearby he knew the boys would love—it had an arcade with over fifty different games. If he remembered correctly, Melody was a champion foosball player, and he wanted to impress her with his own skills.

Melody stood and placed a hand on his arm. "Actually, Brad, I think we should see if there's a flight back to Newark tonight."

What? They'd just arrived and she wanted to leave already? "You guys just got here... I thought you might want to stay for a few days." He'd expected them to stay at least until New Year's Eve.

Melody shook her head. "We shouldn't. I mean, you already spent so much on the plane tickets. Another night in a hotel is unnecessary."

Yes, it was. They could stay with him. He hadn't even been thinking about a hotel. "I've got space..."

"We really should get home." Her voice was tight as she glanced at the boys. "It's been an exciting day, but..."

"But?"

"But it was just a day. And it has to end sometime."

He moved closer and examined her face

for any indication that she wanted to stay. "Says who? Every day could be like this, Mel—following your dream, pursuing music again..." *Being with me,* he didn't add, unsure if he could handle personal rejection on top of rejection of the opportunity he was trying to offer her.

"I told you this was a one-time thing, Brad. I'll keep writing music...sell more songs, maybe," she said. "But this will be the only song I record."

He'd done all he could. He'd convinced her to give music another try and she had, but he could only do so much. She didn't want this life anymore...she didn't want a life with him. Clearly the past couldn't be forgiven.

MELODY GLANCED AT the ringing cell phone in her hand and silenced the call.

"Another one?" Heather asked several days later at the bowling alley.

"Yes."

"Wow, I guess it's true what they say. People come out of the woodwork when you're famous."

"I'm hardly famous—it's just one song. I

don't even know how everyone found out so quickly." Melody filled the bar fridge behind her with bottles of champagne for that evening's New Year's Eve celebration.

Heather busied herself with wrapping the cutlery in paper napkins. "Yeah, weird." Her guilty expression said it all.

"Oh, Heather! Tell me Brookhollow hasn't gotten to you, too."

"Sorry, Mel. I couldn't help it. I squealed so loud the other day when you texted to say you were on your way to Nashville to record the song. I couldn't have kept the information to myself if I'd died trying. I'm sorry, but I was so excited for you."

"Fine, but the next time this phone rings, you're answering it." She tossed the cell to her friend. Since she'd been back, her phone hadn't stopped ringing. She enjoyed when former friends and family members called to offer congrats, but the press was killing her. The constant attempts to secure an interview with her were shameless. One reporter had even dared try to use the single-mom-turned-country-star angle. She didn't like publicity, least of all publicity that included her kids.

Heather caught the phone just as it rang again. She glanced at the caller ID. "Not a Brookhollow number. What do I say?"

"'Not interested,' or any other version of that. Be creative." She was so done with these calls already. She'd had to unplug the home phone because the calls had been disturbing the boys. The last thing she wanted was for a reporter to try to solicit comments from one of them.

She wasn't as worried about David. Her more practical son seemed to understand the severity of revealing any information to strangers on the phone. But poor Josh was still floating in the clouds over the whole experience. He kept the local radio station on in his room all day long, waiting to hear his mom on the radio. All he could talk about was how cool the recording studio had been and how much he now wanted to be a singer. One day in Nashville and her little boy had been completely bitten by the industry bug. She couldn't blame him. They'd visited Music Row before going into the studio, and that industry hotbed had been a sight. She hadn't wanted to leave—which was exactly why she'd had to do it.

She refused to even think about how hard leaving Brad had been. But there hadn't been any way for her to stay, not with him. Their history was…their history. It didn't matter that she'd fallen in love with him or that he'd fallen in love with her—it was a love that never should have happened. That never could happen. Going forward, they would be friends, and that was all.

"Oh, hi, Brad!" Heather said into her phone a second later.

Melody's heart raced. Sure, friends. Who was she trying to fool? He'd texted her the night before just to see that they'd made it home safely, but she hadn't expected to hear from him again. At least not so soon. She knew she'd hurt him by leaving. His teary eyes at the airport had nearly destroyed her. To her credit, she'd waited until both boys were sound asleep next to her on the plane before she'd allowed herself to cry.

"Yeah, she's here. She's just avoiding the media." Heather paused, and then laughed. "You're too cute."

Melody tried to pretend she didn't care that her friend was flirting with the man she loved. Heather and Brad would make a great couple. Heather was carefree and loved adventure. She had nothing tying her to Brookhollow. Melody's stomach turned at the thought of setting the two of them up. She reached for the phone. "Here, I'll talk to him."

Heather moved the phone out of reach and covered the mouthpiece. "Oh, I see. I get to handle the annoying reporters, but you get to talk to the handsome country star?"

"Give it," Melody said, hating that her friend could see right through her. There was no point denying her feelings for Brad to Heather. The savvy city girl knew her too well.

"Please hold for Melody Myers," Heather said into the phone before handing it over.

Melody took a deep breath. *Act nonchalant.* "Hi, Brad." Her higher-than-normal pitch was anything but nonchalant.

"Hi. How are you?"

"Good."

"I'm sorry if the press is swarming you. Arnie kind of went crazy promoting the single…that's why I'm calling. You're at the bowling alley?"

"Yes. Just setting up for the New Year's

Eve party." The thought of the party once again made her wish she'd be celebrating the occasion with him. Working the event here and seeing the happily dancing couples celebrating the countdown was going to be torture. She remembered how it had felt to be in his arms at the mayor's holiday party, the way his lips had felt when he'd kissed her on the sleigh ride…

Suddenly a loud screeching sound on his end made her cringe and hold the phone away from her ear. "Where are you?"

"At the stage in Times Square. It's crazy here."

That's right. He would be performing with a group of other musicians when the ball dropped that evening. It made her miss him even more, although she was hopeful he'd be too busy singing to kiss anyone that evening.

"Anyway," he said, "turn on Nash FM."

That was a radio station in New York she could get in Brookhollow. "Okay." Approaching the radio behind the bar, she turned the dial until the familiar radio DJ's voice came through the speakers.

"…Next up we have a new single from Brad Monroe…"

Monroe?

"…and a new up-and-coming country star, Melody Myers."

She covered her mouth with her hand. Heather's squeal could surely have been heard in Beach Haven. Up-and-coming country star? They'd gotten it wrong. "Brad…"

"I have to go. Listen to it. You deserve this moment. Say happy New Year to the boys for me. I'm going to try my hardest not to wish I was kissing you tonight at midnight, but I make no promises."

"OKAY BOYS, HURRY…I have to get back to the bar." Melody gathered their overnight bags for their New Year's Eve sleepover at her parents' house. By the time the party crowd rang in the New Year and they kicked everyone out and cleaned up the mess, it would be well after three in the morning. She couldn't think now about how lonely coming home to the empty house would be. Hopefully she'd be too tired to notice.

"Can I bring my air hockey table from Uncle Ethan to play with Grandpa?" David asked.

Melody threw their overnight bags over her shoulder. "Can you carry it?"

"Yeah."

"Then sure. But hurry, okay?"

Josh appeared in the hallway with Patrick's guitar over his shoulder.

"You're taking the guitar?"

"Yeah, I have to practice. Brad said if I can learn to play, I can go on tour with him when I'm older."

She wanted to go on tour with Brad, too. "Take me with you, okay, buddy?" she said, affectionately tousling the boy's hair as he moved past her into the hall.

"Hey, Mom, Grandma's here," he said a second later.

"She is?" Had she gotten it wrong? She thought she was dropping the boys off. Josh opened the front door and Delores entered. Oh, the other grandma. "Hi, Delores. I'm sorry, we're just on our way out."

"I won't keep you. I just wanted to make sure you and the boys were still coming for lunch tomorrow."

Shoot, she'd forgotten. The only thing she had planned for the next day was sleep. After the excitement and whirlwind trip to

Nashville, she was already exhausted and she hadn't even worked her shift yet. "What time? You see, I'm working the New Year's Eve party at the bowling alley tonight, and the boys are sleeping at my parents place… so if it's early…"

"It's whenever you get there." The woman took a step closer and handed Melody a long, thin white box.

"What's this? You already gave us our Christmas gifts."

"I saw it in a window of the pawnshop yesterday and I stopped to check…"

Oh, no. Melody's heart stopped as she opened the lid. Her U 47 microphone was inside. She swallowed a lump in her throat. "Delores, I didn't want to sell it, but I had to."

"To take care of your family—I understand completely. I would have done the exact same thing. But after I saw it, I couldn't leave it there. It belongs to you."

"I don't know what to say. Thank you." Her gift from Patrick was back where it belonged.

"My son wanted you to have this because

he believed in your talent. I heard your song on the radio this morning…and I do, too."

Melody was rendered speechless.

"Your voice belongs to music, Melody."

She shook her head. "It was just one song. I don't plan on returning to music…"

"I've come to believe that no one plans anything important or significant in life. Music returned to you, Melody. Dan and I didn't support Patrick's decision and it's something we will never be able to forgive ourselves for, but we are here to support yours. Go after what you want, honey, because with your talent, you're sure to get it."

MELODY SAT AT the stoplight on Main Street even after the light had turned green. Delores's words had struck a chord and her mind was reeling. Go after what she wanted. Could she really do that? For the first time in a long time, she was thinking about what she wanted, and that was Brad and a career in music…but mostly Brad.

A horn honked behind her and she hesitated just a second longer before pulling the van to the side of the street. She waited until the truck passed, and then she swung the van around. The boys were with her parents for the evening. New York City was three hours away by car.

This was crazy. Well, maybe crazy was a good thing. For years she'd been playing it safe, afraid of falling, afraid of making the wrong choices, afraid of living. Now was her chance to change that. Brad had said he would try his best not to be wishing he was kissing her that evening. Well, she was going to do everything in her power to make sure he was.

THE CROWD IN Times Square was unbelievable. Despite the bone-chilling weather and the falling snow—which was giving Brad the feeling of being inside a shaken snow globe—the radio was reporting record numbers at the New Year's Eve event. Brad had arrived at the festivities before six o'clock to witness the raising of the ball to the top of One Times Square's roof. This was his first time attending the annual event, and he'd been mesmerized by the flurry of activity and coordination involved in corraling thousands of spectators into different viewing sections. Party favors—balloons, hats and noisemakers—had been distributed as the crowd had gathered, and he couldn't help but think about how much Melody and the boys would love all of this excitement.

Now, ten minutes to the ball drop and eleven minutes to his group performance of the iconic "Auld Lang Syne," he paced the backstage area.

He took his phone from his pocket. If he called her, what would he say? Would hearing her voice make him feel better or worse? It was 11:53. By now she would probably be distributing glasses of champagne to the locals gathered in the club as everyone got ready to ring in the New Year. He'd never been sentimental about the occasion, but this year, he wished he wasn't about to perform in front of millions of fans worldwide. He wished he were at the bowling alley with the other two hundred or so celebrants…and he wished he had his arms around one woman in particular, his lips on hers at midnight, and every midnight after that.

"Hey, no one is allowed back here," he heard the event security guard say behind him for the millionth time so far that evening. Three hundred pounds of solid muscle, the hired guard wasn't someone anybody wanted to mess with. Brad's safety wasn't in question.

"But, I need to see Brad," a female voice said.

"You and about thirty thousand other women. Sorry, no fans allowed back here."

"You don't understand—"

"Miss, I have to ask you to step away," the guard said.

Brad needed to see who was daring to go up against the menacing guard. Turning, his breath caught in his throat. Melody. Rushing toward them, he said, "It's okay. She's okay."

"Mr. Monroe, I'm under strict rules not to allow anyone back here." The guard wouldn't budge.

"She's a…friend." Love of his life was more accurate.

"I don't care if she's your mother. Safety first," Darryl said.

Melody shrugged as their eyes met around the guard.

She was here, so close, yet he still couldn't touch her, hold her… "Okay, she can't come in, but can you let me out?" He jiggled the thick ropes separating them.

"No, sir. Once you're in, you have to stay in unless you have a guard with you."

Fame sure had its downside. "Okay, fine," he said, gesturing for Melody to move over. He reached across the barricade for her hands, which she extended toward him. He smiled at the sight of the gloves he'd given her for Christmas. Their fingers barely touched, and he stretched even farther. "What are you doing here?" he yelled above the deafening noise in the Square.

Her response was drowned by the crowd's applause. The mayor and his special guest had taken the stage for the ball drop behind them. He frowned. This wasn't going to work. Reluctantly letting go of her hand, he reached for his cell phone and quickly called her number, which was still on his screen from when he'd been contemplating calling her moments before.

She gave him a puzzled look.

He gestured toward her purse and mouthed *your phone.*

Quickly she retrieved it and answered. "Hi."

"Hi."

"I had to see you."

"What about the bowling alley? The boys?"

"Pretty sure I'm fired from the alley, and the boys are with my parents. I just needed to tell you something and it couldn't wait."

"Brad, we need you on cue," a stagehand said, coming up behind him. The rest of the performers had already taken their places.

"Just a second," he said. He turned back to Mel. "Tell me." He held his breath. She'd come all this way. Did he dare hope she was about to tell him what he longed to hear?

"I love you," she said, her voice barely audible above the roar of the crowd around them. But he heard her.

His reached for her hand again. Damn barricade. He wanted to hop over it and take her in his arms. "I love you, too, Mel," he said bringing her hand toward his chest but falling several inches short. *Oh, come on!*

"Brad, we have to go." The stagehand waved at him from the top of the stairs leading onto the stage.

Brad ignored him. "I wish I could kiss you," he told Mel.

"That would be nice," she said with a small laugh. Onstage, the ball dropped.

Sixty seconds until midnight. Here she was, his dream come true, and he wouldn't be able to share a New Year's kiss with her. This was just too cruel. The clock in the distance read thirty seconds.

"Brad, let's go!"

"Oh, all right!" the guard said, coming toward them. Leaning over the barricade, he lifted Melody effortlessly over it and set her down in front of Brad. "Kiss your girl," he said gruffly before moving away.

"Thanks," Melody said.

"I could have done that," Brad said, moving closer and wrapping his arms around her. He shoved his phone into his pocket.

"Brad!" The stagehand's voice was but a distant annoyance as he stared at Melody's rosy cheeks, her snow-and-confetti-covered hair.

"Say it again," he said, brushing a stray lock away from her cheek.

She didn't hesitate. "I love you."

He wanted to accept it, hold her, kiss her, never let her go, but his mind still plagued him. "Melody, I'll never be Patrick."

She ran a hand along his jaw, and then cupped his cold chin with the warmth of the cashmere. "I loved Patrick, and I lost Patrick. Now what I need, what I want, is you."

"Then be with me, not just right now, but always. You and the boys can come be a part of this life." He gestured around him. "A part of my life."

"Ten, nine, eight…"

"Okay," she said softly.

He couldn't believe it. Overjoyed, he lifted her off her feet and spun her around. "Okay!"

"…seven, six, five…"

"But I'm not changing my name to Jackson," she said.

"How about Monroe?"

"…four, three, two…"

"Melody Myers Monroe. I think I like…"

He didn't let her finish. His lips met hers in a soft, tender kiss as the bell sounded midnight and the sound of "Auld Lang Syne" filled the air around him, a song he was supposed to be singing.

She wriggled out of his arms, her eyes wide. "You need to get up there." She nudged him toward the stage.

"Come with me."

"Not on your life…not this time, anyway."

"But someday?" His expression was hopeful and she smiled at the man she loved.

"Definitely. Someday…"

* * * * *

LARGER-PRINT BOOKS!
GET 2 FREE LARGER-PRINT NOVELS PLUS
2 FREE GIFTS!

✦ HARLEQUIN®

Romance

From the Heart, For the Heart

YES! Please send me 2 FREE LARGER-PRINT Harlequin® Romance novels and my 2 FREE gifts (gifts are worth about $10). After receiving them, if I don't wish to receive any more books, I can return the shipping statement marked "cancel." If I don't cancel, I will receive 4 brand-new novels every month and be billed just $4.84 per book in the U.S. or $5.24 per book in Canada. That's a savings of at least 19% off the cover price! It's quite a bargain! Shipping and handling is just 50¢ per book in the U.S. and 75¢ per book in Canada.* I understand that accepting the 2 free books and gifts places me under no obligation to buy anything. I can always return a shipment and cancel at any time. Even if I never buy another book, the two free books and gifts are mine to keep forever.

119/319 HDN F43Y

Name	(PLEASE PRINT)	
Address		Apt. #
City	State/Prov.	Zip/Postal Code

Signature (if under 18, a parent or guardian must sign)

Mail to the **Harlequin® Reader Service:**
IN U.S.A.: P.O. Box 1867, Buffalo, NY 14240-1867
IN CANADA: P.O. Box 609, Fort Erie, Ontario L2A 5X3

Want to try two free books from another line?
Call 1-800-873-8635 or visit www.ReaderService.com.

* Terms and prices subject to change without notice. Prices do not include applicable taxes. Sales tax applicable in N.Y. Canadian residents will be charged applicable taxes. Offer not valid in Quebec. This offer is limited to one order per household. Not valid for current subscribers to Harlequin Romance Larger-Print books. All orders subject to credit approval. Credit or debit balances in a customer's account(s) may be offset by any other outstanding balance owed by or to the customer. Please allow 4 to 6 weeks for delivery. Offer available while quantities last.

Your Privacy—The Harlequin® Reader Service is committed to protecting your privacy. Our Privacy Policy is available online at www.ReaderService.com or upon request from the Harlequin Reader Service.

We make a portion of our mailing list available to reputable third parties that offer products we believe may interest you. If you prefer that we not exchange your name with third parties, or if you wish to clarify or modify your communication preferences, please visit us at www.ReaderService.com/consumerschoice or write to us at Harlequin Reader Service Preference Service, P.O. Box 9062, Buffalo, NY 14269. Include your complete name and address.

HRLP13R

LARGER-PRINT BOOKS!

GET 2 FREE LARGER-PRINT NOVELS PLUS
2 FREE GIFTS!

HARLEQUIN

super romance

More Story...More Romance

YES! Please send me 2 FREE LARGER-PRINT Harlequin® Superromance® novels and my 2 FREE gifts (gifts are worth about $10). After receiving them, if I don't wish to receive any more books, I can return the shipping statement marked "cancel." If I don't cancel, I will receive 6 brand-new novels every month and be billed just $5.69 per book in the U.S. or $5.99 per book in Canada. That's a savings of at least 16% off the cover price! It's quite a bargain! Shipping and handling is just 50¢ per book in the U.S. or 75¢ per book in Canada.* I understand that accepting the 2 free books and gifts places me under no obligation to buy anything. I can always return a shipment and cancel at any time. Even if I never buy another book, the two free books and gifts are mine to keep forever.

139/339 HDN F46Y

Name   (PLEASE PRINT)

Address   Apt. #

City   State/Prov.   Zip/Postal Code

Signature (if under 18, a parent or guardian must sign)

Mail to the **Harlequin® Reader Service:**
IN U.S.A.: P.O. Box 1867, Buffalo, NY 14240-1867
IN CANADA: P.O. Box 609, Fort Erie, Ontario L2A 5X3

**Are you a current subscriber to Harlequin Superromance books
and want to receive the larger-print edition?
Call 1-800-873-8635 today or visit www.ReaderService.com.**

* Terms and prices subject to change without notice. Prices do not include applicable taxes. Sales tax applicable in N.Y. Canadian residents will be charged applicable taxes. Offer not valid in Quebec. This offer is limited to one order per household. Not valid for current subscribers to Harlequin Superromance Larger-Print books. All orders subject to credit approval. Credit or debit balances in a customer's account(s) may be offset by any other outstanding balance owed by or to the customer. Please allow 4 to 6 weeks for delivery. Offer available while quantities last.

Your Privacy—The Harlequin® Reader Service is committed to protecting your privacy. Our Privacy Policy is available online at www.ReaderService.com or upon request from the Harlequin Reader Service.

We make a portion of our mailing list available to reputable third parties that offer products we believe may interest you. If you prefer that we not exchange your name with third parties, or if you wish to clarify or modify your communication preferences, please visit us at www.ReaderService.com/consumerschoice or write to us at Harlequin Reader Service Preference Service, P.O. Box 9062, Buffalo, NY 14269. Include your complete name and address.

HSRLP13R

LARGER-PRINT BOOKS!

GET 2 FREE
LARGER-PRINT NOVELS
PLUS 2 FREE
MYSTERY GIFTS

Love Inspired®

Larger-print novels are now available...

LILPDIR13R

Reader Service.com

Manage your account online!

- Review your order history
- Manage your payments
- Update your address

---

*We've designed
the Harlequin® Reader Service
website just for you.*

Enjoy all the features!

- Reader excerpts from any series
- Respond to mailings and special monthly offers
- Discover new series available to you
- Browse the Bonus Bucks catalog
- Share your feedback

Visit us at:

ReaderService.com